STAGE SEPARATIONS

THE COMPLETE SCIENCE FICTION STORIES 2013-2018

RAYMUND EICH

TABLE OF CONTENTS

LOVE AND DEATH IN THE CITY OF BONE

Perhaps our only sickness is to desire a truth which we cannot bear rather than to rest content with the fictions we manufacture out of each other.
    – Lawrence Durrell
    Clea *(The Alexandria Quartet, Book 4)*

My footsteps echoed under the high ceiling of the spaceport's arrivals gate. Plastic shrouds wrapped all but one of the interview stations. At the last open interview station, the guard's frizzy hair and long ears reminded me of Nesbitt, Juliette's husband. I held out my ALECS passport and let the guard take a fingertip scraping and a retina scan to confirm my identity.

After a few seconds, the machine gonged and a green light glowed on its panel, sequencing of my DNA complete. The guard gestured at a gray plastic frame, two meters fifty tall, one meter fifty wide, thirty centimeters thick. Under the center of the frame, bee-striped lines marked the outlines of feet.

"Stand there until released," the guard said.

I raised an eyebrow at the frame, then at him. "Brain activity scanners are voluntary at any ALECS arrival or departure point."

"The rules have changed. Stand there until released."

He set his fists on his hips. The gesture set a crease into the ALECS patch on the guard's blue sleeve. Under the patch, no doubt, lay the logo of United Sodalities of the Galaxy, soon to be the only human organization allowed to remain on this planet. I could waste time with his superiors, arguing protocols they knew and disregarded, with little hope of evading the scanner. Or I could comply. In one inhalation I planned my thoughts, then did as he bade.

The guard moved around the frame and faced me. Motors spun up and fans whirred in the plastic frame as he scowled at my passport. "What's the purpose of your visit, *Mr.* Lee?"

I let slide his willful refusal to use my honorific. "The Way in the West has sent me to supervise the withdrawal of its personnel and assets from Elard, according to the Indigenous Autonomous Council's decree." A sense of purpose filled in behind my eyes. Sadness at our mission's end hung from it like icicles. He would expect the scanner to pick up both those feelings.

It helped I felt them.

His scowl shifted targets to my face. "Is that your sole purpose?"

"I might look up some old colleagues," I said. Stolen hours with Juliette returned from memory and touched my inner senses. The glow of afternoon sun flooding the opacity of the window near my narrow bed. The texture of her kisses. The grinding of our pelvises against each other. The public trysts, in her jitney, that one in the women's restroom at the café on Gregory Dialogus Street, sneaking out with disheveled hair and untucked shirts only to find Purcell waiting for us—

Mustn't think about Purcell—

"Step forward," the guard said. He snapped shut my passport and held it out, pinched between his thumb and forefinger. "Your papers are in order. I cannot deny you admittance. But here's some advice. The rules you might remember from your previous stay, when the ALECS administrators ruled the human settlement and the wishes of our native brethren were ignored, they've changed. The natives have decided your doctrines are false. We abide by those wishes. You'd be wise to do the same, Mr. Lee."

I took the passport from him, lifted my shoulders, and turned away. I had a month on Elard to learn her secrets. Secrets I had missed on my posting here decades prior.

The planet's secrets. Not Juliette's.

Outside the arrivals gate, a robotic flatbed cart waited with my suitcases. Its front structure bore shoulders and head, eyes level with my chest. A smile formed on its cartoonish features when I approached. "A jitney waits for you outside," it said.

I trickled my hands over the barely-visible seal in the uppermost suitcase. Cool to the touch. No sign of forced entry by the security guards. "Follow."

My heels clacked and the cart's tires whispered on the tile floor. I alone had arrived today. The only other sounds and motions on the concourse came from cleaning robots. Chairs and tables gleamed in the glow of lighted ceiling panels and waited for passengers never to come. A cleaning robot, the size of a tiny dog, clung on gecko-like feet to a poster saying *The United Sodalities of the Galaxy and the Indigenous Autonomous Council Welcome You to Elard.* A lighted strip in the frame above the poster glinted on the robot's carapace. With a raspy sound, the robot licked the face of the Sodalities's local operations director. An augmented reality server pushed his name to the video screens in my contact lenses. Vainqueur. A name I'd never heard before.

A dozen paces further, a light had burned out over a poster with the ALECS logo and an array of smiling humans diverse in race, sex, and attire. Their puffed hair and narrow, starched lapels resembled decades-old images of the four of us on the soft synthleather couches in a back corner of the café. *The Apostolic League of Earth Communities of Spirit. Many Manifestations, One Truth.* Thick lines of dust marked the edges of the poster frame.

I rounded a last corner and entered the spaceport atrium. My footsteps echoed off the concrete walls and vast front windows. My pace remained constant but my heart sped up. Across kilometers of scrubby desert, the human settlement thrust its bony fingers toward the sky.

The most important three years of my life had been spent in and around those living buildings and the wide boulevards between them. I had been a callow boy, deluded by my recent diploma and my accepted application for an extrasolar posting into believing I was a man.

Three years of fruitless missionary work humbled my naive certainty in both The Way in the West's teachings, and my own abilities to persuade the natives. *Alien Lifeforms Extremely Contemptuous of Salvation,* Purcell had said with his customary cynicism, and Nesbitt had narrowed his eyes.

A few months in Juliette's close orbit demolished my masculine pretense of control over my surroundings and my emotions.

She lived still among those bony towers.

The doors to the loading zone parted to reveal a single jitney waiting along a hundred meters of curb. On its side, the ALECS logo, the white sun of the Transcendent pouring out the rainbow-colored waves of the different spiritual communities. A standard vehicle from the motor pool. The baking air desiccated me, pulled recollections of field work out of the depths of my memory. I shaded my eyes and squinted at the cloudless sky under noontime Elar. Quick steps to the jitney, and I sagged into the rear seat before ordering the air conditioning vents to aim themselves at me. I stepped down the windows' opacity to give myself a sepia-tinged view of the spaceport and the landscape. Thumps came from the trunk as the robotic cart loaded my luggage.

Minutes later, the jitney hurried down the road toward the human settlement. Straight as a crow's flight, the same low, mounded median of rocky soil and sparse Terran shrubs divided the two inbound lanes from the two outer. To the sides, new boundary fences ran parallel to the road, ten meters from the paved edges of the shoulders. Atop the barbed wire, concertina coils angled toward the road. In the old days, the ALECS concession stretched five kilometers to either side, marked by a fence a person could climb. Beyond the fences, rocky desert tufted by a few Elardian plants stretched to the edges of the plateau. The natives rarely strayed this far and high from the great narrow sea stretching halfway around the planet.

My thoughts turned to the hidden one of my purposes. Three days before I left Earth, my superiors sent me to Prague, where I met the executive committee of The Unneeded Hypothesis, Purcell's sponsors.

We never learned his fate on Elard. In the decades since he disappeared, our leadership focused on more urgent matters. But our stature declined anyway, and our number of adherents has shrunk. Learning Purcell's fate would be one of the last victories we could win. Now that the United Sodalities of the Galaxy has cajoled the natives into expelling the rest of us, our chance at even that victory is slipping away.

Three kilometers outside the window, across a city of midrise apartment buildings housing tens of thousands living mostly in virtual reality, gray-bellied clouds brushed the spires of St. Vitus' Cathedral. *Where do I come in?* I asked.

The executive winced. *We can't afford to send an agent to Elard. Your superiors in Calgary agreed we could partially fund your trip if you do this for us.*

Calgary didn't tell me—

His eyes grew imploring. *We ask for a pair of reasons. First, yes, our spiritual paths differ, but they are more consonant than any others. We both strive to see the universe as it is, yes? Unlike the USG, and the Universal Church of Christ, both telling pretty lies of the universe as it could be, if only the masses would bow down to the USG's historical dialectic, or the UCC's god.*

All that is true. I knew the answer before I asked my next question. *And the other reason?*

In his reports, Purcell called you his friend.

A sign announced a thousand meters to the settlement's gate. To the left, beyond the road's outbound lanes, the boundary fence turned a right angle away from the road. The airfield looked little changed. The aircraft hangar and liftpad were as I remembered, shimmering in the heat. No one was about, and on a pole near the hangar slumped the ALECS flag.

Between the airfield and the settlement, a few jitneys rolled over rock and packed sand between several new buildings. Extruded like giant sausages, only narrow, translucent windows and recessed doors broke up their smooth shells. Near each door was a building number and the spiral-galaxy-and-all-seeing-eye logo of USG.

The jitney slowed for a sallyport arcing over the inbound lanes. A curtain of air buffeted it and it stopped under the sallyport's shade. A guard tapped the window and I told the jitney to open it. "Yes?"

He leaned his head in and slid off his sunglasses. A speaker bud like a white chrysalis showed in his left ear, and flesh-toned discs on the sides of his Adam's apple marked his subvocal microphones. "Traffic control verification. Your destination?"

"The Way in the West, Elard Headquarters, 14 Laozi Street."

"Thank you." He angled his head to his left and got a faraway look, listening to his earbud. "May your stay be productive. Good day."

The jitney rolled forward, through another air curtain, and back into the glare of Elard at midday. Dark shadings and the outlines of pried-off letters marked shut-down shops along Guru Nanak Boulevard. A few remained open under unfamiliar names. Harvard Square Poetry Slam, Portland's Finest Coffee, Park Slope Brewery & Pub Grub. All had windows tinted against the harsh light. The boulevard lacked any traffic other than me.

A few minutes later, I arrived at our headquarters. A glimpse up the front facade showed little change in the three floors of white bone and reflective windows. Our banner hung slack above the vehicle entrance. The banner bore the *taijitu*, its light side shaped roughly like the Americas. I turned into the parking garage entrance and shade swallowed the jitney.

I climbed out near double glass doors leading into the building. Though attenuated by the garage structure, Elar's glare still forced me to shield my eyes with my hand to widen my pupils enough for the retina scanner mounted on the wall. I pressed the thumbprint scanner and said, "Darren Lee, *daoshi* of the third rank."

The doors shuddered as the magnetic seals gave way.

I went in, savored the cold air thick like a hotel's, and followed a virtual arrow to the elevator. It debouched me on the top floor.

Silence reigned throughout the floor, broken only by a few low voices at the far end of a cubicle layout. Beyond the voices, lights glowed in one of the offices around the perimeter. I presumed the lighted office belonged to Scobee, the director of local operations. Between the elevator and the voices, the cubicles stood empty save for a few empty snack wrappers and abandoned datachips in their back corners and deep in their footwells.

In his office, Scobee stood behind his desk, arms crossed behind his back, shoulders high and rigid. His right eye drooped, and both eyes had heavy bags. I waited in the open doorway until he greeted me. "Welcome—back—to Elard, *Daoshi* Lee."

"You seem displeased to see me."

A moment of alarm flashed wide his eyes. "No, *Daoshi*, certainly not. The chance to meet and share the Way with a *daoshi* of the third rank, I can only be pleased—"

"Perhaps *you* can, but what about all the other parts of your psyche?"

"They, yes, they are pleased to. I—part of me, rather—wonders, though, why Calgary sent you. And without warning, that's what puzzles—me." He cleared his throat. "My reports to Calgary have made clear our evacuation is on schedule. Haven't they?"

"I can't speak for Calgary, but they must see it differently. After all, they ordered me here."

"We'll be down to ten percent of our complement when the ship that brought you takes off. There are only four remote sites left and I shouldn't have any more trouble shutting them down—"

"Brambles in the path."

For all our claims of relying on inner wisdom, we regurgitate our share of mantras. *Brambles in the path? Go around them. That's all you need. Don't bother asking, 'why are such things made in this world?'*

Scobee's head jittered, then stopped. "Of course, Marcus Aurelius said it so well, and so long ago." His shoulders slumped. "*Daoshi*, I'm sorry, all the difficulties in wrapping up our presence here are getting to me. I've been doing well closing down our operations, and still Calgary doubts me...."

"The handbook on withdrawing a mission from an alien planet was all theoretical," I said, tone chummy, "until now. Mind if I sit?"

He nodded, gestured at a chair facing his desk. He dropped into his. "The handbook came close enough. I've had to cut a few corners—I think my results will show those were good decisions—"

"I'm sure they will. Yet even if the handbook gave your team good advice, the logistics of packing up our facilities and shipping out hundreds of people must have kept you up at night."

"The logistics are just details. We're on top of them." He backhanded the air, confident and nonchalant, but his hand soon fell to the glass desktop. A dour look filled his face and he retreated deeper into his chair. "The United Sodalities is the difficulty."

"How so? USG won over the vast majority of the natives; the natives ordered the rest of us to leave. What am I missing?"

He looked haggard for a moment. "You know those aren't ALECS security personnel at the spaceport and the settlement gate."

"Yes. So? USG security is running a victory lap." I peered at him. "Have they interfered with your operations?"

He rocked his chair back and forth in a slow but agitated tempo. "Not directly. Yet. Much. Mostly they just watch and jump on our every transgression. Did you see where our logo used to be on the building? No, of course not, it's on the side away from the street."

His window faced the same direction. I stood, went to it. The next block held dogtrot stucco houses where married ALECS personnel with families had lived. Beyond lay forty meters of bare dirt, then a barbed wire fence marked the settlement perimeter. Hazy with distance and heat shimmer, past the canyon-carved edge of the plateau, close to the sinuous indigo sea, thick brown piles marked the nearest native villages. "Facing the lowlands," I said. "Visible to the natives. If someone gave the natives a pair of binoculars."

"Exactly. Visible enough to offend their newfound faith in USG-ism, at any rate. We wasted two days covering up the logo and spreading osteoclastic factors to get the building to slough it off."

"At least it was only two days."

Scobee shook his head. "They forbid access to some of our old field posts. They're uncrewed, we scrubbed anything sensitive when our people last left them, so maybe it doesn't matter, but the handbook says we should double-check those sites and remove anything which might affirm our tradition." He looked at me for approval.

Purcell's unoccupied airmobile had been found in the high desert two hundred kilometers to the north. To give our allies at The

Unneeded Hypothesis all the answers they sought, I would have to find his remains.

Scobee expected a reply. "That's a corner I'm glad you didn't cut," I said.

"I've been haranguing them for flight plan approvals twice a day for the last week. We're still on schedule to evacuate, but that could slip if they delay us much longer and one of those field posts has more stuff left behind than we expect."

"I'll talk to the High Arbiter at ALECS local headquarters, and someone up in the ranks at USG. I was friends with Nesbitt Edmondson, and his wife Juliette, when I was first posted here. If he's still around—"

"He died."

"What?" I peered at him. Did he misspeak? Did I mishear? "I didn't know."

Scobee nodded his gaze down to his desktop. Death comes so unexpectedly these centuries. I read his avoidance of my gaze as a grant to me of privacy for grief and shock.

It also meant he saw no trace of a boyish longing shooting up the inside of my chest. *Her husband was dead, her other lover was dead, she might now turn to me—*

Scobee inhaled loudly enough for me to know he readied to speak. "It happened about five years ago. Some task in the wilds went wrong and he came back to the settlement in a body bag."

"If I see his wife, I'll give her my condolences." I forced my voice to sound casual. "Did she stay here after he died?"

"Last I heard. I can look her up for you."

"No need. She probably wouldn't remember me."

A knock on the open door turned my head. The woman looked to be in her twenties, hair thin and sandy-blond. She dressed like an office worker, in a white blouse and a pleated skirt hemmed just below her knee. A glance showed she lacked Juliette's depths.

She looked puzzled. "Are you *Daoshi* Lee?" She had an Australian accent, thick with earthy casualness, heightening the lack of depth.

"I am."

"Sorry, *Daoshi*, from your name, I was expecting you to be ethnically Chinese."

"I get that sometimes. You are?"

"Clio."

Scobee cleared his throat. "Clio will be on the final ship out. Her skills are too valuable to let her go before then."

To Clio, I said, "You do field work? Liase with ALECS local operations?"

"No, *Daoshi*. I'm in counterintelligence."

"We've been granted a flat for you," Scobee said, "on John Maynard Keynes Street a few blocks off Guru Nanak Boulevard. Clio will accompany you and get you situated."

"Thanks," I replied, then turned to her. "—but babysitting me seems a waste of your talents."

Clio held my gaze for a second. "*Daoshi*, I wish it were."

A few minutes later, my jitney drove from the depths of the garage and parked outside the double glass doors. It opened for us as we hurried into it. I let the vents blow cold air at my face for a few seconds before I turned to Clio. She held her finger in front of her lips and her eyes implored me. I nodded and she moved her finger away. "*Daoshi*, tell me news from Earth."

"You must get plenty of news already."

Muscles trembled in her neck. The jitney apparently picked up her subvocalization: the windows opaqued as if thick curtains had been drawn closed. For a moment, the cabin seemed dim, cool. She reached between two pleats of her skirt and pulled from some hidden pocket a case about ten centimeters long and three deep and high. A thumbpress flicked open a lid. Four rounded black balls, each smaller than the thumbnail of my little finger, lay in foam. "I've been too busy to follow it."

"You can't have left that long ago."

"I've been here two years. Please, *daoshi*, tell me news from Earth." She gave me a look urging me to comply.

"There's no news. Ninety-five percent of the human race takes their charitable allotment…"

Clio lifted a ball from the case. A half-ball, actually, its missing hemisphere previously hidden by the foam. She tapped its flat face and pressed it against a lower corner of the window on her side of the jitney. It clung to the window after she pulled her hand away.

I subvoked to her, "Are you worried about eavesdroppers?"

"I am," she replied the same way, her voice lilting through my earbuds. "But speak aloud."

I did as she asked. "…twenty kilograms of nanoassembled products and five hundred kilowatt-hours of fusion electricity every day—"

"Hasn't changed, then." She stuck another half-ball to the front window.

"A little. For the worse. Virtual reality games and immersive stories gain more popularity every day, and engagement with the real world drops in proportion. Except for our adherents, and those of the other ALECS spiritual communities, we're becoming a species bounded by nutshells and counting ourselves kings of infinite space."

Clio reached across me to press the next half-ball to the window on my side. Halfway there, her chest over my lap, she blushed and her eye visible to me widened. She left the seat to crouch on the floor, skirt covering more of her legs then I would have guessed possible, and I shifted my legs further from her. Her stare bored into the window where she pressed the half-ball. "You've talked enough for the system to calibrate your voice."

"Why does it need to do that?" I filled my voice with languid humor.

Once more on the seat next to me, she turned her back to press the last half-ball against the rear window. Between her shoulder blades, sweat formed a dark drop the size of a large antique coin. "The rattlers are an eavesdropping countermeasure."

"That implies an eavesdropping measure."

"Set off, please," she said to the jitney, aloud for my benefit. The jitney rolled forward. She crossed her legs, angling a knee toward me. Her face showed professional poise over traces of embarrassment. "When we speak, we create pressure waves in the air. When they hit a window, they set it to rattling. Not so much as we could notice, but aim a lidar—a laser rangefinder—on that window, and you could hear what we're saying."

What might USG security have heard during my ride from the spaceport? "The rattlers disrupt that."

"Yeah, but the two easiest rattler techniques give the game away. Easiest is a jitter pattern to feed the eavesdropper a white noise. That doesn't happen naturally. Next easiest is an interference pattern to cancel out our sound waves and feed the eavesdropper silence. But who ever is utterly silent for ten minutes in a jitney?"

"The rattlers are sending interference with an audio track."

"Exactly. Same principle as a noise-canceling earbud." Clio tapped her left ear. "We coded the system to improvise the audio track based on the jitney's passengers...." Her cheeks reddened. She turned away but forgot to subvocalize. Her inadvertent whisper came to me over the rush of air from the vents. "Is the system running a hook-up—?" Her cheeks grew even more red and a moment of alarm bulged her eyes.

Old habits stirred in me. I needled her embarrassment. "We wouldn't want that, would we?"

Her back stiffened and she half-turned away from me. I picked non-existent lint off my pants while the mood eased. I didn't have time for romantic encounters, especially not with the extra complications arising from crossing rank levels within a workplace.

And especially especially not if Juliette had no other man in her life.

We pulled up to a two-story walkup on John Maynard Keynes. "I'll double-check, but we've already secured your flat."

Flat like the flight deck of an archaic aircraft carrier. My new space was twice the size of my apartment on the downtown Calgary riverfront, and ten times the cramped apartment I'd shared with Appel-Ball during my first posting on Elard. The few pieces of furniture stood on spindly carbon nanotube legs and made the space even larger. Clio put her finger to her lips, then slid a device smaller than her palm from another hidden pocket of her skirt. She paced around, checking some visual data projected to her contact lenses, while the building's robots set down my luggage. After the robots left, she scanned my luggage, then blew out a breath. "I've spoofed their cameras and microphones, but I wager they'll try to plant more when you're out. I've set up intrusion sensors on the doors. Vibration detectors on the floor, in case they try to feed a device in from the flat below. You'll be free to speak here, in our headquarters, and in one of our jitneys. Anywhere else, assume you're being overheard."

"I will."

She nodded. "One last thing, *Daoshi*." She handed me the palm-sized device. I twirled it between my fingers. "That's yours till we leave. I'll do ongoing scans, but you're the first line of defense."

After Clio left, I rode my jitney down John Maynard Keynes to Guru Nanak Boulevard. I passed through the shadow of a tall building, taller than I remembered, at the corner. USG headquarters. The front facade showed only a bone-white brilliance dappled with reflective windows. I checked the upper floors for the joint of new growth, saw none. Impermeable to the eye, USG kept its secrets.

ALECS local operations stood half a kilometer further down Guru Nanak, at the intersection with Gregory Dialogus. Despite the addition to USG headquarters, ALECS local operations remained the tallest building on the planet. I waited on the top floor, where transparent interior walls combined with wide windows to give a view across dozens of kilometers, from far south out to sea to the lifeless gray mountains separating the plateau from the high desert to the north. Snow dusted the highest peaks like a dip in coarse salt.

Heavy footsteps sounded behind me, followed by a voice full of delight. "Darren! I knew you had come back, but I hadn't expected you to visit so quickly!"

I turned to Appel-Ball. He wrapped me in his burly arms and kissed my cheeks. "I didn't know I would have to," I said.

His jocular front faded. "Come to my office."

Appel-Ball's office occupied the southwest corner of the floor. From paintings hanging on the interior walls, English toffs from a bygone age judged us with their stares. The top of his wide, broad desk could sleep three and, knowing him, quite likely had.

I remembered Clio's warning about USG's eyes and ears. The windows lacked rattlers. I sat facing his desk. My chair's leather squeaked and the nailhead trim was cool under my fingertips.

"You've come up in the world, High Arbiter."

His solemn moment in the lobby had disappeared. "As have you, old friend. A *daoshi* of the third rank? Almost high enough not to be sent interstellar on a pointless venture."

"I had the bad luck to have Elard on my resume."

"This planet is a curse upon us all." A drawer of his desk slid open and a telescoping arm extended a tray bearing two glasses and a bottle of Scotch. He affected an accent, badly. "A wee nip?"

I nodded. The cork thwoomed from the bottle. I sipped peaty amber liquid and said, "Curse or not, while I'm here, I will do Calgary some good. Our man Scobee tells me USG security forbids him access to some of our remote sites. You know that's a violation of ALECS protocols."

He shrugged. "What does that matter? You have some empty buildings in a desert no natives ever cross. There's no need to visit them. What, you think some native might stumble on them and happen to be literate enough in English to read the *Meditations* of Marcus Aurelius, the *Tao te Ching*, or those other titles—" He squinted, swatted the air with thick fingers. "—*Self-Therapy, The Trading Tribe*?"

I gave him a level look. "I have to make sure our remote sites are scrubbed, or we'll be in violation of ALECS protocols. We won't stoop to USG's level."

With a wry grin, he shook his head. "The West keeps getting in your way," he told me, for the hundredth time. He referred to all the archaic notions—the rule of law, respect for contract and custom, fair play, the rise and fall of individuals on merit rather than family connections or disparate impact regulations—that had propelled the human race a few thousand light years from Earth, then run out of fuel.

"You've become USG's tool, I see."

Ever the actor, he mugged a hurt look. "I still am the supreme human authority on this planet. But let us look at reality. I will strike ALECS' colors in a month. What would I gain by ruffling USG's feathers? Were I to tell them, 'you must abide by the rules,' they would just say, 'what is permitted to the gods is forbidden to oxen.' Not as eloquently, of course. Regardless, were I to repeat my demand, their agents would meet privately with the ALECS Executive Committee back on Earth, and I would be punished with an assignment even more inglorious than Elard."

"I understand the USG offices here are run by a newer arrival, named Vainqueur?"

"Don't bother." Appel-Ball gulped whisky.

"USG can't blow me off too much. If their agents try to meet privately with Calgary, the *daoshis* of the fourth rank would ignore them in retaliation."

Another wry head shake. "You are ever so naive. USG is strong and growing stronger, not just here and on other ALECS planets, but on Earth as well. You must know that better than I. They could make life difficult for The Way in the West by a thousand cuts."

Appel-Ball had it right. Parts of my subconscious shifted. "A shame Nesbitt died."

"You think were he still prominent with USG, he would pull strings to ensure his security personnel would give you passage?" His face softened. "Perhaps you are right. You two were part of a close circle, with Juliette and Purcell."

He stared at his Scotch for a time. Formerly he spoke frankly when in his cups, and rare is the man who grows out of that habit with age.

"What did you hear?" he asked. "About his death?"

"An accident, out in the wilds."

Appel-Ball sniffed out a breath. "Suicide."

I lifted my glass and held it front of my mouth. Nesbitt had been capable of many things, but suicide? "Why would he kill himself?"

"Because he could no longer take Juliette's ailment."

I frowned. Ailment? Any disease of the body could be treated. Likewise, any disease of the brain.

But a disease of the spirit… "What ailment?"

"She is a nymphomaniac."

My voice worked while the rest of me sat stunned. "The clinical term is 'sex addict.'" I took a swallow of Scotch. The whisky glowed down my throat. "You're serious."

"I had it from Baldassare. The official psychiatrist, recall him from our annual checkups?"

"Vaguely."

"He returned to Earth about ten years back. The night before he left, as the afterparty ran down, I pinned him in a corner and plied him with more drink. He was loose with many a person's secret, but hers was the only one that lodged in my mind. Juliette had all manner of affairs, and though she told him Nesbitt had no idea, Baldassare sensed from Nesbitt's checkups that he knew. Those hard edges, those steely eyes, Nesbitt repressed many emotions. Would you agree?"

What did Appel-Ball know about her affair with me? I blinked a few times. "I can't speculate."

"Her affairs dated back to your time on the planet. With hindsight, Baldassare realized Purcell had probably been one of her lovers. You did not notice?"

"No."

He leaned back, squinted. "I always assumed you were her emotional tampon. Someone she could use to satisfy her need to talk about her feelings, without caring about yours."

"'Dickless friend' would be pithier."

Appel-Ball spread wide his hands. "I've offended you. My pardons. We were all much younger and knew fewer of the ways of the world. I can tell you have grown as a man. When you meet her this visit, you will be free of the foolish hope she will open her heart and legs to you."

I angled my head in conciliation. "You were right about my relationship with her then. And what it would be if I met her now."

"But she never spoke of…?"

"The men she cheated on Nesbitt with? No. What woman in that situation would? Her words would stir up her male friend's jealousy. Either he would break off their friendship and take away her emotional tampon, or she would give him sexual sops out of guilt." Juliette, of course, had done the latter. Realizing that a few months after I left Elard had been one of the clearest moments of my life.

"You have indeed grown as a man." He raised his glass to me.

After I finished my Scotch, I rode back toward my flat. I could spend the rest of the long afternoon reviewing files from Scobee, and from the Unneeded Hypothesis, while Elar crawled toward the horizon. An early night, a fresh start in the morning—

A new message alert chimed in my ear. I subvoked, "Play."

Her voice, like old honey: sweet as ever, but gritted by time.

"Darren. Just the sound of your name takes me back to our younger days. You must meet me for dinner and catching up. The old café, twenty-five o'clock. The name has changed, but you recall the address. I'll get the table in the—in our—corner. Till then."

In my subconscious, my younger self jumped up at her command and ran to the old café. He thrashed within me while I sat immobile. The jitney continued down the scorched street. My younger self gave a confused, plaintive note and then sank back.

Presumptuous. Demanding. Flattering when it served her purpose. Juliette hadn't changed. But as Appel-Ball had put it, now I knew more of the ways of the world. She could wait in the café till closing, craning her long neck at each clang of the entry bell, while she found for herself what powerlessness felt like.

A wisdom from the Way passed through my awareness. If I avoided her to show I finally held some power over her, she still held power over me.

My thoughts ran more clearly. Her organization, the Universal Church of Christ, had long been in partnership with the United Sodalities. She might be on good enough terms with her late husband's friends at USG to give Scobee's field teams the clearance they needed to scrub our remote sites.

And me clearance to find Purcell's remains.

I subvoked a reply message. "Till then."

After styling my hair and changing into slacks and a blazer, a few minutes before twenty-five, my jitney rolled along Gregory Dialogus. Elar lay two hours under the horizon. The lights of shops spilled out of transparent windows and pooled at the feet of strolling pedestrians. Jackets shielded the pedestrians against the cloudless desert night and the dregs of sea breeze that struggled up to the plateau. By day, I could have pretended the settlement kept its old crowds, and everyone lurked indoors until sunset. Not now. *Closed, please come again* slid and jumped around the opaque windows of half the shops. Most pedestrians had USG or UCC logos on their jacket sleeves. The transparent windows of restaurants and social clubs revealed unused tables and empty dance floors. Serving robots crouched at the doors like patient dogs.

My jitney took the parking spot immediately in front of the café. I climbed out and the artificial lights and the chill dry air dredged the sounds of talk, laughter, clanking plates, clinking glasses from the murk of memory. The structure remained unchanged, save for a scarred area of newer bone, roughly eighty centimeters wide by a meter twenty tall, to the right of the recessed doorway. In the past, the scarred area had held Greek letters in blue glass, forming an old poem, *The God Abandons Antony*. Now, float-mounted over the door, lighting strips formed Japanese characters in an icon of a wooden box.

The interior had been redone also, in red leather chairs and black lacquered tables. Near the door, three tables of USG and UCC personnel glanced up, eyes flat. A pale walking stick of a man came forward and bowed. "*Daoshi* Lee." His English had a Continental accent, and he comported himself in a manner more Japanese than a Japanese. We live in an age when the best sushi chefs are Dutch. "She arrived a few minutes ago. She said you would be able to guide yourself."

My mouth grew dry as I rounded the broad spur of bone shielding our usual corner from the USG and UCC personnel.

"Darren!" she said from an end of a bench, near a corner of the table.

One of the old writers had said, at fifty, a person has the face they deserve, and so much more true now. Age no longer leaves a mark. Only our social masks, and the emotions innervating our faces despite our wills, sculpt our expressions. Juliette remained beautiful, with brown hair now curling past her shoulders. But the decades had shaken her assurance. Something haunted her eyes. Perhaps Nesbitt's death—

—you finally feel guilt for all the men you toyed with?

I reseated my social mask. "A delight to see you." I leaned toward her and kissed her cheeks. Benches ringed the table on all sides. I'd always sat in a padded armchair to the right of where she sat now. My mind started down the trail of habit, but I resisted. I went to her left, on another bench, with a corner of the table between us.

She glanced down at the ebony point of the table corner, said nothing.

"I just heard about Nesbitt," I said. "My condolences."

"Thank you."

Drink orders. She took sake. The only draft beer was a lager from Park Slope. "Don't answer unless you want to, but how did it happen?"

She winced. "A cultural misunderstanding. He went out with a team of USG personnel and some natives representing the Indigenous Autonomous Council, to oversee humanitarian work at a distant village not yet fully acceded into the IAC. The bulls still trampled other bulls' offspring, other backward cultural practices like that. He said something wrong to a villager. No one around even heard what. But the villager took it wrong and fractured his skull before the other team members could intervene."

I studied her. She shrank away at first, but soon opened up, giving me a straighter look at her face and neck.

"You don't know what Appel-Ball says about it?"

"That old lecher? Of course you spoke to him, one has to call on the High Arbiter, that's the protocol. I always have admired your respect for protocol. Was he sad the sacred prostitutes of Ishtar shipped out two weeks back?"

I plowed through her chaff. "He says Nesbitt killed himself."

After a moment, she rolled her eyes. "You know you can't take everything he says at face value. Sometimes he puts the laser on the center of the target, other times he ablates a chunk of wall downrange. Nesbitt's death was the first sapient native attack in decades. It was an accident and we treated it as one."

"So Appel-Ball was wrong."

"Utterly. Nesbitt died in a good cause. Hard to believe it's been five years." Her hand crept across the table toward me.

I pulled my hand back, lifted my beer glass. "Did Nesbitt ever know about Purcell? Or me?"

Her shoulders stiffened. "Let's not talk about that."

"No? I left the planet because you let slip Nesbitt had hunted down Purcell out of jealousy and he'd do the same to me if her ever found out about my affair with you." I air-quoted. "'Let slip.' With Purcell gone missing, you were no longer torn between two lovers. You didn't need to unburden yourself to me anymore. With the choice between your husband and me, you chose your husband, and got rid of me by claiming to love me so much you wanted to see me safe on Earth."

My cramped apartment. Her plaintive look. *It's too dangerous for you to stay. I couldn't live with myself if you got hurt.* The memories ached, and the pain on her face failed to dull them. But the feelings pushed up by the memories washed away as part of me heard what I'd said. Why shouldn't she choose her husband? Why shouldn't she get her last surviving lover to depart? Before she'd lied to me in my cramped apartment, she'd known I would do as she told. If she'd spoken the truth, I would have stayed, and the three of us would have formed an unstable triangle that would eventually have shattered into fragments.

Juliette studied my face, then gathered herself with a breath. "You never spoke so harshly to me, before. I deserve it. I'm sorry. I should never have lied to you. After Purcell disappeared, my guilt about cheating on Nesbitt made me imagine he had killed him. I reached bottom. A moment of clarity—"

"We should never have been lovers." I softened my tone. "We were friends before that. Let's reconnect on those terms, if we can."

"Let's."

Dinner arrived in wooden boxes, styled like the icon above the front door. Inside, sliced bricks and logs of sushi rice encased tuna-flavored strips of uncooked protein and omega-3 fats. Fabricated in the settlement's nanoassembler within a few hours. d-chiral amino acids made up the native animals of the Elardian sea. They would taste rubbery and inflict diarrhea if eaten by terrestrial life.

I talked about my postings over the decades. Earth, Prawub, Olnosc. In the latter, as The Way in the West's director of local operations, I'd commissioned linguists to translate our recommended texts into three native languages. Then a promotion—

"So *daoshi* of the third rank is higher than it sounds." Juliette glanced at my left hand. "Are you—were you—married?"

"No. When lifespans are indefinite, there's always time later." I remembered my first stint back on Earth, late nights in the bars along the Calgary riverfront. My pose, aloofness masking a tortured Byronic soul. More women than I now cared to count had deluded themselves into bed with me. More times than I now cared to count, I'd exulted that seducing them punished their sex for having Juliette as a member.

From reading her face, I felt certain she sensed my thoughts.

She looked over my shoulder. Male banter came from behind me. Two USG men, one speaking in a tipsy, mentoring tone. "Remember, we don't want the natives to keep higher fidelity to their customs. We don't want them to keep lower fidelity to their customs. We want them to keep *United Sodalities* fidelity to their customs."

Once they left earshot, I said, "Nice friends you have."

Propped up by her elbow, her hand unfurled like a blooming flower. "What's wrong with USG?"

"What's wrong?" I scowled at her. "As a member of their sister organization, you might not see it. They encroach on the rest of us every chance they get. Today they scrutinized me at the spaceport and on my way into town, in violation of ALECS protocols. Worse, they've denied Scobee access to some of our old field sites—"

"They have? Where?"

"Half a dozen places off to the north."

"That explains it." She paused while the two men walked past us back toward their table. "USG and UCC have ongoing missionary work among the native tribes along the coast where the sea curves around to the north. The Indigenous Autonomous Council wants to minimize the risk of further missionary work by disapproved spiritual communities. No offense."

"I'd take none, if the natives actually chose that and their human allies simply relayed the message. Yet how are the rest of us to know?"

Juliette angled her head and lifted her chin, exposing more of her neck. "If they scrutinize you so much, should you be talking about such things?" Her voice sounded playful, but for a moment, her tone did not match a tightening of the fine muscles around her eyes.

I drew in a breath and held my mouth open to imbue my next words with a meaning some electronic eavesdropper would not pick up. "It's been a long day of travel and meetings, and my frustration with the denied access to our field sites is spilling out. Of course USG earned approval from a quorum of native polities. Of course the natives want the rest of us gone. I feel frustrated because we're trying to do that. If the natives want a full cultural decontamination, we have to go out to our old sites, pry up the metaphorical floorboards, and if we find any of our recommended texts we left behind, toss them in the nanoassemblery's recycling bin."

"I understand your frustration."

Another glass of beer arrived. I hadn't noticed my first one disappear. Time to slow down. "That's all you can do?"

"What do you mean?"

I quirked an eyebrow. "You've been on Elard longer than anyone else, except possibly Appel-Ball. Your organization is the only one staying here with USG after the rest of us head back to Earth. I suspect your rank is higher than you're letting on."

She leaned back and hugged herself across her upper abdomen. "You want me to push USG to give you access to those field sites."

"Friends do one another favors. We are friends, right?"

"Are we? Do friends ask friends to push against the new order of the world?"

I mimicked her earlier tone. "If they order your world so much, should you be talking of such things?"

She fixed me a look I'd never before seen her give me. Notes of admiration, respect, even a little fear, all leaking out from her brown eyes. I gazed back, unblinking, until she spoke.

"It will take a few days. Be patient. I'll contact you."

I expected the next few days to drag by, and at first they did. Every morning promptly at ten o'clock, Scobee briefed me on the previous day's results and the new day's plans. He anticipated my questions about the day's plans and always reported completion of the work of the previous. His right eye drooped more and the bags under his eyes grew thicker and more purple. When I left my large, nearly empty guest office at twenty o'clock, he might hold his head low over data on his desk, or his voice on a call to some subordinate might spill impatience out his door.

From the polarized southerly windows of my guest office, Elard crawled up and down the sky. I could do nothing to help The Way in the West shut down its operations. Perhaps I could help the Unneeded Hypothesis find answers about Purcell's disappearance.

I reviewed the files given to me in Prague, for the dozenth time. In the last months before his disappearance, Purcell reported multiple field trips to native villages near the north coast. As it happened, not far from the sites USG kept us from visiting. Purcell's final flight plan repeated a journey to a village he knew, but for some reason, he veered off course near some badlands about two hundred kilometers to the northwest of our settlement. Traffic control lost sight of him a few minutes later. Rescue teams soon found his empty airmobile, then traversed hundreds of square kilometers of jumbled terrain for three weeks, until simulations indicated he would have run out of water and food.

Trained rescuers hadn't found him, and my odds were even worse than theirs. I checked and double-checked the files, looking for something to track him from the abandoned airmobile. On my own, I found nothing.

Scobee inadvertently gave me the answer I needed. In his office one morning, my gaze ran down the day's to-do list, overlaid by our augmented reality contact lenses on our views of the wall near his door. "This is a lot."

"We'll get it done." He sounded tired. "Just like we got a lot done yesterday, and the day before."

My gaze stopped at an entry. *Review physical effects at ALECS lost & found.* I pointed at the task. "I'll take this one. Your team saves a person-day looking through boxes in a warehouse, and I don't sit in an office playing solitaire."

Scobee grunted. "Knock yourself out."

ALECS Unclaimed Property occupied a warehouse on the east side of the settlement. Near the front corner of the building, a single door faced a shaded parking lot. An awning stretched from the building to poles on the far side. I climbed out of my jitney. The mid-morning air baked me and the awning's fabric rippled in a faint breeze.

Inside, my eyes adjusted to a dim, shabby room. Years of use had scuffed the gypsum board walling the room off from the bulk of the warehouse. The leatherette of chair-arms in the waiting area had cracked, and a strip of unglued veneer dangled outward from the edge of a table.

In the far corner, a chair creaked. A throat cleared. "May I help you?" A male voice, labored with breaths.

"I'm Darren Lee, with The Way in the West. I'm here on behalf of our operations-suspension team, to review any physical effects of ours you might have in custody."

The man stayed in his chair. He looked as if his body had molded itself around it. "Have a seat, *Daoshi* Lee, and I'll see what we have of yours." He subvoked a few commands, then shut his eyes. "You just come out from Earth?"

"I did."

"I'm Olivenberg. Is there something important of yours in the warehouse?"

"Important?"

"Your bosses sent you here from Earth to look at unclaimed property?"

I chuckled, then shook my head in the manner of exasperated employees. "I'd be astonished if there's anything of interest to anyone in your warehouse, but you tell that to my headquarters."

"They want to keep their laundry lists out of USG's hands. Can't blame them. USG thinks a fingerprint from a blank chip could be an exploit." He shut his eyes again. "You've got six boxes."

"How are they labeled?"

"Organization, last known individual's name, location where found, date logged in. They'll be filed under W. If you still can't find them, message me."

"I can't just wave for the cameras?"

"We don't have any inside the warehouse."

I raised an eyebrow. "*You* don't."

"The changeover hasn't happened yet."

I nodded. "Will you stay on?"

"And work for USG? I'm heading back to Earth. Twenty years was long enough. Time to claim the matter and energy minimum while I figure out what to do next."

Sounded like he already claimed a minimum lifestyle. But like any bureaucrat, he succored himself with self-delusions of his job's importance. "Thanks for all you've done. You're a credit to ALECS."

He shrugged and gestured over his shoulder at a door into the warehouse. "I leave at twenty o'clock. Be back here five minutes before."

My footsteps echoed through the warehouse. Huge lighting strips wandered across the ceiling. At the warehouse's far end, daylight, dust, and heat leaked around the roll-up door of a loading dock. A breeze rattled the door against its track. Shelves bolted to the floor held plastic boxes, and larger crates stood on racks mounted to the straight, lower reaches of the walls. The space smelled of aged plastic, and d-handed native biomolecules borne in by the wind.

A set of long tables, beige tops on flimsy-looking, but sturdy, carbon nanotube legs, filled a central clearing. I nudged a chair with my foot to claim a table, then set off for shelves labeled *W-Z*.

A robotic cart whispered to a stop near me as I found the first of our boxes. "Would you like some assistance, sir?"

I yanked the box out and held it against my hip. Clio's admonitions trumped my middling confidence in Olivenberg's words. "I'll walk with it. And a few others. Every little way to maintain muscle mass helps," I added, for the sake of any USG security personnel who might be listening through it.

"As you wish, sir. If you change your mind, I'll be at the recharging station in the southeast corner." It rolled away.

I carried the box to the table, then went after the next. I repeated the process for the remaining three boxes. The five formed a pyramid on the table.

Five? Olivenberg's database lookup had returned six.

I returned to the shelf. Not there. Not behind a solitary box owned by Zoroastrian Revival. Where, then, was the sixth box for Way in the West, The?

The question gave me its own answer. I checked the signs on the ends of each shelving unit, looking for *T*, then found it. My path took me past *U*. I slowed my steps and glanced at the shelves for *Unneeded Hypothesis, The*. None there.

I took my next steps even faster than before.

A box stood on a lower shelf. I knelt and pulled it toward me. *The Way in the West*, its label read. Behind it stood another box. The only sides I could see were blank. I tugged and turned it.

Organization: The Unneeded Hypothesis

Last known owner: Purcell, Ward

My heart thudded. I pulled the box out and stacked it on the other one. I grasped the long sides of the lower box to keep Purcell's name hidden against my chest, then carried them both to my table.

After setting them down, and rearranging them to hide Purcell's name, I returned my mind to my official task. Yet all morning, while I sifted through the forgotten belongings of my fellow *daoshis* and acolytes, my mind wandered to Purcell's box. At the old café, he often sat back with an archaic sketchbook, its pressboard cover flipped onto his knee, and scratched a pencil over nanoassembled paper, with occasional pauses to say something caustic to the rest of us.

Finally, after I filled a recycling bag with unwashed coffee cups, cracked flying discs, a bag of sand accompanying a desktop zen garden, and other leftovers of my distant colleagues' lives, and collected our few data chips for secure destruction at our offices, I opened Purcell's box. Stacks of sketchbooks greeted me.

I'd only ever glimpsed his drawings at steep angles, in passing. Seeing them straight-on, with time to study them, amazed me. Lines and shadings of graphite did more than represent us as we had been. They revealed aspects of us I had never before so clearly noticed. A manipulative streak tightening the skin between Juliette's eyebrows and upper lid. Nesbitt's flat look of loaded, cocked criticism needing only a squeeze of the trigger to fire. My callowness slackening my cheeks. I had not seen that look since the shaving mirror in my old, tiny quarters. If I'd even seen it then.

I flipped through more sketchbooks. Each drawing showed in the lower right corner a date and a location, in block letters whose strokes never quite touched, as well as a scrawl of his surname. Each sketchbook as a whole focused on a single topic. The three of us in the old café—Juliette, nude under rumpled sheets in Purcell's apartment—

from field work, closeups of natives showing emotions I could not read.

In the latter, he came to focus on one individual. A bull, with a scar down one of its cooling crests and a thousand-yard stare in its hawed eyes. After a dozen pages of this bull came the torn stub of a page ripped out.

Sketchbook after sketchbook, page after page, I flipped. The specificity of each sketchbook to a topic meant often the latter pages showed only creamy white, virginal and dead. I flipped anyway, in case he had some secret purpose. While going through blank pages in a sketchbook of buildings around the settlement, the last date about eight months before his disappearance, my fingertip found an edge folded over by a couple of millimeters.

The next page had nothing to do with ALECS architecture. It showed a map. The settlement, the slender curving sea, the mountain ranges and types of desert stretching from our location a thousand kilometers to the north. The margins held cryptic notes—"the red canyon," "the bull leaning on the cow," others even more obscure. Squares with curt abbreviations depicted Unneeded Hypothesis field sites, I surmised.

Circles dotted the map, scores of kilometers from any other habitation, human or native. Around the circles, latitude and longitude coordinates. Xs marked some of the circles, with dates overlapping that of this book's last sketch. The latest X's date was two weeks before his disappearance. The circles and Xs bore no pattern that I could see.

I recalled the files Purcell's colleagues had given me, and matched their maps to this one. Purcell's final flight had landed about eight kilometers from an unmarked circle.

I hid the sketchbook under the packet of data chips to be securely destroyed back at local operations. Most of the boxes, now empty, I broke down and tossed into the recycling bag. The two sorted by *The* I took back to their shelf of origin.

I knew where to go. If I could leave the settlement.

The possibility of being trapped in the settlement soured my mood for the rest of the day. I went to the fitness club and tried to fight off the mood by attacking a kettlebell routine, more sets of more reps than usual of swings and get-ups. Sweat left a salty rime under the arms and on the lower back of my wicking shirt. Heart knocking, I kept going, twenty-four kilos, another fifty swings—

"Darren?"

I managed to safely settle the kettlebell on the mat between my feet. "Juliette, what's?" I toweled sweat off my face and caught my breath.

"Pilates class." She dressed the part, black spandex clinging to her legs and torso, hair pulled back to cast her cheekbones in sharper relief. Her gaze slid over my upper arms and chest. "I was going to call from my jitney, but when your software assistant showed you were here, I decided to tell you in person. I explained your situation to Vainqueur and he cleared your people to revisit your last four abandoned sites."

"Thanks." I had more breath now. "I'd offer to do you a favor in return, but we both know there's nothing I can do for you."

She drew a breath. "Don't be so sure."

I peered at her. Did she still have some hope of rekindling our long-gone tryst? I gave an exaggerated look down and to the right, to let her know I checked the time in the corner of my augmented reality display. "Don't miss your class on my account."

"Okay. One last thing. Would you have time to meet again before you leave?"

"Probably. Just one condition: no sushi." I nodded to her, then reached for the kettlebell.

I went out the day after with our first field team, to the surprise of its leader, a narrow-chinned man named Kapodistrias. As our van waited at the entry gate for the airfield, Kapodistrias asked me questions about how the team should work and nodded at my responses. Once we were airborne, he gave the team instructions he had already planned. I spent the next hour staring out a window at the jumbles of sand and rock, dune and scarp, defining the high desert north of the settlement.

What had Purcell looked for out here?

Had Juliette's long-ago hint, that Nesbitt had killed Purcell, been true? Out of jealousy? Or did it relate to something else?

We landed. Before Kapodistrias raised the airmobile's rear hatch, we donned and double-checked our polarized face shields, air-conditioned cloaks, water packs, drinking tubes, and sunblock lotion on the backs of our hands. Over the protests of some acolytes, I slung a portable air conditioner over my shoulder as the hatch lifted.

Outside, the day seemed brighter, hotter, dryer than it ever did in the ALECS settlement. The exhaust fans mounted on the others' backs poured out streams of broiling air. We walked in line, not column, to the old site.

Up a slope, three structures hunkered, half-burrowed into the rocky soil. Double layers of thick plastic covered each structure's windows and doors. A reprogrammable sign still held our logo and the name of the station, but the pigment molecules, long fixed in position, had faded in decades of sunlight. Beyond the station, the granite peaks of the last mountain range before the sea jutted into the pallid blue sky.

Team members parted the double layer of plastic covering the main building. Radio chatter called for the portable air conditioner and I hustled up. They opened the building's front door before I got there. Slightly cooler air, thick and stale, slithered under my face shield. One person aimed the air conditioner down an interior hallway, while another routed its vent out the part in the plastic, and a third sprayed temporary solar cells on the building's roof. Soon the inside had cooled enough for us to turn off the cooling function of our cloaks.

The main building held offices and a store'n'cook kitchen on one side of the interior hallway, and a meeting space on the other. Same layout as other field sites, where I'd led spiritual retreats with The Way in the West personnel and a few natives, bachelor bulls all. The chairs and couches in the meeting space formed a circle, as if the site had been abandoned in the middle of a retreat. Team members surveyed the room, looking for forgotten data, especially any eye-readable text. My interface projected deepening shades of green over my view of the meeting space as the probability forgotten data eluded us dropped toward zero.

The smaller buildings, accessible through shaded tunnels lit by thin, near-opaque windows near the ceilings, held sleeping and recreation quarters. The air conditioner could not reach so far, but Kapodistrias had ordered the team to keep their cooling units turned off. Sweat stung my eyes and ran down my neck as the team searched. The departed personnel had been sloppy. Data chips with broken cases lay forgotten under unmade beds.

"Remember," Kapodistrias announced over the team's radio net, "if it looks like it might be proprietary, bag it for local ops and—brambles in the path."

I shared a puzzled look with the other team members in the room.

Kapodistrias spoke, more urgently. "*Daoshi* Lee, please join me at the front entrance. Quickly, if you please."

I found him just outside the front door. The roar of the air conditioner's exhaust fan echoed off the plastic. Outside, partially clouded by the plastic, a trio of airmobiles had landed near ours, and armed humans in desert camouflage waited in line.

"I thought you'd cleared us, *Daoshi*."

"You're not the only one. Let's greet our guests." I turned on the cooling unit in my cloak, spread my fingers wide, and went out the parting in the plastic, palms-first.

Once clear of the plastic, I spread my arms wide, like Jesus—no, that was not a name to conjure USG with. Certainly USG had its martyrs, but I did not know their names. I took three steps, squinting despite my face shield. Kapodistrias' footsteps crunched the rocky soil behind me.

"Stop there," boomed an amplified voice from the figure in the center of the line. "Identify yourselves."

"Darren Lee, *daoshi* of the third rank, of The Way in the West. I have a dozen colleagues with me, ten inside, two staying with our airmobile."

"What are you doing here?"

"Complying with ALECS protocols by eliminating ideological or spiritual data from our facilities, prior to withdrawal from Elard. We're unarmed. I'm going to lower my hands now."

Behind my shoulder, Kapodistrias muttered, "*Daoshi*—"

I dropped my hands to my sides. The USG security personnel shifted their weight and glanced toward their spokesman. For a moment, confusion showed across his shoulders. Finally, he set his hands on his hips and jutted his chest toward us. "As a gesture of goodwill, we'll take your word for it, for now."

Security personnel? Was not my spiritual community dedicated to seeing the universe as it was?

I stared at a line of soldiers.

Their spokesman—squad leader, I corrected myself—said, "Are you aware the Indigenous Autonomous Council has decreed this region is to be free of unauthorized human activity?"

"So I've heard. Are you aware we have to scrub any record of our beliefs from all our sites?"

The squad leader shrugged. "How you put a round peg in a square hole is not my problem."

"Vainqueur granted us permission. I mean, the IAC granted us permission, and Vainqueur relayed that news to us."

A wave of agitated body language rippled through the line of soldiers. The squad leader swayed away from me and shifted a foot backward to plant his weight. "Vainqueur."

"Yes. Did I mispronounce his name?"

"Relayed that news to you."

"Not directly, but I have his authorization from someone who has his… ear."

The squad leader stepped forward. "Be that as it may, Mr. Lee, at first glance, you and your subordinates are in violation of an IAC decree. You and your subordinates are hereby directed to return to your airmobile, pending investigation of your claim. If you truly have IAC permission, you'll be allowed to resume decommissioning this site. If not, we'll escort you back to the settlement, and any of you found leaving the perimeter again will be locked in the brig until the last ship lifts off."

Kapodistrias grunted.

"Throw away the bitter cucumber," I told him, "and get the team back in the airmobile." To the USG soldiers, I said, "We'll wait in our vehicle."

Sealed up in the airmobile, many of my team members grumbled about the delay. One young man, red-haired and ruddy-cheeked, even asked me, "Do we really have clearance? Or do you think you can waltz in from Earth and bluff those thugs?"

The conversations around us froze.

"I don't," I said. "We do." I stared at the redhead until he blinked and turned away.

Time passed, until an armored glove rapped on the rear hatch. Our cooling units roared to life as Kapodistrias opened up.

The squad leader stood with hands on hips, and a glum set to his shoulders. He craned his neck and searched through the crowd for me. "Your authorization is confirmed, *Daoshi* Lee. My apologies for the delay. If my team can assist you, here or at another site—"

"We welcome your offer, but there's no need. Good day."

The squad leader trudged away while my team lifted its equipment to return to the site. I reached for the portable air conditioner, but the redhead lunged past me, then hoisted the unit to his shoulder. We returned to the site in high spirits, which remained with us as we finished our work. Twilight darkened the sky as we flew back to the settlement. I pulled a flask from my pack and handed it around.

When we landed, I boarded the same van as Kapodistrias, and took a seat next to him. "You should have no problems on your future missions. You won't need me to accompany you. But I reserve the right to fly out on my own and snap inspect your team."

The next morning, after meeting with Scobee, I went to my office. A few minutes to write a brief report on the previous day's actions, then hours to spend studying Purcell's map—

"*Daoshi* Lee," said the building, "you have a guest in the lobby."

"A guest?"

The building sent a camera image to my contact lenses. Juliette, her eyebrows crinkled, mouth tight.

"What does she want?"

"She would not tell me," the building said.

I closed Purcell's sketchbook, slid it in a drawer. "Let her in."

"I will relay your authorization to Clio. Scobee has ordered that she accompany any guests at all times in the building."

"Sounds like I'll see them both." I locked the drawer with my thumbprint and waited for them to come.

Clio's accent heralded her approach. "...We're truly honored *Daoshi* Lee came out from Earth to help us decommission our facilities. I've learned a lot from him."

Juliette paused a moment. "I'm sure you have."

They halted in the doorway. Clio knocked. "*Daoshi*? Is now a good time?"

"As good as any. Come in." From my seat, I waved across the desk, at two chairs. "Sit, please."

Juliette paused halfway between standing and sitting. She lifted an eyebrow at Clio. "My business is with *Daoshi* Lee."

"Since I'm his assistant, I ought to sit in."

Seated, Juliette said, "My conversation with your boss is private."

I cleared my throat. "Clio is the soul of discretion."

Juliette turned to me a cautious gaze. "You can tell her to take ten minutes."

"I can. But I won't. What brings you by, in person?"

She crossed her legs and enmeshed her fingers into a double fist of prayer on her lap. "I heard about your difficulty yesterday with a USG security flunky. I want to apologize."

"Apologize? We suffered a two-hour delay. An inconvenience, nothing more."

"You shouldn't have had to suffer even that." She pressed her lips together before speaking her next words. "I spoke to Vainqueur and he promised you would be cleared to visit your old sites."

"You did all I asked of you. On top of that, he honored your promise. I seek no apology." I narrowed my eyes. "You expected him to tell everyone in USG security to stay out of our way? That's a high expectation to pile on yourself."

Juliette stretched her neck. "I rank highly in UCC's local operations. My requests to USG are always honored to the full."

She remained lovely, despite having a vulnerability to her now that I had not seen in our past. I shoved the thought away. "Clearly not *always*," I told her. "Yesterday, Vainqueur didn't tell everyone about his approval of our trip. Maybe he didn't see the need to honor your request to the full by relaying it to all his subordinates. Or perhaps he did, but his subordinates dithered about informing all of their underlings. Or, simply, it's a bureaucracy, and the left-hand official doesn't know what the right-hand one is doing."

"None of those are acceptable excuses—"

"What bothers you about this? You thought you had more influence over USG's local operations? You don't. You did once? We've all gotten older, and the worlds have changed out from under us. Thank you again for putting in a word with Vainqueur, and my team and I are walking around the settlement today instead of cooling our heels in the brig, so your word to Vainqueur was enough. Is there anything more? I have the rest of my day's work to get to."

Her eyes widened before a social mask returned to her features. "You're busy. I understand." She glanced sidelong at Clio, then stiffened her shoulders to exclude the other woman from our conversation. "Maybe we can meet some evening. The sushi place?"

"I hated the ambiance."

"A café, a bar?"

Had I ever sounded so needy, asking her for trysts? *Now she knows how I felt* and the thought's pettiness shamed me. "I'll check my schedule. Take care."

Clio led Juliette from the room. Juliette, vulnerable and confused. None of us would have imagined it, during my first tour on Elard. She had known the rules of the world, and how to apply them to her benefit. But the rules had since changed, and her skill at applying them had ossified.

My petty thoughts returned. She was mortal, after all. Yet those petty thoughts brought with them sympathy. She was human, and capable of making a mutual connection. That capability had been beneath the Juliette of decades ago.

Even so, it didn't matter. I had a duty to The Way in the West that trumped any wish to try reconnecting with her.

The next few days I worked in the office, except for one snap inspection of the field team. One hour airborne each way, with no one to talk to but the autopilot. As expected, all was in order, but any USG spies watching me would now think nothing of me flying alone into the desert. Late each afternoon, I talked with Kapodistrias to find his plans for the next day, then hurried back to my office to match the flight path I would be expected to take on a "snap inspection" against the circle on Purcell's map nearest his point of disappearance.

The evening of the second day before our withdrawal, I found they were bound for their final site, two hundred kilometers past the site of Purcell's disappearance. I checked the time. A few minutes after twenty o'clock. On my way down the elevator to my jitney, I sent a message to Appel-Ball. "Do you have time to meet?"

He called as the jitney rolled toward my flat. My augmented reality engine projected his image onto my contact lenses so that he seemed to sit on the rear-facing seats across the jitney's cabin. "I'm not in the office."

"I guessed. I have an unofficial purpose. A few minutes over drinks. I wouldn't be keeping you from anything?"

"No. Other than your blonde Aussie-ette, almost all the ladies have gone. I'm at the Anfield, on Guru Nanak Boulevard, across and half a block down from ALECS headquarters."

I parked in a mostly empty multi-level garage shared by a number of shops. After a short walk through turbulence flung by fans taller than me, I entered the pub. Dim lights, cool air, walls decked with pennants of European soccer clubs. No sound but the antique audio-video displays chattering with British-accented play-by-play of a match played on Earth two months ago.

While the bartender drew for me a glass of stout, I asked, "You're staying?"

He had some flavor of British accent. "Them USG blokes need a place to raise a pint, yeah? Besides, they like football. I see their five-year-old kids on the covered field near the primary school, running through drills." He set my glass on the bar. Its head was as stiff as a crystallized cloud. "Your mates are at a back table. Can't miss them."

Deeper in the pub, Appel-Ball sat at the head of a table with three younger-looking ALECS men along the sides. Shouts of displeasure erupted from all four of them. The monitors replayed a shot glancing off the outside of a goalpost. "How could he miss that?" Appel-Ball said, then noticed me. He waggled a finger at me. "I don't want to hear that Marcus Aurelius bit from you."

"If I told it to you, I'd be asking, 'why were such things made in the world?'"

He frowned and bobbed his head from side to side, then shook his head with a wry smile. "You think too much, old friend. Sit, drink."

The first half ticked by. Appel-Ball and his colleagues cheered and booed the action while I sipped my beer. Soccer is like hockey, but slower, and with prima donnas.

When the referee's whistle announced halftime, I said, "I'll take those few minutes now." I aimed a hitchhiker's thumb at an interior corner, far from the windows.

His eyebrow flexed upward, but he pushed back his chair and went with me. He leaned his elbow on a high table. "What do you need, Darren?"

"Do you still run air traffic control? Or has USG already taken charge?"

"The crew is still all ALECS."

I mirrored his posture, elbow on table. "I'll be flying out tomorrow, around twelve or thirteen o'clock. Once I'm a hundred kilometers north, I want air traffic control to log me as following my flight plan."

"Where will you be going that the rest of us cannot know?"

"I want a few last hours alone on Elard. In the wilds, total solitude, just me and my thoughts."

"You could have that while following a flight plan."

I looked him straight in the eye. "I'd rather not."

He chuckled, a single exhalation broken into a series of sniffs. "You are a poor liar, Darren. Relax. It makes me no mind why you want this. And we are old friends, so I'm inclined to grant this. But since this matters so much to you, I would disserve ALECS if I gave it to you without getting something in return."

"I'm sure we can come to an arrangement."

He wetted his lips. "I will be on the same outbound ship as you and the blond Aussie-ette. Her name again?"

I stood tall and folded my arms over my chest. "I wouldn't pimp her out, even if I could, which I cannot."

He chuckled again. "Of course. If you haven't already pierced her defenses, you have your own plan to do so on the trip to Earth. You need only have told me."

"She's a fraction of my age. Yours too."

Appel-Ball shook his head. "You are a gentleman from a golden age, sent by accident into our age of brass. What then can you offer me?"

From the displays, the announcers recapped the first half's highlights.

"The last few weeks, I looked into how you came to be high arbiter. By default. No one wanted to come from Earth to be a caretaker of the inevitable handover to USG. So you received a promotion you would not have gotten anywhere else."

"If you're attempting to flatter me—"

"I'm telling you about the universe as it is."

"Rare is the man who wants to hear *that*."

I went on. "And you already know the truth of what I say."

"The man who wants such a thing dragged into daylight is rarer still. But go on."

"Returning to Earth means a demotion for you. Either an office job in ALECS headquarters or a minor role in an interstellar mission. Your best chance of a position more suitable for your present status is to cultivate an ally. Do this and I'll make sure The Way in the West puts its thumb on the scale for you in meetings of the ALECS personnel committee."

A display over his shoulder showed teams returning to the pitch. Appel-Ball scraped his fingers over his smooth cheeks. "What guarantees can you offer?"

"Beyond my reputation, and The Way in the West's? None, but what can you offer me?"

He chuckled again. "You have a deal. Before I return to the match, one thing. Would that thumb on the scale be denied me if I attempted to charm the blonde Aussie-ette on the flight to Earth?"

"She can make her own decisions." Especially if I soured her on Appel-Ball.

"Betimes your West shows you your way. You shall have what you ask."

"We'll remember your willingness to work with us. Enjoy the second half." I clapped my hand on his shoulder and left.

The next morning, I went to the airfield at ten-thirty. The USG security men at the settlement exit and the entrance to the airfield asked me my name and organization, then waved me through. Their impending triumph made them lazy.

At the operations hut, the clerk fed my interface the hangar location of my airmobile for the day. A sleek gray runabout. Years of desert travel had abraded the ALECS logo on its side. I palmed Clio's scanner and walked around the vehicle.

USG security had glued a tracker inside the cargo bin. Clio's scanner had a sharp enough edge for me to pry it off. I dropped it to the hangar floor and crunched it under my boot heel, then climbed in and took off.

Thirty minutes later, a thousand meters up, my airmobile slowly circled the coordinates of one of the circles on Purcell's map. The terrain rose and fell. Hills partially masked lower ground behind them. Salt pans glared at Elar. A few large boulders lay about.

Aha. What appeared to be one large boulder, when seen from a good angle, was really two. A pillar of rock had slumped down on a rounder one.

A bull leaning on a cow.

Just beyond them, a fold in the terrain turned out to be a narrow canyon. Its floor was red as dried human blood.

Two runs along the red canyon showed it to be banana-shaped, about eight hundred meters long and a hundred-fifty wide. A scarp formed its south face, and a steep but walkable slope, its north. The top of the north slope merged into rolling terrain climbing up to a line of hills about two kilometers away. No sign of human or native activity.

I told my airmobile to land in the canyon. The engines' roar echoed off the scarp. I touched down on the canyon floor, about three hundred meters from the rock formation and a hundred meters from the scarp. The engines cut out.

An irregular pattern of jagged holes showed along a section of the scarp wall. They could have passed as natural, save for several elongated holes reaching down to the depression floor. Most were the size of a standing human or native. One would allow an airmobile to enter, or two off-road jitneys abreast.

I donned my water bottle, cooling cloak, face shield. I subvoked to the cameras in my contact lenses and the microphones in my earbud to *record*, checked the time- and location-stamps were on, and went out.

The cooling fans in my cloak whirred at full speed as I set out into the hot midday air. Despite the insulation in my boot soles, I hopped from foot to foot across the red canyon floor. The shade along the foot of the scarp cooled my footing, but the cooling fans remained at full speed.

I went in the largest hole. My guess of jitneys seemed even more right. Through a layer of dust on the floor showed the white lines of empty parking spaces. I walked on.

Deeper in, large, empty rooms. Holes in floors and ceilings suggested bolts holding long-gone furniture. The dimensions of the bolt holes could have meant bunks, kitchens, dining halls, storerooms, tall upright racks like the ones holding cues in the poolhalls down by the downtown Calgary riverfront…. Dozens of sapients, and their equipment, could have dwelled here at a time.

Outside, I stood in the shade and looked around. High above, an airmobile flew to the north. I double-took and peered at it. Its line of flight continued on, seemingly oblivious to my airmobile parked on the red canyon floor.

I let out a breath. What I sought would be at ground level. There, on the depression's slanted north slope, a couple hundred meters away, was that…? I trudged through the heat. The cooling fan's whine became a roar.

I sucked water through a straw as I studied the item. A line of eight bone-white plugs, each as thick as my forearm, extended about ten centimeters above the ground. Decades of wear had rounded each plug's edge. I stooped for a closer look and a drop of sweat stung my eye.

From the center of each plug's top surface rose a few millimeters of metal showing the smooth cut of a laser saw.

Behind the line of plugs, a long, narrow mound of brown and tawny rocks, gravel, and pebbles ran parallel to the line of plugs. Too straight, and too different from the red rock of the canyon floor, to be natural. A firm touch on the mounded particles told me the mound had greater cohesion than a first glance would have guessed. Spray-on adhesive? My gloved fingers traced the smooth surface of the adhesive coating the outside of the mounded rocks—wait—

Something had spalled chunks the size of a baby's fist from large rocks, and torn pockets about the same size from regions of the mound formed from gravel and pebbles. The spalled and torn regions occurred in vertical lines, each line about as far from its neighbors as the plugs in the canyon floor were from each other.

From one damaged area in the mound, I drew a line in my mind's eye through the nearest plug, and extended it across the canyon floor. About a hundred meters away, another line of eight bone-white plugs jutted just above the ground. Nearby, an L-shape of more bone suggested the foundation of a building.

I did not know where Purcell's body lay, but I had a strong inkling why he had died.

From the mound, I hiked up the canyon's northern slope. Loose particles slid under my boots and skittered downslope. The northern rim of the canyon gave good views of both the dwelling dug out of the scarp and the line of plugs in front of the mound. Near the canyon rim sat a large boulder, roughly teardrop-shaped. Slivers of daylight showed under the boulder's sides, where shallow depressions looked scooped out by decades of wind.

I went around the boulder, then stopped. My breaths roared inside my face shield.

Behind the boulder, another shallow depression marred the ground. What stopped me were its contents.

Half-buried by wind-blown dirt, a corpse lay face up. I did not know for certain it was Purcell, but of *corpse* I lacked all doubt.

I knelt next to the dead man. My face grew clammy.

Purcell. His face shield had been pushed up, exposing his desiccated features. His lips had pulled back from a mouth locked in his dying agony. Narrow, shallow slits went through the flesh of his ears on both sides of the canals, and two more had opened his eyeballs to the elements. I looked for earbuds and the thin clear discs of augmented reality contact lenses, but failed to find them.

The front of his cloak hung loose, its seam sliced by a sharp knife. I flicked the fabric panels aside. His shirt had been shredded to reveal his thin chest, tufted with a few hairs over his breastbone. Thick flaps of skin had been cut open in the upper right and left of his chest, about five centimeters below each collarbone. I tightened my mouth and poked a finger under each flap. The processors and local storage for Purcell's augmented reality hardware had been cut out, and with them, any data stored in it after being copied from the cameras in his missing contact lenses.

What did you see? His killer had wanted to ensure, even in death, Purcell could not answer my question.

How had he died? The knife wounds looked too shallow to be fatal, and the front of his body lacked other signs of violence. I moved next to his torso and pushed up. With little effort, his dried-out body rolled onto its side.

A laser rifle fired from a shallow angle had struck the back of its head. The seared edges of a tear in his cooling cloak slumped over a killing wound the size of my hand. His occipital lobe had been vaporized in an instant. Gray powder drifted out of the wound and fear stirred deep in my subconscious. *That gray powder is his brain, is him—*

I sat in the dirt next to his corpse and took a deep breath. Purcell had ceased to exist when the laser sheared off the back of his head. He existed in my memory, no less now than he had the moment I'd heard of his disappearance decades prior. Whatever happened to this bundle of dry meat, shrunken skin, and desiccated brain could change nothing.

I pulled a DNA sampling kit from inside my cloak and scraped the collecting tip across his chest. I could identify him, but any greater victory was denied me. I knew what the red canyon had housed, but without the evidence lost with Purcell's missing subcutaneous data storage unit, I lacked any ability to prove it.

But Purcell had been killed! By human hands! Despite the USG's hegemony, that alone would be enough for an ALECS investigation committee to come back to Elard. I let the cameras in my contact lenses take in Purcell's mummified corpse. The tamper-proof time- and location-stamp would verify where and when I had seen this.

I sat for a moment, racking my memory for quotes from Marcus Aurelius or Laozi appropriate for commemorating a murder victim, then realizing my error. The world as it was had led him to violent death and a shallow grave, and led me to find him. The best I could do was set mantras aside and remember him, as he had been, and as he was.

Weighted down with solemnity, I stood, stretched my arms, turned my body, opened my eyes to look for Nesbitt's firing position—

Juliette stood a few meters away.

I looked to each side. If USG security wanted me dead or confined, it would have acted minutes ago. The desert terrain held only rocky soil and jumbled boulders. "Where are your friends?" I told her.

"I'm alone. USG doesn't know I'm here. Appel-Ball did me the same favor he did you."

I raised my eyebrow. "Clearly he didn't." A breeze stirred the loose sleeves of my desert cloak. "Why did you follow me?"

She stepped closer. Through the polarization of her face shield, her eyes implored. "Because I have to tell you something, before you leave tomorrow. I love you."

Anger washed like ice water down the inside of my chest. The wisdom of The Way chased it with pity, then calm. "You loved me so much you wanted me to leave for my safety. You thought better of an affair with me and sent me away to salvage your marriage. You're a nymphomaniac. Or nostalgia has you in its grip and I'm the only man from your younger days left here to ease it. I don't know what the true story is, and I do not care."

More steps brought her within a forearm's reach. She gripped my hand. My glove transmitted insistent warmth. "I'm so sorry I told you so many lies. I didn't know my own feelings for so many years. You were the man I should have chosen. Oh how I wish I'd known when you were still here—"

I pulled my hand from her grip. "You should have stuck with your first story. It was Nesbitt, wasn't it?"

"Nesbitt?"

I aimed my thumb over my shoulder. "Who killed Purcell."

Her eyes glistened. "You mean—?" Her lower lip curled.

"Take a look."

"Purcell's body. There. Killed." Her eyes looked glassy for a moment and I shifted my weight to catch her should she faint. She staggered back a step and leaned her hands on her knees. Her breaths rocked her torso. "How can you know he was killed?"

"A laser vaporized the back of his head. Take a look."

Juliette shut her eyes and breathed deeply. "I will," she said as she stood and sloughed out her breath. She went and crouched near Purcell's corpse.

I waited. After a time, she whispered a few words rendered indistinct by the rustle of our cloaks' cooling fans. A prayer, I assumed. For herself, not him.

Juliette stood and brushed dirt from her knees. "I didn't know. After Purcell disappeared, Nesbitt carried himself with a brooding mystery. He gave me the most dire looks when he thought I couldn't see. I realized he'd killed Purcell."

She only told half the truth. I stared back.

"I meant what I said to you. I wanted you to be safe. I didn't know I loved you, then, but I knew I didn't want you to die—"

"What was this place?"

Her brow crinkled. "What?"

"Jealousy had nothing to do with it. Nesbitt killed Purcell because he came here looking for something Nesbitt couldn't let him see. What was it?"

"What are you talking about?"

I gestured at the dwelling dug out of the canyon's far wall. "There's a dormitory and storehouse. Over there—" I pointed at the mound of spalled rock. "—is, well, perhaps you could tell me."

Her hands waggled in the air. "Some missionary field site. How should I know? Maybe Purcell came here to sketch and Nesbitt tracked him down."

"To sketch."

"Darren, he died with a pencil in his hand. Didn't you see?"

I subvoked, and my augmented reality hardware played video of

Purcell's corpse on my contact lenses. She told a truth I hadn't noticed: a stubby pencil poked between withered fingers.

Why would he sketch the site below? Only video with an unforgeable time- and location-stamp would give Purcell the evidence he would have needed. A sketch would convince no one.

I remembered his sketchbooks. He never sketched to convince. He sketched to better understand what he saw. If what he saw ran counter to every ALECS protocol, then he might well have turned to a habit promising order and control over his inner world. It also explained why the sketch itself was gone. Nesbitt would have taken it for destruction, to close the final open loop.

I had as much evidence as I could find.

"He came out to sketch," Juliette said. Her tone, and the repetition, made the words more believable. "Nesbitt was jealous. Nesbitt followed him here and killed him. But now Nesbitt's dead too. It's just you and me. I know you have to leave tomorrow. My duty to the UCC means I have to stay. But we still have tonight. Let's spend it together so you can know I love you. How I wish I'd said it earlier, when we could have had a life together. But let's at least have one night, and a lifetime of memories."

I longed to believe her. Then I recalled the cut flaps of skin on Purcell's chest.

"You toyed with me," I said, "while your husband and your other lover played a game ending in death. All my memories of our intimacies—more than the sex. The sex was a tiny fraction. The emotional connections were far more important—are steeped in the wormwood of your motives. One night cannot cleanse those memories. Take care, Juliette. We shall never meet again."

She extended her hands. "There must be some way you can forgive me."

"I fell under your spell because I did not see the universe as it was. I cannot forgive myself."

I turned and stared into the red canyon. Time ticked by, counted by my deep and ragged breaths. A gust whistled through the vacant windows of the dwelling. Footsteps crunched on the rocky soil, grew quieter, faded from hearing. One last rustle of sound came from over a rise half a kilometer to the north. I looked up as her airmobile rose on a straight path toward the settlement.

I had evidence, but would it be anything more than a nuisance to USG? Before an ALECS investigation team could arrive, USG security would scrub the site and dismiss the data copied from my augmented reality sensors as fabrications. Give up. Let them win.

I took a centering breath. If USG had done what I suspected, I could not let it rest in its criminal victory. A few hours remained before I had to return to the settlement. What more evidence might still exist?

Sketches. Purcell might have made several drawings of the scene and Nesbitt might have missed one.... which the wind would have long since carried away, and Elar's harsh rays long since broken down its graphite streaks to dust.

Purcell's implanted hardware? Maybe he'd added a data chip to some other location in his body. Or Nesbitt had tried to destroy the hardware he'd cut out by smashing it against the rocks and been incomplete. Hardware was more robust than most people thought... and I still grasped at straws.

Yet I had no other chance of finding the evidence we would need, and hours with nothing better to do. I trudged downslope to my airmobile, pulled an object detector from a cargo bin, and returned to the boulders.

As I approached, I thought through Nesbitt's steps that day. He had reached his firing position unseen by Purcell. If he had flown directly from the settlement, he would have landed out of sight, just as Juliette had, and returned to his vehicle by the same route. If he had worked that day in the facility below, he would have looped wide to stay out of Purcell's sight, but gone back straight downslope. He'd been at the café with Juliette, Purcell, and me the night before, but I hadn't seen him after about twenty-eight o'clock. Nesbitt might have flown out here that night, or early the next morning, but how would he know in advance Purcell's destin—

How many lies had Juliette told me, then and now?

I shook off the question. Perhaps Nesbitt had tailed Purcell from the city and tracked him here. If Nesbitt had tossed aside a smashed piece of implantable hardware on his way to his vehicle, it would be between the boulder and his landing site. I would start along that line, and if nothing turned up and I had time, I would check the slope leading into the depression.

I stopped next to the boulder, then breathed into my abdomen and started off. I soon developed a rhythm of detector sweeps. Draw a line from the crevice to the small boulder I guessed to be Nesbitt's firing position, go five meters to left and right of the line, find nothing, step closer to the firing position, repeat. Doubt gnawed at me. Nesbitt could have taken Purcell's implanted hardware back to USG headquarters for secure destruction. He could have thrown them ten meters beyond the limit of my scan. I remembered an archaic joke, a drunk on a nighttime sidewalk, looking for fallen keys—the physical kind, metal with a jutting, notched shaft—but only in the light cone cast by a streetlamp. *Over here, the light is better.*

The doubt kept gnawing as I worked my way from Nesbitt's firing position to Juliette's recent landing site. In truth, I had no idea where he might have landed. A dozen swells in the terrain could have hidden his landing from Purcell. My chances of success shrank with each step. Though Elar crept from the zenith toward the western horizon, like a sticky ball on a gentle slope, the shadows still grew longer.

I stopped amid the pattern of swirls her airmobile had left on the rocky soil. Nothing. My shoulders slumped. Forty-five minutes remained before I needed to return to the airfield. Not enough time to scour the slope in front of the boulders. But I would go until time ran out. I would sleep a little more soundly, recriminate myself a little less, in the days and weeks and months to come, if I looked as much as I could.

My detector had plenty of charge, so I left it on as I walked back to the boulder. I circled around to the right. Purcell had probably hidden in one of the low spaces between the boulder's underside and the wind-scooped dirt and rock. Which side of the boulder?

I knelt and craned my neck to look under the boulder. Against the shadowed rock, my camera picked up a spatter pattern. The detector's wand found the spatter enriched in iron, calcium, and l-amino acids. Nothing else.

Give it up, urged part of me. I checked the time. Five minutes before I needed to fly back to the settlement. Keep looking.

I went along the front of the boulder, then waved the detector at the other gap between the boulder and the ground. The detector squawked in my ear and dim smears of fluorescent green appeared in my field of vision, projected onto a low pile of dirt at the front of the gap.

The pile of dirt hid an object of plastic, metal, and glass, the latter just barely buried.

I crouched and clawed my gloved fingers at the rocky dirt. The smears in my field of vision grew more intense, more defined. I dug deeper, and struck something round and thin. I pulled on the object, scraped dirt with my fingers, pulled, scraped, then pulled it free.

A cracked plastic box barely big enough to hold a few petabytes of data. Two small lenses. Optical cables coupling the lenses to the box. I held the cables across my palm and let the box and cameras droop. A sudden fear of being seen whipped my head around. Only lifeless, rocky soil showed itself, and the cloudless sky held nothing but air.

I slipped the video recorder into my cooling cloak, then into a pocket of my cargo shorts. To my airmobile I hurried, pebbles scrabbling down with each step.

Two hours later, I returned to my flat. In the living room, I stepped past my half-packed luggage, checked the opacity of every window, and ran Clio's scanner over every surface.

Once convinced of my flat's security, I pulled the video recorder from my pocket and set it next to an induction charger. Despite the cracked housing, the ready light on the box flickered on, then glowed a steady green.

My augmented reality hardware interfaced wirelessly with the recorder. An authentication window popped into my vision. My chest tightened around my breath.

User: wpurcell

Password: |

Wherever I turned my head, the blinking cursor taunted me. Purcell seemed the type to use long alphanumeric strings of mixed case for his passwords. Given what he'd been looking for, he must have set the recorder to wipe after several failed logins.

I could let it go. Take the equipment back to Earth and let a data forensics expert in Calgary or Prague extract what could be gotten. But a part of me wanted to be certain what Purcell had found, and why Nesbitt had killed him.

I called Clio. "Could you come over? I need you to do something for me."

She blinked a few times. "*Daoshi*, you know we're packing up the last of the office today."

"Knowing Scobee, you finished in mid-afternoon."

"Well, yes, but I'm on duty until twenty o'clock, then those of us in the office are going for last drinks and dinner at that sushi box place on Gregory Dialogus—"

"You don't want to go there. Too many USG and UCC people."

She angled her head and dipped her chin to look up at me sidelong. "*Daoshi*, is it really necessary? Could it wait till the flight back?"

"No. I need you to do this as soon as you can."

Her head bobbed. "Of course, *Daoshi*. I'll see you about twenty-fifteen."

She arrived at the promised time. I hid the recorder in my pocket to mask any view a USG camera in the stairwell might see over her shoulder, then let her in. "Great to see you, Clio."

She hesitated at the threshold. "Are you sure we need to do this, *Daoshi*?"

I realized what she expected, then. "Absolutely," I said for the benefit of any hidden microphones. "But you have to come in."

The insistent tone from my baritone voice pulled her in. I shut and locked the door behind her. "Does USG security have bugs in the public spaces?"

"It does."

"With luck we sold them on this being an amorous encounter. Can you set the rattlers to send the same message out the windows? That should sell a cover story while we get to work."

Clio looked both relaxed and disappointed. "So what sort of security matter do you have for me?"

I pulled the recorder from my pocket. "It's password locked."

"They had passwords back then?" She lifted it up, ran her fingertip over the brittle plastic. "Where did you find this antique, *Daoshi*?"

"Out in the field. Its owner is long gone."

She squinted at a label on the underside, then blew away dust. "Says its owner is The Unneeded Hypothesis. They had personnel here?"

"Decades ago. Around the time of my first posting. I'd like to spend my last night on Elard reminiscing about my first posting, and whatever video might be on here would help."

"You need me to live boot it?"

"However you can get me through the password lock."

She gave me a cautious look. "Are we going to cause an intra-ALECS incident?"

USG would never know— Not what she meant. "The Unneeded Hypothesis doesn't even know this recorder exists, let alone what might be on it." I quirked an eyebrow. "If you don't think you can crack it—"

"I can crack it, *Daoshi*." Her eyebrows arched in return. "Was she a pretty woman?"

My head jittered, my eyes widened. Oh, she didn't mean Juliette. "Like I said, I don't know what video might be on there. I just want to find out. Nostalgia does funny things to someone my age."

She studied my face for a moment. "You don't seem so old as that, *Daoshi*." She took the recorder and sat at the desk. I went to the kitchen for a glass of water. I needed to rehydrate after my day in the desert, and I wanted to keep my mind unfogged by alcohol. Through the door I glimpsed her profile as she worked. Stares at the box, fingers tapping keys on a virtual keyboard projected onto the desk by her augmented reality hardware, frowns at the wall. "He closed all the easy exploits, didn't he?" she muttered.

I downed the glass, poured another, let her work in peace.

After a time, she turned to me with a pleased look. "We're in, *Daoshi*."

I went to the next room. I dug through the directory tree overlaid on my vision until I reached two video files, both the same length, about twenty minutes.

Clio said, "I'll go ahead and launch the viewer—"

"No. I'll take it from here. Go join the rest of the team for sushi boxes." I held my left hand behind her elbow, not touching, and gestured to the door with my right. Once she started that direction, I pocketed the recorder and followed. At the door, I reached around her for the knob—

"Not yet, *Daoshi*." Her voice held an odd tone. She came closer and turned her face up to me. Her lips parted. "We have to sell it, right?"

I grasped her wrists and gently guided her forearms between us. "You will live a happy life with a good man." Gently but firmly, I said, "I'm not him."

She blinked, and allure melted from her features. Quickly, though, she saved face. "What I mean, *Daoshi*, is we need to—" She broke free of my grip and ruffled my hair. "—look the part."

"Yours too," I said. "And smudge your lipstick."

A few gyrations of her head disarrayed her hair. She nudged her mouth with the back of her hand. "Farewell, *Daoshi*. I'll see you at the spaceport tomorrow."

I shut the door behind her, then thumbed the lock. I hurried back to the desk and pulled the recorder from my pocket. Quick jabs of my finger at the air, and the videos started playing in tiled windows overlaid on my view of the wall.

The red canyon, looking toward the mound, looked similar to what I'd seen that afternoon. But the bone-white plugs in front of the mound held rigid metal frames about two meters tall. Hanging from the frames, rippling in a faint breeze, thin sheets of material bore the outline of a humanoid torso and head, each decorated with concentric circles.

Targets.

The other line of plugs walled off firing pits. The L-shaped remnant of foundation supported a building with walls open from a man's waist to the roof. Three men in USG security uniforms stood in the building, working at control panels just out of sight below the tops of the walls.

The USG security men looked toward the scarp, just as the other window showed individuals filing out of the barracks. A man at the front, a man at the end, and three men walking in cluster near the middle. One of the cluster, from his body language the leader, spoke with one of the line's eight natives. The latter wrinkled his snout and rolled his shoulders, gestures I recalled from my first arrival orientation as showing submission. The human leader took it in as if it were his birthright.

Every native, and the men at front and end of the column, carried a laser rifle.

The line of natives soon entered the firing pits. One of the men from the leader's cluster paced behind the firing pits, mouth moving and arms gesturing. A black box hanging on a lanyard around his neck was presumably a translation device. The recorder's microphone picked up a few indistinct words. English or a native language? I couldn't tell.

The next sights, and a few muffled sounds, removed all doubt. Capacitors crackled like distant firecrackers. Hazes of ablated target fabric and kicked-up dust came from the targets and the mound between them.

USG violated the core principles of ALECS.

Juliette must have known.

The video continued. Capacitors crackled. Dust hazes drifted up from the targets.

Another capacitor crackled, much louder.

The firing range fell still. The natives craned their necks and the men shaded their eyes with their hands as they looked toward the top of the slope. Agitation hunched their shoulders, until a few seconds later, the USG leader raised his hand in a question.

"Pest control," Nesbitt shouted a few meters from the recorder. I hadn't heard his voice for decades, but I knew it as if I'd heard it yesterday. "We can't let Terran life become an invasive species, right? Go back to work."

The USG leader nodded and gestured at his men and the native trainees. The firing range soon returned to normal.

The video ran on. After a while, the microphone picked up the sound of a nearby shovel biting the rocky soil.

Knuckles rapped on the door. I started. USG security? Had they outplayed Clio? I put the recorder into an unprotected sleep mode and hurried to the kitchen. A paper napkin, wadded as I walked back to the desk, thrown over the recorder—it would hide it enough if no one came in.

I slowed my steps and my breath as I neared the door. "Yes?"

"Darren."

What did Juliette want?

"I need to see you."

My heart thudded. I lifted my thumb toward the biometric lock and cursed myself as a fool before I opened the door a dozen centimeters.

"I'm still packing," I said. "I don't have much time."

Red rimmed her eyes. "Make the time. Please. You have to. I'll never see you again." She raised her hand to the outside of the door. Her fingertips brushed the nanofabbed wood.

I opened the door just wide enough to pull her in. I slammed and locked it before turning to her.

She started speaking before I fully faced her. "Are we alone?"

"I'm not hiding a lover in the bath—"

"Secure. Are we? You have to tell me."

"To the best of my knowledge."

She looked thoughtful for a moment. "USG security has no idea where you were today. Whoever on Scobee's staff is in charge of securing your facilities is well skilled." She exhaled and shivered. "Get us both a drink and meet me in the living room. I have to tell you the truth."

The poorly-masked recorder on the desk hovered in the corner of my eye. I kept my gaze on her. Part of me wanted to believe she meant what she said. "Have a seat."

I went to the kitchen and told the store'n'cook to make two strong martinis. With my back to the living room, I listened for her footsteps near the desk, and glanced that way every few seconds. She seemed to stay on the couch across the room until I returned with our drinks.

Juliette stared at the wall, her knuckles white on a clutch purse. She set the purse down to take her drink. She sipped from her glass and for long seconds her gaze watched the dance of room lights in the olive-tinged liquid. She took another sip before she spoke.

"It all began about nine months before Nesbitt killed Purcell.

"You wouldn't remember the night. We were in the old café on Gregory Dialogus. Purcell was always cynical about those of us who professed belief in something more than the universe's uncaring laws, but that night, after a few drinks, he was downright nasty. 'If Voltaire hadn't said it, he should have. Your UCC is neither Universal, nor a Church, nor of Christ.'"

"Sounds like Purcell," I said, "but you're right. I don't remember."

"Nesbitt was spoiling for a fight. Maybe he already intuited Purcell's suspicions. 'That's my wife you're insulting.'

"Purcell ignored him. He gave me that haughty look. 'Come now, Juliette, you know all that as well as I do. How often do your sermons mention Christ by name? Four times a year? You're more likely to celebrate your centuries of lesbian pastoresses who bravely protested every war the Americans ever fought, except those against Germans or white Southerners.'" She studied my face. "You still don't remember."

"Tense moments always popped up. Though more toward those last nine months."

"Of course, it would seem like any other. But when Nesbitt and I got home that night, we stayed up till three, talking about what Purcell might have already known and what he might find out."

"Might know—" The video of the firing range in use remained my secret. "—about?"

"USG sent Nesbitt out here to arm one tribe of natives with laser weapons."

"What?" With luck, I faked surprise well enough.

"USG headquarters on Earth had decided to reject the ALECS standards of cooperation with other human organizations and non-interference with native cultural development. Elard was an experiment. USG would back some faction of natives, who would then make USG the sole human advisors on the planet. But USG was only willing to do it while maintaining plausible deniability. All the weapons were built on-planet, do you remember the first USG workshop out by the airfield? And if caught, Nesbitt would be denounced as a rogue by USG headquarters."

"What was your role? You meaning UCC, and you meaning… you."

"UCC headquarters didn't know about USG's plans when I married Nesbitt and it sent me here with him, but it did want to build a collaboration with USG. USG would pay lip service to our gospel of social justice, and we would preach a doctrine of 'render unto Caesar.' He didn't tell me his mission until a year after we arrived. But when he told me, he'd gauged me accurately. At the time. I agreed with him. It was God's plan to bring social justice to the Elard natives." She shook her head and a haggard look filled her eyes. "You can't make an omelet without breaking eggs, a million deaths are a statistic. Christ forgive me for thinking that."

"That's your judgment now," I said. "You were telling me about then."

"That night, I had a hunch Purcell had guessed something about USG's plans, and by three in the morning, Nesbitt agreed with me. Also that night, I realized how I could investigate Purcell."

The affair. "How did Nesbitt take *that*?"

"Do I look stupid? No man would accept his wife's suggestion to cheat on him. I kept quiet that night, and spent the next month dropping hints until he came up with the idea on his own. I put up enough sham resistance to make him think he had full control of the situation, then I 'went along' with his request."

A question came to mind. Did I really want to know the answer? Yes. "Where did I come in?"

"Deep down, Purcell was always aloof. His suspicions about USG's and Nesbitt's activities made him even more wary of me when I started coming on to him. A sex addiction cover story was the best thing I could come up with. A few hookups here and there… a fling with you, and me arranging for Purcell to come across us in a compromising position…."

I breathed deep into my belly and held it for a five count. My emotions softened enough for me to think. "It worked."

Juliette crinkled her face and avoided my gaze. "Like I knew it would. A few days later Purcell let me into his flat—"

A part of me exulted that I had taken pleasure from her flesh before Purcell.

"—and within a month, I knew all his secrets. I wriggled out from his arm as he snored and flipped through his sketchbooks until I found the map."

She met my gaze then. "How did you find it? I destroyed it five minutes after Nesbitt called me from the training facility to tell me he'd killed Purcell. And we cracked Purcell's computer security and found no electronic copies."

"I have my ways. So Purcell had evidence pointing to a few different sites out in the desert, and he sneaked off to spy on each one in turn. He didn't realize how well you were tracking him. When he went to the red canyon, Nesbitt followed him."

"And you know what happened next."

"Why have you told me this?"

In passing, a swallow of her martini bulged her neck. "Because Nesbitt and I were evil and I have to atone somehow. We violated our ALECS vow. We sent tens of thousands of natives to their deaths. We lied to Purcell and we killed him."

All true. But. "What triggered your change of heart?"

Juliette turned her gaze to the floor. In her eyes welled tears. Perhaps the first honest ones she'd ever cried in front of me. "I meant every word I said at the red canyon. I'm alone. While Nesbitt lived, I off-loaded my conscience to him. His end justified all our means. But after he died—and he was killed fighting native rebels holding out against the Indigenous Autonomous Council, you guessed that already?—I couldn't deny my responsibility any more."

More tears welled in her eyes. Juliette threw her arms around me and burrowed against my chest. I returned the embrace and held her close for a time. Choked-back sobs spasmed through her torso, and her breath came fast and ragged, but she did not cry. Her breaths slowed and her body relaxed. I kept holding her close.

She looked up at me. Her face was composed despite the red of uncried tears like a mask around her eyes. "Take me."

"Juliette—"

"Give me this. If you want to think of it as revenge for how I used you, think that. I would deserve it. But you're the only man alive I ever might have loved and ever could love and after tomorrow I'll never see you again. Give me this."

She reached up to the back of my head and pulled my mouth toward hers. I resisted for a few seconds, but then the warmth of her lips and the memory of our long-ago trysts stiffened my penis and I chose to give her what she wanted.

I walked her backwards to the bed. Moments later our clothes fell to the floor. I attended to her pleasure, but when the time came to take mine, I held her wrists to her pillow and pounded my body against hers. Her hips soon rocked in time with mine. When a woman chooses to submit to a man, she can take a pleasure in his vigor she would never admit in the cool light of day. Never admit, to him, or to herself. She moaned and grunted, then gasped when our orgasms struck us.

As we lay next to each other, catching our breaths and letting our sweat dry, I thought of the sleeping recorder under the napkin in the next room. Was that enough? If USG could muddy the water, with accusations of forgery and lies, could it escape the punishment it deserved?

"If you want to fully atone for Nesbitt's crimes, come to the space-port tomorrow."

Sadness returned to her eyes. "Don't say that."

"If the ALECS Executive Committee had your testimony, USG would be crushed—"

"Darren, don't you see? I can't leave Elard. I know too much."

Gooseflesh covered my cheeks and neck. I should have already known.

She went on without noticing my reaction. "USG security would stop me before I got to the departure gate. And they would stop you too. They might let me live, but you? I can't let them do that to you. I already sent Purcell to his death. Don't ask me to send you to yours."

"There has to be a way," I said. "We could smuggle you on-board somehow."

"I'm not petite enough to fit in someone's luggage."

"We could nanofab a life support crate overnight and have Scobee declare it privileged—"

"Does The Way in the West have its own private assemblery? No? USG would know what you nanofabbed. They would scan it despite the privilege. And Scobee's blood would be on my hands too." She lifted her hand to my cheek. "I can't leave. You must. You have to find a way to expose what USG did here. That, and my memories of tonight, will be enough for me. Let them be enough for you."

We could disguise her and give her false papers as a member of The Way in the West... and USG had a list of every one of our members still on Elard and could take DNA from her to hunt for matches in the ALECS personnel database.

Next plan. We could....

I let out a long breath. She was right. If she tried to leave, USG security would stop her, and then stop me. The evidence I had from Purcell's camera would have to be enough to bring about justice.

"They are," I said.

We lay for a time, the only sounds our breaths and the rush of cooled air through the vents. Eventually I fell asleep.

An alarm clock blatted. I stopped it, then lurched awake.

Juliette was gone.

A message from her bounced on the bottom of my vision until I subvoked it open. *My memories of last night are so powerful, I couldn't risk my saying something to spoil them. Perhaps you feel the same. Take care. J.*

Disappointed, I shook my head. I had an hour before I needed to leave for the spaceport. No time to ponder her flightiness. Showering, dressing, packing Purcell's recorder—

I scrambled into the living room. The napkin tossed over the recorder was still there, but what was underneath—?

The recorder. It remained in power-save mode. After a few breaths, I carried it back to the bedroom and stuffed it into my attaché case.

By nine o'clock, robots had loaded my luggage into my jitney. I started down the street toward Guru Nanak Boulevard. The boulevard held more traffic this morning than I had seen over all daylight hours of the last month. People squeezed by fives and sixes into jitneys and robots packed and repacked luggage into the cargo compartments. USG security personnel in black cloaks and opaque face shields stood at major intersections, laser rifles slung over their shoulders. Traffic crawled past their unreadable gazes.

My jitney sped up as we neared the exit of the settlement proper. The air curtains remained, but USG security had broadcast an all-clear appearing as a green icon in my field of vision. A glimpse at the gatehouse showed two security men with relaxed poses and crossed arms chatting to themselves.

At the spaceport, a robotic cart and the envious looks of people dragging their luggage waited for me. Rank had its privileges. Anxious faces and bickering couples surrounded me. Only the few USG personnel returning to Earth showed anything resembling delight, tinged with the cruelty of boys not yet grown up.

Eventually I reached the line for the security checkpoint. At the head of the line stood a gray plastic frame, two meters fifty tall, one meter fifty wide, thirty centimeters thick. I shuffled along with the queue. The morose faces around me repelled any urge of mine for small talk.

At my turn, the guard gestured at the brain activity scanner. I waited on the outlines of feet, breathing deep and trying not to think of the previous day and night.

The guard squinted at my passport while motors and fans in the scanner whirred at high speed. "What was the purpose of your visit, *Daoshi* Lee?"

"Supervising the withdrawal by The Way in the West of its personnel and assets from Elard."

"Hmm." He peered at some detail shown by the brain activity scanner. "What's in your luggage?"

A chill stole over my neck. "My personal effects," I said in an offhand tone. Think of Juliette. Think of last night, in bed, after we talked on the couch in the living room near the desk—

"The Indigenous Autonomous Council has forbidden the export of native artifacts and recordings of cultural performances."

The natives in the firing pits in the red canyon. I called up memories of Juliette's body as quickly, held them as firmly, as I could. "I haven't seen a native this entire trip," I said.

Two more USG security personnel came toward the scanner and

stopped between me and the concourse leading to the departing ship. The guard at the scanner's control panel cleared his throat. "These men will guide you to a lounge while we check your luggage. It shouldn't take but an hour."

"It had best not. If I'm held here against my will out of some power-trip of yours, the ALECS Executive Committee will have much to ask your masters about."

The guard gave me a flat look. "If all is in order, you'll be on board well before launch."

One of the security men led me away from the concourse to the ship. The other fell in behind me. Part of me longed to sprint away from the guards and toward the ship. A rabbit or squirrel might feel the same, when a trap snared its leg. But flight would do no good. Even if I made it to the ship, USG's security personnel could deny the ship freedom to launch until they found me.

A door unsealed itself and we descended an echoing stairwell. Without a word, the security men showed me a small lounge containing two ugly armchairs and stark white light. I squinted and sat. In an animated poster on the wall in front of me, Vainqueur posed with members of the Indigenous Autonomous Council. I crossed my arms over my chest to try to hide my heart's slamming.

If Clio had been able to crack the recorder's password protection, couldn't USG?

I took deep breaths and meditated on a native's cooling crest. The exercises calmed me enough to think how I might talk myself out of their discovery of the data.

I found that old thing, oh, that's what was on it?

There are a hundred copies on board the ship already, and you can't arrest everyone before departure time.

Am I going to have break cover and call Vainqueur?

More deep breaths. What a mediocre set of cover stories. Still more deep breaths—

The two USG security personnel knocked before coming in. "You're free to go," one said. "We'll lead you back to the concourse and you can find your way to the ship from there."

"That's it? Where's my apology?"

The second USG man frowned. "You mean, the apology you owe us, for thinking we're drones of some police state when you go through the scanner?"

After a tense silence, the first one said, "Follow us."

A few minutes later, I stood alone on the concourse with the robotic cart holding my luggage. My legs wobbled the first steps toward the ship. How had I eluded them? Had Juliette gotten my name onto a whitelist? I clamped my face over feelings of relief and good fortune.

At the end of the concourse, the robot lifted my luggage onto the conveyor leading to the ship's complement of cargo handlers. I opened my eye and pressed my thumb for the biometric scanners and a small chip with my stateroom assignment clacked out.

Ten minutes later, my luggage all stowed in my stateroom, I fell back on the bed and shivered. I had dodged a bullet. Once we lifted off, nothing could touch me. Within a day of my return to Earth, the ALECS Executive Committee would have a copy of Purcell's evidence.

A dark intuition snapped open my eyes. I lunged for my luggage.

Clio's hack of the recorder's login responded to my biometrics. Heart thudding, I checked the directory tree.

The recorder's images had been wiped.

For some long time, I couldn't move, couldn't even think. When my thoughts finally did flow, they bobbed along a sea of anger. *How could she have done this? Miserable lying—*

She saved your life—

'Don't bother asking, "Why were such things made in this world?"'—

I threw away the bitter cucumber. I had lost the most valuable evidence I'd found. That couldn't be helped. What evidence remained? A sample of Purcell's DNA. What I had seen. What I had heard. The latter two items backed up on a datachip.

She could have destroyed it too.

I went to my attaché and pulled out a gray datachip case with a biometric lock. I sagged into a chair and my hands trembled as I thumbed the lock and pushed open the lid. The case sprang open to reveal two datachips.

Two?

I subvoked to my augmented reality hardware, then held the second datachip close to my chest for a low-latency connection. A window appeared in my vision.

User: dlee

Password: |

I stared at the blinking cursor for a moment, before the obvious password occurred to me. A virtual keyboard appeared across my thighs. I typed *juliette*.

A file browser opened. At the root of the datachip's directory tree I found several folders and a file named VIEWME.

I opened the file. A video window popped up, overlaid to the right of a closet door on the stateroom wall.

Juliette in her living room. Alphanumerics in the lower right time-stamped the recording at about two hours after she met me at Purcell's corpse.

Come to gloat? I extended my arm to backhand the video window into the trash. But another, calmer part held me back.

"Hello Darren. If you're still on Elard, stop watching now. All I'm going to do is reminisce about our affair in the old days." Haunted eyes belied her words for three slow beats of my heart.

"I assume you're past the brain activity scanners. USG on Elard cannot stop you from getting to Earth. You might not thank God you're safe, but let me thank Him for you." Her eyes grew moist. "I wish I could have met you before Nesbitt. But all I can do is choose you now, when I'm a prisoner who knows too much and you're the one chance I have to reveal USG's crimes. You're the one chance I have to atone for my role in those crimes. Go, to Earth, and live."

She lifted the datachip I now held. "I copied all Nesbitt's files right after he died, before USG security scrubbed all his sensitive data from our flat. I held onto them in case this chance might come. Use them wisely.

"Good-bye, Darren. Know you go with all the love I'm capable of giving."

The video stopped and the window shut itself. For a few seconds, I stared at the now-blank wall where her face had been shown. Then I navigated through the files she had copied.

Perhaps not all Nesbitt's files, but thousands, with created and modified dates spanning decades. I skimmed them while heeding the pre-launch instructions from the ship with half my mind. Strategy papers from USG headquarters. Video from the first laser rifle fab out by the airfield. Logs of personnel working in weapons fab and native military training. Maps of the firing range in the red canyon, and others Purcell had never known about. Video of natives posing with energy weapons. Far away, the fusion drives rumbled to life, and acceleration pushed me into the launch couch. Nesbitt's reports, with frank description of military training of his native allies, their combat operations against other native factions, and his killing of Purcell.

Twenty minutes later, the ship announced we could unstrap from our launch couches. I copied the files to my other datachip and to a memory implanted under my skin, then sealed Juliette's datachip back in the case.

I left my stateroom and asked the ship to guide me to Scobee and Clio.

PRIVATE KEYS

Now that I am dead, I can tell you everything about my husband's assassination.

Are you wondering why I chose you? According to my archived calendars, we have only officially been in the same room four or five times over the decades, mostly during American Historical Association meetings. I don't remember you from those. But much else recommends you. First, although your research on bureaucratic subornation of democracies in Latin America during the '20s and '30s was outside of my specialty, it ranks highly for both quality and relevance, according to the search engines. I'm sure you know your term *technocratic pronunciamiento* recently entered the official databases at Merriam-Webster.

Second, though you are two decades younger than me, by the time I write this message, we are contemporaries, and will only become more so in the decades before you will read this.

Third, that you have risen in university administration, in our age when most growth of organizational hierarchies is downward, indicates you are adroit at political and social games, and suggests you will be capable of bringing this message and the attached files to the public in a manner most advantageous to our cause.

Because, fourth, and finally, I know you share our cause. I referred to *official encounters* before and I'm sure you know why I used that term. If I remember a freshly-tenured associate professor overheard in a hotel coffee bar over three decades ago, you must remember the First Lady.

I don't recall where '55's AHA summer meeting took place, and it's not important enough to look up. After dinner, I sat in a high-backed booth, catching up with an old friend from my grad school days at Harvard, while my Secret Service detail fanned out to various tables. You walked in with colleagues of yours and your voice carried. "President Fletcher is coddling the striking adjuncts! They don't deserve job security! We could bring in a million replacements from India and Latin America! He's a fool—"

I suspect at this point you realized the nature of the men in dark suits scattered around. My friend and I shared an amused glance, then returned to our conversation, reminiscing about our FDA-disapproved visits with our husbands to the life-extension clinics in Singapore in the '20s. In the back of my mind, though, I mused about you. I knew all along I was bound, as politicians' spouses have been since time immemorial, to never express public disagreement with my husband's policies. I did not know you, and could not communicate with you as we do now, through a set of public and private keys. All I could do was prepare a wry nod to nonverbally say *I agree, my husband is wrong to negotiate with the adjunct professors*; but when I left, you studied the lid of your drink and would not look up.

That was less than six months before Rod's assassination.

The script that checks the output of my medical monitoring implant runs daily at midnight Central time. It will send this message soon after. I assume you will not read it until the following morning, by which time I expect you will already have seen news stories about my death. I'm certain our generation's news outlets will show, over and over, the shaky footage shot by other skiers as they ran to us. I can see comparable images from my memory when I close my eyes. The contrasts! The cloudless turquoise sky, the sun-dazzled snow, the deep green spruces, our black and gray attire, and my husband's blood, spattered across the ground by the sniper bullet and bubbling from his mouth as he died.

I also expect the newsreaders will remind you that Andrew Phillip Younger had been a student of mine one semester. I remember the questions one reporter asked me in the scripted, staged interviews those first weeks after Rod's assassination. *You knew Andrew Phillip Younger. Did you have any idea he was capable of this?*

Artfully I had spent most of my tears by that point of the interview. *He was just another student from one of the many semesters I taught at Nebraska. When his transcript was leaked to the press after Rod's murder, I was surprised he'd been a student of mine. I don't know how he could have done*—I stopped holding back the last tears—*this.*

True, as far as it went. But the other two times I encountered him gave me reason to suspect.

But before I get to that, I don't want to be accused of glossing over the semester I taught him. At least one reporter, a fresh-faced girl from a new new new media startup, sandbagged me to get an interview and then sprung questions about the course. "The UNL course catalog lists POLS 251 as 'Coups d'État, Assassinations, and Armed Revolutions: Successes and Failures of Violent Regime Change.' Wouldn't you expect that kind of subject matter to attract people contemplating assassination? Or, worse, lead normal people to consider assassination as a valid way to bring about political change?"

I formulated my answer as she spoke, and delivered it coolly. "Not at all. Thousands of my students over decades at Nebraska and hundreds over my last few years here at Georgetown have taken my course. Everyone—except my husband's killer—finished the course knowing that assassination is a counterproductive way to affect regime change." My press secretary soon ended the interview and rousted the girl from my office. I mentioned the girl's trickery, and the name of her startup, to all of our peers that I could. Her name and her employer's have since fallen off the radar of the search engines.

The lectures and discussion sessions on assassinations were always the toughest part of the course. Students, besotted with idealism as the young usually are, were unwilling to believe me at first when I explained how assassination doesn't simply fail to bring about the ends sought by the assassin. Almost always, the social structure that propelled the victim to high office will backlash against the assassin and his faction.

I pounded home examples. I always started with John Wilkes Booth. Almost no students knew that President Lincoln had supported a mild Reconstruction: ending slavery with compensation for slave-owners and second-class citizenship for freedmen. After Lincoln's assassination, the Radical Republican backlash maintained a decade of military occupation of the South and gave freedmen the vote and high offices.

Cassius and Brutus stabbed a dictator whom they feared would establish a hereditary tyranny. Fifteen years later, their victim's heir, Augustus, became Rome's first emperor.

The list went on: the Narodnaya Volya movement and Alexander II; James Earl Ray and Martin Luther King; Guillaume Saint-Martin and Georges Boucher; the New Taiping movement and Zhou Pufang. Between the weight of repetition, and students' tendency to repeat what they think the professor wants them to say, most acquiesce.

Not all. When I checked my archives a few days after the girl was forced from my office, I found, from spring '39, an annotated copy of Andrew Phillip Younger's course paper on an assassination and its outcome. He picked Oswald and Kennedy, and filled five pages with the Arab oil embargo, defeat in Vietnam, '70s stagflation, and the botched hostage rescue in Iran as Oswald's desired outcomes. I reread my note to him and nodded at my wisdom. *Oswald knew nothing about Vietnam or Iran. His only political position was pro-Castro, and normal relations with Cuba came fifty years after the assassination. You can disagree with my lectures, but present strong evidence if you do. B-*

Andrew Phillip Younger faded from my thoughts as soon as the semester ended. Rod was reelected governor yet again, and we decided to put more and more effort into wooing party bosses for his eventual run at the Presidency. My job was to look coiffed and proper, smart but not too smart, while Rod called in chits from the favor bank. My second encounter with Andrew Phillip Younger emerged from that.

In September '48, we attended a banquet fundraiser in Omaha for

Senator Page's presidential campaign. After Page flew to his next campaign stop, one of the party's gray eminences took us aside. "Rod, I think you'd be a great candidate in '52." Everyone knew Page was too smart for his own good and expected him to lose, leaving the '52 nomination open for the taking. "I know some people think, 'what can a man who's spent twenty years as governor of a state full of life insurance companies and organic free-range buffalo know about foreign policy,' but you're lucky to share a bed with an expert—" Lust showed in his gaze for a moment, and then all three of us pretended it hadn't. "If only the voters could know how Miranda would be your unofficial Secretary of State...."

Rod and I made our decision in the elevator riding down to our car, and I outlined three popular political science books on the futility of violent regime change before we returned to Lincoln. The summer of '49 saw me touring to support the first book, *Peace For All Time.*

We were in Austin, my reading and signing just completed, when the doors opened and the hot Texas night and the protestors' chants hit me at the same time. "Retire at eighty! Make room for us! Retire at eighty! Make room for us!"

I ignored the protestors and strode to the parking lot. The Nebraska State Patrol officers accompanying me took action, one on point, another at the wing, and a third at my left elbow. The last nodded toward blue uniforms standing between the rental car and the protestors. "Austin PD tells me they're from an intentional community on a ranch east of here. They're abiding by city, county, and state laws. Too bad."

"Let the kids squawk," I said. "They're powerless to bring about change."

The chant continued and I kept on ignoring them. My administrative assistant held the rear door for me when I heard one of the protestors shout, "If Oswald had triggered a backlash, Goldwater would have been elected in '64!"

I looked up at that. I assumed the speaker had been a former student of mine, but I didn't recognize him. Five years later, after seeing his mug shot broadcast over and over, it occurred to me it must have been him. Sandy-brown hair cut within a half-inch of his scalp, and a T-shirt showing a video loop of some long-dead Marine general and a word balloon, *War is a Racket*. The protestor's face showed the belligerence of a naughty boy, surprised at getting caught.

"You should have written that on the paper," I called. "Last semester's grades are final." I climbed into the car and we soon drove off.

I would have completely forgotten the incident, except a car in the parking lot, in hindsight clearly his, caught my eye: an old, rusty hybrid station wagon with a Nebraska plate and an expired registration transponder. Stickers smothered the car's bumper and rear hatch with the usual ineffectual student protest. A half-decade later, the FBI file showed me the clues I missed that night. In addition to the usual messages like *I Went $1 Million Into Debt and All I Got Was This Lousy Diploma* and *No Blood For Photovoltaic Electrons*, the rear hatch bore *Make Precision Tools Not Undocumented Loans* and *US Army Long Range Marksmanship—Reach Out and Touch Someone*.

But at the time, the then-unknown protestor proved my thesis in miniature—in '52, Rod won Austin and the surrounding county with nearly 65% of the popular vote.

Once we reached D.C., and the pinnacle of Rod's career, a truth I'd known for a while came back to me in full force and refused to let go of my attention. Rod was a skillful politician, adept at trimming his sails to the wind of public opinion. Wait, why am I protecting his reputation and mine? Let me be blunt. He had no principles. That hadn't mattered in an underpopulated, homogeneous state, but it mattered on the national stage. When crises came, and the worst forceful action would be better than indecision, then principles, any principles, would have galvanized him to action. Indecision was his default. The adjunct's strike was only one of many times he wavered and earned a worse outcome than he should have gotten. Do you remember the EU-backed coup in Mauritania? The debate about extending life-extension benefits to people under forty who'd never attended college?

And, of course, December '55. The Million Entrepreneur March had occupied the National Mall and staged a sit-in at the Lincoln Memorial. The blizzard of administrative actions that drowned the leaders in legal fees and bad press, served by Park Police in paramilitary gear, did not come until after Vice-President Osorio succeeded Rod in January. In December, Rod had dithered, negotiating one day and staying firm the next. He almost canceled our vacation to Aspen, and did work late the day we arrived, on the phone past one o'clock from the office in our guest house. I surprised him by staying up to talk with him when he emerged.

"Did you make up your mind about those ungrateful brats?" I asked.

"Those 'brats' are our fellow citizens. They have legitimate grievances and don't give me that look. You know it too. At UNL and Georgetown, how old are the youngest tenured professors? Sixty-five? It's the same for Fortune 500 executives, senior civil servants, and Hollywood directors."

He often let his fancies run when alone with me late at night. "Rod, if you float any kind of mandatory or even encouraged retirement—"

"I'm not. I know I need those executives and bureaucrats to butter my bread for next year's campaign." He never sounded less principled in our half-century of marriage then at that moment. "I won't let young people rise to the tops of existing businesses. But, Christ, do you know how difficult it is for them to start new ones? Labor regulations, licensing requirements, environmental regulations, anti-AI inspections, ten million clauses in the tax code. How can a startup navigate those mazes?"

I raised an eyebrow. "We have to do what's right for the country as a whole."

"Which happens to be what's right for our generation? I'm not talking about just random strangers here. I'm talking about our grandchildren too."

"Rick Jr. will make partner at Fletcher & Edelstein—"

"Speaker Ramachandran, Senator Vasquez, and Bill and Mustafa from my staff discussed a compromise." Rod's tone now reminded me of small-town Lutheran pastors I'd heard far too many times over the decades I lived in Nebraska. "A noble experiment. The first week of January, they'll introduce a bill to give tax breaks and reduced regulatory burdens for businesses owned by people under the age of 50."

"Breaks…?"

He raised a hand. "I'm not talking *laissez-faire* here. That would be an insult to all the hard-working Federal employees who voted for me. But we'll give young entrepreneurs a fighting chance."

I thought about the politicians he'd named. "The Speaker and the Senator both agreed?"

"I made my case," he said.

I shuddered. How could Rod trust people to act responsibly when given so much freedom? He didn't even talk about people wise with age, but instead, the foolish, heedless young. He stepped closer to me, oblivious of my reaction, and exuded the charisma he'd used to win fifty million votes for President in '52 and my one vote for husband half a century earlier.

I touched his cheek in the way I used to deflect his advances. His shoulders slumped as I said, "We're booked on the ski slope tomorrow morning. Time to turn in."

Rod gulped a glass of Scotch and fell asleep half-dressed while I brushed my teeth. I stood in my nightgown and watched him snore on the king-sized bed. Finally, here in the middle years of the 21st century, the adults had regained control of American society. Somehow he failed to see how precious a thing he was about to throw away.

Before joining him in bed, I checked my email, and encountered Andrew Phillip Younger for the third time.

From: Alek J. Hidell ajhidell@sicsemperstruldbrugs.com

PublicKeyEncrypted=Yes

PrivateKeyDecrypted=Yes

Subject: Merry Christmas, Dr. Fletcher

Tomorrow I will prove you wrong.

—ajh

In hindsight, clearly, Andrew Phillip Younger sent it. The Hidell name was one of Lee Harvey Oswald's aliases. The domain name combined Brutus and Cassius', and Booth's, premature cries of triumph with the never-dying Struldbrugs of *Gulliver's Travels*. But I thought nothing more of it and deleted it, sending it to the trash and then emptying the trash. A prank, clearly. No real assassin would make a death threat. Alerting the Secret Service would only encourage the sender to keep acting out. Ten minutes later I was in bed, and within half an hour, asleep.

You know what happened the next morning. I was five yards ahead of Rod—as a native of the Great Plains, skiing was not his element—when Secret Service men shouted around me. I stopped and turned as the crack of the rifle reached our slope from Sievers Mountain. Rod had collapsed and slid downslope, trailing blood behind him.

I had to get to him. My peripheral vision fell away. All I saw was Rod's gray ski jacket daubed with red. I herringboned a few strides uphill when a Secret Service man interposed himself between me and the sniper's location. "Ma'am, you're in danger!"

I wasn't, but it wasn't even worth telling him. I pressed forward.

"Ma'am!" He reached for me, then gave up.

I dropped to my knees next to Rod and flung my gloves aside. The front of his jacket was soaked and blood gushed from his mouth with each breath. I pulled off his goggles. His eyes had lost focus and I knew, deep in my gut, nothing could save him. I felt love and pity, and grief was a caged monster which I knew would someday escape.

"Rod." I could barely see him through my tears. I groped for his hand with mine. "I'm here. I love you." That much of what I told the interviewers later was true. But the rest of our final conversation, overheard by no one, will remain in my confidence until you read these words.

He looked my way. I don't know whether he really saw me. "Miranda." He coughed, and blood burbled. "The noble experiment. Will happen now. I'm a martyr."

I still felt my prior emotions, but added to them in that instant came a cold, spiked nugget of anger. Forty years I had taught my course, with its message of the backlash triggered by assassinations. Forty years I had talked about my course over the breakfast table, from my vanity in the bathroom, and pillow-to-pillow. In his zeal to grab the next brass ring, he had never listened to me.

I shoved the anger down to a cell near my grief. "You're right," I said.

That was the last lie I ever told him.

CARNIVAL IN SORGENBACH

Hans lifted the beer mug to his mouth when the vision hit.

The rabble-rouser, lank strand of hair falling down his apoplectic face. The hooked cross, black on white on red. The rumble of engines high above, from aircraft far larger than the Fokkers and Sopwiths of the war. A rubblescape stretching for miles, punctuated by skeletal walls and smothered with the stench of innumerable corpses.

Hans' awareness returned to the beer hall. The glass mug lay sideways on the wooden table. Lager pooled on the tabletop and dripped down the edges. It soaked the thighs of his best pair of pants.

He stood up and brushed at the sodden line across his thighs. A fool's task, it would not dry them in time. Why had a vision struck him now? He'd ordered a beer to keep the visions away during the job interview, not bring them on.

He caught his breath, then remembered the other people in the tavern.

The women and the old men looked wary. A few glanced searchingly around, hoping someone else would have an explanation. In a corner, Schmidt came closest to showing understanding, through eyes too old for his youthful face, and jacket cuff pinned to his shoulder. Yet even Schmidt wouldn't know. He would assume Hans had been plunged into memories of the year before, not into premonitions of greater horrors in the years to come.

The bartender came out with a rag and a pail. "Hans, let me help you." He sopped up beer along the table's edge.

Hans stared glumly. Part of his dwindling money wasted, when he needed a job and every penny was precious. "I hadn't even taken a sip."

"As I said, I'll clean it." The bartender wrung beer into the pail. "You fought hard for us. You deserved better than getting stabbed in the back."

A never-ending supply of fresh-faced doughboys, joining British and French soldiers reinvigorated with American munitions and tins of bully beef, had done a good job stabbing the army in the front. The emptiness of his pockets returned to Hans. "I mean, all that beer, wasted."

The bartender paused his motion of the rag. "Times are tough for all of us, with the British keeping up the blockade. But you'll find some free beer in a few days, once Carnival starts."

Hans trudged toward the door. Out of habit, he reached into his jacket for his notebook and fountain pen. If he recorded every detail of each vision, perhaps he could understand the future they predicted and, Mary full of grace, keep it from coming true.

But a glance at his wristwatch told him he had to leave now for his interview. Understanding the visions would not fill his belly. He took his overcoat and hat from their racks and hurried out.

Clouds clotted the late-morning sky. Hans' breath steamed as he walked from the tavern toward the town's market plaza. The St. Boniface Church, clad in brick and rough stone, stood near the half-timbered, half-plastered face of the town hall. A cart pulled by two blinkered horses waited, as workmen off-loaded bunting and effigies of springtime spirits to dress the town hall for Carnival.

Hans took the shortest route to Müller's watch factory, straight down toward the Rhine and then along the street serving its docks. The river's gray-green presence buoyed him. It would flow on, even if all the disasters he foresaw would come about, and Sorgenbach joined the weed-covered Roman ruins on nearby hilltops.

The watch factory looked alive. Its beige brick face bore rounded windows, and whiplash curves of wrought iron moldings. Hans took firmer steps as he approached the factory. Müller would not notice the spilled beer on his pants, nor the visions sometimes gripping him. Müller would give him a job.

A rumbling sound came up the street behind him. Hans stepped aside and glanced over his shoulder. A large truck with a tarpaulin stretched above the cargo area, and the French army's tricolor roundel on the side. A driver in a horizon-blue greatcoat and Adrian helmet, next to an officer wearing a visor crusted with braid. The driver glowered at Hans as the truck passed.

In the cargo area, colonial soldiers huddled for warmth. Their dark faces contrasted with their greatcoats and the orange-red tips of cigarettes. One stared at Hans with an unreadable look while the truck faded into the distance.

Hans resumed his earlier pace and soon reached the watch factory. Inside, the tick of a large clock echoed off the brick and tile of the main reception room. A few minutes before eleven, he'd made it on time.

A receptionist, with a long gray dress and a careworn face, spoke. "Herr Müller is ready for you." Time and sorrows sapped her voice. He wondered how many of her sons had been plowed into French soil. "Please follow me."

The only sound came from her heels clacking the tile. It echoed down underused hallways as they went to Müller's office. She announced Hans, then withdrew.

Müller had a ruddy face and a firm handshake. "Hans, it's an honor to meet you. You are one of our heroes, undefeated on the battle-field." He gestured at a chair facing his desk.

Hans sat. "I don't consider myself a hero, but thank you, Herr Müller."

"I regret I must be curt. The French have sent a squad of Negroes and I can only stall them a few minutes."

The truck overtaking him on the street. "Why?"

"We served the war effort by making shell fuses," Müller said.

"When the French occupiers first arrived in town, they confiscated every fuse remaining in the warehouse. Now, though we have retooled the factory to manufacture watches, they think we still have fuses hidden away."

Desperation and hope leaked into Hans' voice. "Your watch business is growing, then."

Müller looked pained. "I wish it were. You see, our best suppliers are outside the Rhineland. When shipments meant for us reach the French checkpoints, they delay them until they get their bribes. If they don't steal them outright. The same happens when we ship finished product out."

Müller sighed. "I don't have enough work for the men already on the payroll. I cannot add a bookkeeper. Not even one as heroic as you."

Hans sloughed out a breath. "I see. Thank you for your time, Herr Müller." He rose from his chair.

"Wait, please. Though times are dour now, they will change someday. Carnival is a harbinger of that change. It is a season when the dark spirits of winter are expelled and the fertile ones of spring are admitted. I am the president of the Fools' Republic, the Sorgenbach Old Carnival Club. Most of the leading businessmen in town are members. We are looking for new blood, younger men of merit. Younger men such as you. Would you join us?"

Businessmen who might be hiring. The company of other men without thunderclouds of steel rumbling at the horizon. Raucous laughter, foolish costumes, and flowing beer to push the visions away. "You flatter me, Herr Müller, but I have little to offer. I can't afford—"

Müller came closer. "We'll provide you a costume for our parade. Don't worry about that. Hans, please, join us."

"Thank you. I will."

Müller beamed. "Wonderful. Meet me in the market plaza on Thursday at noon to watch the women seize the town hall. After that, our club gathers on Sunday night for a final meeting before we march in the Rose Monday parade. We tell our wives we're putting the final decorations on the wagons, but—" His eye twinkled. "—mostly we'll be drinking."

The twinkle faded. "I must go deal with my unwelcome guests. Can you find your way out?"

Hans had navigated zigzag trenches in darkness. "Yes."

"Till Thursday!" Müller held his office door for Hans, then hurried toward the factory's rear.

Hans headed toward the reception area. Or thought he did— unmarked cross-corridors and unfamiliar stairs led him on a meandering course past empty offices. Relief touched him when brightness at the end of a hallway indicated a side door. Not ideal, but it would get him out of the factory.

He went through the door. Wrought iron lengths with post finials in the young style fenced off a picnic area. The clouds had thinned. Cold light seemingly encased wooden benches and tables in a brittle shell of winter.

Not completely. A young woman sat at the furthest table, closest to the river. She leaned over an oversized block of paper. In her hand, a pen's nib skipped over the paper like a flat rock on water, and though she faced almost fully away from Hans, the facet of her cheekbone revealed intense concentration.

Her hand slowed. She looked around, started when she saw him. Blond strands curled from under her cap. Cold air rouged her cheeks and the tip of her nose. Her blue eyes showed a wisdom unexpected in a youthful face.

She stood and her breath streamed out with her words. "Hello, I'm Liesl Müller."

He stepped forward. "Hans." He reached for her hand.

She offered it, but when he raised it to his lips, she resisted. Ink smudges dotted her thumb and first two fingers. "I'm sorry—"

"They make your hand even lovelier." She relaxed her forearm and he kissed the back of her hand. "What does your father think of your art?"

"He approves it. He thinks it will repel the coarser sort of suitor, when the time comes to marry." She glanced playfully at the looming wall of the factory. "Though he may disapprove me shirking my duties in the filing room right now."

"I don't think so," Hans said. "I understand business is slow."

Liesl's gaze darted, taking in his arms, his upright carriage, his unscarred face. For a moment, warmth showed on her face, but then paused. Perhaps she sensed the war had wounded him in places she could not see. "You sought a job and Father could not provide you one. You aren't the first. I wish we could do more, for all of you. For our sakes, you went through a hell on earth which I cannot imagine. All we can offer in recompense is cold comfort." Gently, she touched his shoulder.

Warmth stirred in his chest, like an iced-over pond responding to the rays of springtime. Liesl understood enough to know she couldn't understand the trenches. Her voice and touch conveyed sympathy, not pity. But another part of him prayed for another vision to come, of her pinned beneath a collapsed building's rubble or some half-Asiatic brute under the red star. The war had broken him. Better to divest himself of dreams of healing himself by connecting with another.

"I don't mean to interrupt your drawing," he said. Through the fabric of his coat, his fingers traced his notebook's outline. "If you wouldn't mind, I'll sit across the way for a few minutes."

Disappointment glimmered on her face, until she gazed at his tracing fingers, stark against his gray coat. Her eyes grew thoughtful. He glanced down. Though he'd scrubbed away as best he could ink leaked by his pen onto his fingers, they still showed reddened skin overlaid with abraded black streaks.

"I don't know what you must do," she said, "but I can tell you must do it. It was a pleasure to meet you, Hans."

"And you."

Hans withdrew to a table at the far end of the picnic area. With trembling hands, he pulled the notebook from his inner pocket and blotted excess ink from his pen's nib onto an unused page at the back. Then he scrawled notes. *Rabble rouser. Aerial bombardment.* What else had gripped him in the beer hall? He squeezed shut his eyes, then dashed out more.

Eventually the pressure of the vision faded, its contents transformed and diffused across the pages. The ink dried rapidly in the cold air, and Hans soon returned his pen to his inner pocket.

He had not finished. He reviewed his recent words, then flipped through the rest of the notebook. The earliest entries dated to the long retreat of last summer and fall, when he first realized the visions were not hallucinations born in dysentery, undernourishment, and incessant shelling. He squinted at barely legible handwriting, winced at misspellings. A deep breath helped him look past those trivialities. His visions formed nodes in a network, like the different machines on Müller's factory floor, or the wire coils, pillboxes, and machine gun nests of a defensive position. If he could learn all the visions' connections, he might find a point where a single man's effort could keep them from happening.

The words he read called up memories of the visions that had propelled them to the page, memories nearly as intense as the visions themselves. Spurred, he pored over his notes with extra intensity.

Some things were clear. The rabble-rouser, whoever he was, would somehow take the reins of government, then plunge the country into an unwinnable war and devastation not seen in three centuries. The rabble-rouser lacked the easy hauteur of the abdicated Kaiser or the princes now shorn of titles, and neither the empire nor any of its former kingdoms use the hooked cross on flags or crests. Not a monarchist, then. But what did he stand for? How did he seize power?

What could be done to stop him from leading the country to ruin?

Could anything?

Hans lost track of time. His energy faded, leaving him with no fresh insight.

He looked up. The clouds had thickened. Liesl had gone inside.

Time to go home. He found a gate in the wrought iron fence, then a footpath leading to the riverside street. Hans trudged along, his belly hollow. He almost turned toward the market plaza, but it would be busy with pedestrians, and workmen setting up for Carnival. He preferred solitude. He kept going, toward the foundry and the workmen's quarter huddled under its smokestacks.

He turned away from the riverside street at a corner occupied by a timber-and-plaster beer hall. The door opened and three men bustled out. They wore workmen's clothes, patched woolen jackets and rumpled trousers, but their demeanor—the bold, lively face of the leader, and the hard eyes of the two men following him—showed they were not simple workmen.

The leader halted his followers with a gesture. "Hello, trenchfighter." The leader stepped forward. "I'm Becker." He jutted out his hand.

Hans shook it and gave Becker his name.

"You look morose," Becker said. "Doesn't he, boys?"

Becker's followers muttered agreement.

To Hans, Becker asked, "What trouble has befallen you?"

"I'm a bookkeeper. I sought a job at Müller's watch factory and was turned away." He thought of his pockets, nearly empty save for his notebook and pen.

Becker put on a sad look. "That's capitalism in a nutshell. Your comrades die on the hill of expanding monopoly, and you come home to enforced idleness. You're as much a victim of the capitalists as we workers. But fear not, all will change after the revolution is come."

A red flag raised over the ruins of Berlin. "Revolution? Or the replacement of one monopoly by another? How many people have the reds killed in their civil war?"

A dismissive wave. "Lenin and Trotsky seek to establish communism in a country that hasn't even reached capitalism. The vast masses of Russian peasants are not in position to comprehend the Marxist message, never mind embrace it. We won't have those problems here."

Hans stood taller. "Can you be so certain?"

Understanding flared on Becker's face. "Ach, of course your first instinct is to side with the capitalists. You're a bookkeeper and fear you would have no place come the revolution. To the contrary. Even after we abolish money, there will still be a need to keep records, of which supplies are come, of which finished products are shipped out, that sort of thing."

Hans failed to find a rebuttal before Becker went on. "Once we turf out men like old fat Müller, we will have all we want. Employment for every man! His daughter will cleave to me, of course, as the leader of the revolution in Sorgenbach, but there's many more young women than young men now, you'll have a prime pick."

Becker leaned closer. "One more thing. Join us for Carnival. We've taken over one of the parade clubs, the Prince-Archbishop-Elector's Guard."

"An odd club for communists to join," Hans said.

"The club names are all in mock," Becker said. "And by maintaining the tradition of a club, its elder members and the people on the street think we pose no threat to their settled ways. Will you join us?"

Hans shook his head. "I've joined another club."

Becker raised an eyebrow. "One of the capitalists'? Do you know why they admitted you?"

"You do?"

"They want men to brawl with us. They think we can be kept down by a few punches, while the police look the other way. They're wrong about that. We will parade peacefully, unless we must defend ourselves. You would gain nothing but a worker's fist if you parade with the capitalists."

"I appreciate your offer," Hans said. A deep breath filled his torso. "But I've already joined another."

∞

Thursday dawned clear and cold, but warmed enough by late morning that Hans left his garret without his hat. A crowd of men spilled out of the market plaza. Hans craned his neck for Müller. No sight of the factory owner.

Hans accreted to the crowd, but a moment later, a hand landed on his shoulder. "Hans?" The speaker had a fringe of gray hair and a jutting nose. Schneider, owner of the foundry. "Let me take you to Müller."

The crowd parted for Schneider. Hans followed in his wake. Moments later they reached Müller, who stood with half a dozen older, well-dressed men near the town hall and the church. The hands of the clock on the church steeple pointed nearly to noon.

"Hans, welcome!" Müller said. "Here, you need this." He extended a tricorner hat with a white ceramic domino masking the eyes. A leer was baked into the mask. From each side of the domino hung a string.

Men's voices grew louder on the streets approaching the market plaza. Near them, men pulled on dominos, jester hats, full masks. "Quick, quick!" Müller said.

Hans put on the hat, and tied the strings together behind his ears. The first peals of noon rang from the clock.

"And one more thing." Müller handed him a necktie. Hans realized Müller and the men around him each wore one.

"But...."

"Yes. We know what will happen. That's the point."

Hans shrugged out of his coat and lifted his collar. With unpracticed hands, he tied the necktie. The clock's dozenth chime rang out. Hans put his coat back on just as the women entered the market plaza.

They wore black dresses, like widows, or brides who'd previously birthed bastards. Black masked their eyes, mostly in the form of dominos, though a few, the leaders, wore cowls. They glowered at the men, who roared with laughter and shrank back, as they proceeded to the town hall.

The mayor played his part of the ritual with grace. He blocked the main door, fists on hips, and shook his head at the women's scripted requests he yield. After he refused them twice, three women stepped forward and pulled him out of the way. He stumbled on the cobbles, but kept his balance and approached the crowd.

A vision swept over Hans.

A well-dressed man with fear in his eyes, trudging into woods, surrounded by men in black greatcoats and hooked-cross armbands. Old men with missing limbs and boys of twelve or thirteen, wearing ill-fitting field-gray and carrying obsolete rifles, cowering in a ditch as a gigantic armored vehicle rumbled toward them. Corpses, shrunken and shriveled like burnt dolls, in waterless fountains as a conflagration consumed their city.

The vision disappeared as swiftly as it came. Hans sucked in deep breaths of cool air.

The ritual of Women's Thursday had gone on without him. With shouts of triumph, the last of the women entered the town hall.

The clerks soon fled the building through the main door, buttoning their coats and pulling on their hats as they ran. The town hall's upper windows banged open, and the women's leaders proclaimed victory with a viraginous tone and the flinging of papers from some clerk's desk. The papers drifted down like British propaganda leaflets as the women's leaders bellowed their decrees. Neckties were forbidden. A woman's request for a kiss could not be refused.

Hans wished he could slip away and write in his notebook. The shoulders of the surrounding businessmen hemmed him in. When half a dozen young women slipped out of the town hall, he shut his eyes for a moment to preserve the vision's memory, then opened his eyes and squared his shoulders to the women.

Young, indeed. About twenty years of age, give or take. They halted in front of Müller. "What's this?" one called out. She fingered his necktie.

"This?" he said with false innocence. "I have no idea."

"You are in contempt of the Women's Committee's decree. Who witnesses this crime?"

"I do," a second woman said. A third repeated the words.

A grave look crossed the first woman's face. "The punishment shall be meted out. Scissors!"

A fourth woman held out a pair of scissors. The first woman took them, lifted the end of Müller's tie straight out, and cut the taut tie with two snips. She lifted the cut end and the women cheered.

She flung the necktie's cut end over her shoulder. "A fine is also due!"

"Oh, how shall I pay?" Müller said.

She stood on tiptoe and kissed Müller. The other women followed, all but one. By the end, lipstick smeared his face.

"And here," the first woman said, "another violator—" Her eyelids fluttered when she saw Hans up close. Soon, though, she recovered, grabbing his tie and pulling him in for a kiss. Her mouth worked over his, striving to draw out a passion he lacked.

"Make way," a stout woman said. She shouldered the first woman aside and cupped his face in thick hands. Her desperation came through her lips as clearly as had the first woman's. A man their age, alive and seemingly intact—

Which of the shriveled corpses in the dry fountain had been women, middle-aged two decades hence?

More young women took kisses from him. The first woman pushed through the crowd. "His necktie must be sacrificed!"

"Allow me," said a woman heretofore silent. She snatched the scissors and closed on Hans. She had been the one woman to not kiss Müller. "Stand back!" she called to her peers. Liesl's voice.

She stood close to Hans, then pulled his tie far enough to slide one blade between it and his coat. She cut the tie with one long snip.

Her lips touched his tenderly, for a long moment. He leaned into her. His hands rose to her hips.

She broke off the kiss. "I must police the rest of the town, young miscreant."

"I am contrite," he said. The corners of his mouth lifted slightly. Liesl turned away.

The vision remained clear in his memory, but distant, as if behind thick glass. He could regard it as something outside himself.

He blinked, turned his head. Müller looked at him, and despite hat and mask, the factory owner projected an air of knowing humor.

Hans' cheeks warmed and he turned his head. The women drifted down the front rank of the male crowd. Hans studied each line of head and shoulders, in search of Liesl.

∞

Thin clouds like worn strips of cloth hung above a purpling sky, and an orange-red sunset backlit the Roman ruins on the hill above Sorgenbach, as Hans went to the Old Carnival Club's parade preparation site. On the outskirts of town, a barn stood on a hillside. A rough stone wall, its base conforming to the slope and its top even, supported an upper structure of timbers and planking. In the tallest part of the stone wall, facing downslope, yellow light leaked around two carriage doors guarded by two middle-aged men in bright blue coats, white jackets, and tall shako hats.

As Hans approached the barn, one of the men came forward. His paunch puckered his buttoned jacket. Between his hands, he spun a stave carved to resemble an antique musket, then held it horizontally and jutted it in front of him. "What enemy of the Fools' Republic comes?" Breath steamed away with his words.

"Herr Müller invited me."

The other man came up. He stomped his boots tromp-tromp. "Name, rank, and serial number, *citoyen*."

The costumes and words parodied the soldiers of the previous French occupation, Napoleon's, a century before. God knew what the current crop of French would make of them.

Hans gave his name, and that of his regiment in the war.

His interrogator pulled up his furry shako and rummaged inside the lining for a piece of paper. He squinted at it in the dim light, ran his finger down it. "There you are. Follow us, *citoyen*." The men marched to the carriage doors and gave each other commands in pidgin French. One lifted the bar and the other swung open a door.

Inside he found light, sound, warmth, mirth. Men crowded around wagons bearing papier-mâché effigies. War economy and blockade had not hardened the men, but merely shrank their softness. Banter about the last touches needed by the floats combined with calls to harried barmaids, recruited from some tavern, to bring more beer. In one corner, brass blatted and drums rattled as a band practiced the fools' marches. In another corner, men in blue uniforms and shako hats drilled with staves. Spilled lager and paste stained the hard-packed dirt floor. Heat from wood-burning ovens cloaked the space.

Some of the floats enacted timeless themes. Here, men lifted tankards and joined arms in drunken song. There, the Rhine's daughters sunned themselves on rocks during the first days of spring.

Other floats made blatant political statements. A bust of Napoleon, right hand inside his jacket, left lifting sausages and cheeses to his mouth, gluttonous face mustachioed by beer foam. Around him, miniature French colonials, their black faces anachronistic above the blue and white uniforms of his *Grande Armée*, dragged fresh-faced blondes to their emperor's feet.

Hans remembered looting the cellars of French country houses. He turned away.

Another float commented on domestic politics. Two men, a stolid burgher and a soldier under the steel helmet, each stood with one foot between the shoulder blades of a flailing figure. The soldier held his bayonet's tip at the nape of a man with a high forehead and pince-nez glasses. The burgher stepped on a woman whose skirts could not conceal mismatched legs. The trampled figures were Liebknecht and

Luxemburg, dead and presumed dead since the failed Communist uprising in Berlin six weeks earlier.

"Hans, it's good you've come." Schneider clapped him on the shoulder, then gestured at his coat. "It's warm enough to shed this. We have a table, let me set it there."

Hans shrugged out of his coat. Schneider draped it over his arm and led him to table near the doors, heaped with woolen coats. After Hans' joined the pile, Schneider beckoned to a barmaid. "This man is thirsty. For that matter, so am I."

The barmaid brought them beers. From her face below the eyes, and her thick fingers around the mug handles, Hans recognized one of Thursday's kissing women. She bustled away.

Schneider tapped his mug to Hans'. "*Prosit.*"

Hans echoed the word and sipped. "Is Herr Müller about? I wish to speak with him."

"He must be somewhere." Schneider looked around with exaggerated care. "I don't see him. Keep searching, I'm sure you'll find him. And keep your mug full!"

Hans kept wandering. He caught glimpses of Müller around the barn, but could never take more than two steps in his direction before one or another of the older club members, slightly familiar from the market plaza on Women's Thursday, curtailed him and bade the barmaids bring him more beer. The need to speak with Müller grew less urgent, as Hans soon became very drunk.

Much later, outside, he wavered on his feet, stream of piss wobbling over the barn's stone wall, when three chimes rose from the clock tower and climbed the cold hillside. The ringing of three o'clock steadied his head. He hadn't spoken with Müller. He went back into the barn and held his hands out to an oven until its remaining heat dispelled his shivers.

The barn had grown quiet. The band had packed up its instruments and departed. Most of the club guards had left, save for a few protecting the floats. Hans remembered passing several more club guards between the barn doors and the pissing wall. A half-dozen men sat around the room, snoring off their drunkenness.

He could find a chair and sleep here, or walk to his garret and sleep there. The cold night air would sober him.

Not yet. Where was Müller?

The factory owner came to him from around the float of defeated Communists. "Hans. The night has treated you well, I see. Do you have a minute?"

"I wanted to ask you the same. What was your purpose in inviting me to your club?"

Müller nodded gravely. "You are a perceptive young man."

"It's not to drink your beer. You and the other members could handle that on your own." He'd drunk enough to excrete his usual reticence with his piss. "You were right, the floats were fully decorated by the time I arrived. I thought it might be to join your guard to battle the Communists during tomorrow's parade, but the guard finished drilling without speaking to me." Hans leaned forward. "What did you invite me for?"

"What makes you think we want to battle the Communists?" Müller asked. His voice sounded sober.

"On the street last week, I ran into Becker—"

"Becker?" Müller's face twisted in disgust. "That vile spreader of Bolshevik contagion. The workmen of Sorgenbach would be content with their lot if not for his lies. If he seized the reins of our town, every-thing we value would come toppling down on us. Here is one of his tricks. He wants to start a fight, then pin the guilt clause on us to whip up the indignation of his deluded followers. He didn't tell you that, did he?"

"No." Hans remembered Becker's other words.

"What else did he say?"

"The usual rhetoric. And…. he lusts after Liesl."

Müller clamped his lips together. Waves of anger worked through his face until he mastered them. "Like all of history's usurpers, he seeks legitimacy by wedding the daughter of his overturned foe. Even though her choice would be another." Müller managed a smile. "Don't look so embarrassed, Hans. I know she cannot remain my little maiden forever. You've taken a shine to her and her, to you."

Hans' heart thudded. "I don't know what she would see in me."

"Don't be so modest. You're a brave hero. And if you don't know what she sees in you, come to our house on Tuesday, for a last tea-time of cakes and chicory before Lent."

Hans' heart kept thudding. "Thank you, Herr Müller."

Müller raised a hand. "There is one thing, though, before that. That intent of mine you asked about? Let's discuss it, in private." He pointed at a loft above the main floor of the barn.

"Of course."

Hans followed Müller to a ladder guarded by a man leaning against it. The brim of the man's shako half-covered his drooping eyes. He snapped to alertness as they approached and stood aside as they climbed.

The heat of the ovens lingered in the loft. A lantern's dim glow cast the scene in orange light. A few bales of hay occupied the loft's rear. To the front, and in addition to the lantern, a table bore empty mugs of beer and maps of the parade route.

"Wait here," Müller said. Along the wall stood a small locked trunk. Müller went to it, worked a key, and brought out a bundle. He rested it on the table in front of Hans and began untying it.

The cords fell away to reveal an ornate, puffy costume of reds and earth-tones, with matching striped hose and a broad, flat hat. The garb of a *landsknecht*, a mercenary soldier of centuries ago. A black domino accompanied the costume. Amid the fabric was a wooden sword, the length of a man's arm, with a figure-eight hilt guard.

"This is the costume of the Prince-Archbishop-Elector's Guard," Hans said.

"So it is. Down to the cat-gutter—at least at first glance." Müller gripped the hilt with one hand and held the wooden blade down with the other. He pulled his hands apart. With a metallic *scritch* came out a knife-blade. Six inches long, but honed steel. A close cousin to the knife Hans had carried on a dozen trench raids.

"I've made inquiries of your officers. How many tommies and frogs have you skewered?"

The whites of a French sentry's bulging eyes, staring up at the moonless sky as he bled out. "One or two."

"You needn't be so modest. You have used the trench knife against our foreign enemies. Now it is time to use it against a domestic one."

"Becker."

"In this costume, you'll infiltrate the Communist parade, find Becker, and gut him before anyone is the wiser. He'll be near the front of his parade, and we'll have the frog-baiting float near the back. When the French Negroes react to the float, we'll add to the confusion, to give you more cover to work. That's clear?"

Hans nodded, mute.

"Splendid. Let me rebundle this—"

Ships stretched toward the horizon, their shells pounding hungry men in field-gray. Long columns of massive armored fighting vehicles, decorated with the red star, thundering across open fields. A fleet of aircraft, their silhouettes like a hundred crosses against the daylight sky, releasing cargoes of whistling bombs.

"No," Hans said. "No. No!" He ran to the ladder and tramped down. His breaths were shallow, like an unmasked man in a gas attack. He ran to the carriage doors and out, into the chill night, onto the road, a few steps down the hill toward town.

The chill air bit his throat. He shivered, slowed his steps. He had done the right thing. He would leave his killing work behind in the spectral wastelands of France, where it belonged. Killing Becker would not prevent the visions from coming true. He knew this with sudden intuition.

He slowed his steps further. Why was he so cold?

His coat remained in the barn.

In his coat, his notebook.

Hans stopped. Could he go back and face Müller? Yes, he could. Müller had kept the plot a secret from his club colleagues. Some of them would be present and awake. Müller would not ask him again.

His invitation to cakes and chicory—to a sitting room with Liesl— would be revoked.

No. It already had. Hans expelled a ragged breath, then turned back to the barn.

The guards let him in the gate and through the carriage doors. He found the table laden with coats. The shuffling of piles had brought it to the top. He put it on, then tapped the breast above the inner pocket. Empty—

"Hans."

Müller stood at the loft's railing. He held a small, open notebook. "Interesting reading. Would you come up to discuss it?"

"Hand it back."

"I'll be glad to. But, please, come up and discuss it with me. I understand now."

Hans stared at the notebook in Müller's hands and licked his lips. "I'm coming up."

By the time he climbed the ladder, Müller stood at the table. On it, the notebook lay closed, yet Hans knew it had yielded all its secrets.

"Troubling visions," Müller said. "A disaster for us all, should they prove true."

"Killing Becker won't stop them from coming true."

"Are you certain?" Müller peered at him. "Becker is not the rabble-rouser, clearly, but who is that man? What does he stand for?"

Hans racked his memory, a sluggish process in the aftermath of all the beer he'd drunk. "Not the monarchy."

"His banner has a red field. Sounds like a Communist or radical Socialist to me."

Hans shook his head. "The imperial flag has the same red, black, and white as the rabble-rouser's. Doesn't matter. He can't be a Communist. The Soviets will lift their red flag over the Reichstag. Would Communists fight Communists?"

Müller widened his arms. "Whoever he is, he's no Communist. I'll grant you that. I'll grant killing Becker won't stop him. But would keeping Becker alive stop him?"

Hans opened his mouth, shut it.

Müller went on. "Becker is one Communist out of millions. We know from the chaos they unleashed on Russia the last eighteen months, and tried to unleash in Berlin this past January, they wouldn't submit to non-Communist domination without a fight. But if your visions are true, then all their resistance won't matter. Even if we let Becker join his comrades, they would still lose. But think of the wreck and ruin they would inflict on their way to defeat. Think of the wreck and ruin Becker would inflict on Sorgenbach, even if his ultimate fate were sealed."

Müller half-sat on the table. "And if your visions are true, even if the future they show could be changed, what could you do, or I? One man makes no difference in the great struggles of our current age. I didn't see the trenches but I know enough to know *that*. If your visions are our fate, there's nothing you or I could do. We can only act here, and now, to preserve ourselves and the few people most important to us as best we can." Müller smiled. "Have you rethought your answer, Hans?"

He felt drained. Not simply tired, or numbed by drink, but as if his spirit had been grievously wounded and it slumped inside him, cold and babbling from blood loss. Kill one more man, then a quiet life with Liesl, and perhaps the visions would follow Becker into the ground.

"I'll do it."

Müller looked solemn. "I appreciate what you do, for our town, for our country. Here you go." He lifted the notebook.

Hans shook his head. "I don't need it anymore."

∞

The clashing sounds of two bands echoed off the front walls of houses and reached Hans in his hiding place, a stairwell leading down to a cellar. Slivers of torchlight like ground-bound starshells swept over his eye. He covered his mouth and nose to keep his breath from streaming up to street level.

The blue and white uniforms and shako hats of the old club's guard hove into view, as did the anti-French float. The first ranks of the Prince-Archbishop-Elector's Guard came close behind. Hans peered over the top of the stairwell at the street.

A French officer scowled at the float. The colonials behind him did more. They brandished their rifles and shouted at the club members standing near the minuscule effigies.

The officer raised his hand and shouted at them. Perhaps the French simply didn't want to make trouble by interfering in the local tradition. Perhaps the officer recognized the float as a temporary inversion of the new order of things, and the next day the people of Sorgenbach would revert to their inferior status, just as the town's women had after the previous Thursday.

If the officer knew that, he failed to share the message with his men. Especially when townsfolk watching the parade hooted with laughter.

Then a man in the trailing rank of the old club flung a half-empty mug of beer into the midst of the colonial soldiers.

Shouts and screams, and waves of movement spasmed through the two parade clubs. The colonial soldiers swung rifle butts at members of both clubs. Musket-shaped staves and short wooden swords came out, raised to parry, and from both clubs, men flowed toward the colonials. The French officer shouted and blew his whistle to get his men to disengage, without success.

Hans scanned the figures of the Prince-Archbishop-Elector's Guard. All wore the *landsknecht* uniform and a black domino. Stolid workers, most of them. Slay the officer and the men will crumble. But where was—?

A figure, taller than average, with two strapping men standing near him, heads turned to receive his commands. The body language was clear. The commanding figure was Becker. His two bodyguards joined the flow of club members going to resist the French colonials.

While keeping his eye on Becker, Hans put on his domino and broad flat hat. He went up the stairs to street level, unnoticed by the identically-clad men around him.

The tumult on the street masked the *scritch* as he drew his knife from its wooden sheath.

PASE DE UN DÍA

The only displacement booth in San Lorenzo stood between the town hall and the church, where Calle Benito Juárez ended at Calle Progresso. The sky was pale in the east, but the sun had not yet risen over the Sierra Madre, when Chalo ran his hand over sleeping Berto's hair, kissed Adelina, and left their three-room house. Awakening birds chirped behind corrugated iron fences. Chalo's stomach felt hollow. He ignored it. Once he got to work, he would scavenge his morning meal from the previous day's pastries in the break room. His family needed the pesos he would save by doing so.

A few blocks from the displacement booth, he stopped at an intersection, looked left and right, and started across. A car horn blared, startling him, and he jumped back toward the corner. A big, old pickup running on the battery of its hybrid engine had come up behind him and now turned left across his path. The window was down and the driver showed a pudgy face with a scraggly mustache and a medium complexion. "Fucking Indian, you're so short I almost hit you!" The pickup's gasoline engine kicked in and the mestizo roared away, flinging pebbles of crumbling asphalt from his rear tires.

For a moment, a tiny flame of rage burned in Chalo's chest, and he hunched his shoulders and head over it. But rage at the mestizo would not build a better life for his son. He took a deep breath to snuff the smoldering emotion, then looked all ways before crossing the now-empty street.

Soon he passed the private school run by the gray-haired gringo couple. The gate stood ajar. From within came the sound of metal shutters rolling up and English spoken too fast for him to follow. *"Aiden wants us to come for dinner* Friday *to meet Nadezhda,"* said a woman's voice.

Friday. Did she ask her husband about the deposit deadline at the end of next week? Chalo counted days and hours and his wage, then multiplied them together. He would work every day but Sunday. He would have enough to pay the deposit and get Berto away from the incompetent teacher who slept all day at the government school. The Virgin had blessed Chalo with a son of great intelligence, but her blessing demanded Chalo provide Berto with every possible chance for his intelligence to thrive.

The sun had crested the Sierra Madre, but the church's shadow still covered the displacement booth when he arrived. The booth was a glass cylinder big enough for a family to stand together. Its door showed the laser-etched logo of Teletransportes Mexicanos. A ring of lights around the cylinder's top glowed green. When he opened the door, it swung so easily it seemed to push itself against his hand.

He took his trifold wallet from the inner pocket of his jacket. Old when Adelina had bought it at a flea market, the wallet's folds showed years of wear and the bottoms of the inner slots had long ago split, revealing the edges of his debit card and family photos. Mounted on the inner wall of the booth, opposite the door, were a card reader and a touchscreen. Chalo swiped his debit card and alphanumeric buttons appeared.

With one finger, he tapped out *u-s-d-a-y-p-a-s-s*, then *Introducir*. The next screen asked him to confirm the address and the fee. He touched *Sí*.

He flicked into another booth, twin to the first. He turned and stepped out into a broad, high-ceilinged room, crowded with people and echoing with a babel of voices. This place still made him nervous —he widened his eyes and jerked his head—but he had been through here a few days now and knew the routine. He'd flicked into one of a row of twenty booths standing along what guessed was the south wall. Five queues snaked around plastic railings and aimed for a far wall dominated by an immense United States flag. He went to the nearest queue and shuffled forward.

Most of the people around him were mestizos, with a few blacks and fewer Indians. Regardless of race, many were dressed, like him, in dark trousers and matching tee shirts bearing restaurant logos stitched on the front and displacement booth addresses printed across the back. Chalo heard multiple Spanish dialects; a nasal language that almost sounded like Spanish; and lilting English from some of the blacks. The languages of the other Indians were completely unintelligible. Did everyone from all the countries of the Americas who traveled to the United States on the pase de un día, the day pass, come through this border station?

When he was third in line from the checkpoint, Chalo slid his day pass from his wallet. The day pass' white face and red and blue accents were the only things to distinguish it from his debit card. Its English words made little sense to him—he could pick out *United States*, but little else. His printed name seemed to shift in three dimensions when he wiggled the card.

In front of him, a mestiza with a long nose, bunned hair, and a buttoned gray jacket turned her left shoulder toward the turnstile's scanner. *You should consider an implant instead of the card*, the gringo in the consular office had told him in a formal Mexico City accent. *It's more secure.*

Chalo had disregarded his words. If the consular official wanted him to take an implant, it must give the gringos some benefit over him. He understood cards. Even if the card were less secure, he would not lose it.

The turnstile snapped shut behind the mestiza, and the robot torso mounted to the turnstile snaked out its neck and turned its cold, peering face down to Chalo. He shrank from it, more than any morning since his first one through here. His heart thudded and his hand shook as he swiped his day pass through a card reader. *Blessed Virgin, Queen of Mexico, strengthen me....* His hand steadied and he stood a little taller. The robot was only a machine, no different than it had been on earlier days. The near-miss by the pickup in San Lorenzo had made him jumpy.

After a moment, the robot withdrew and a light shone green next to the turnstile. Chalo went through. Around him, a few people strode from the turnstiles toward a row of a dozen displacement booths. The booths looked the same as the one in San Lorenzo, except their doors bore the logos of different companies: Pelton Industries, JumpShift, FARcast, and Portkey Science, alternating in that order. All worked the same, he'd been told, and he'd discovered for himself over his first three days using the day pass. He hadn't yet used a JumpShift booth, so Chalo went to that company's nearest one.

The touchscreen held a swirl of pale blue dots on a darker blue background. It showed three white buttons, each bearing an icon: a red cross for a hospital, a blue shield for police, and a bright yellow dot racing around an outline of the United States. The border police. Going to any of those addresses would waste many of his twelve hours, or worse.

He moved his day pass to one end of the card reader slot. He had been told his debit card, because of its link to an account with a Mexican bank, would not work on the United States network. True or false, he had no need to experiment. He had to get to his job.

Chalo ran his card through the reader. The touchscreen's buttons wobbled and disappeared, and lines of text replaced them.

Destination/destino: The Shoppes at Indian Bend (NW service booth), Paradise Valley, AZ

Latest departure time/Última hora de la salida: 05:49:28 PM MST and the second ticked up to 29 by the time Chalo pressed the button *Yes/Sí.*

He flicked to work. Concrete block and hanging fluorescent lights defined a wide, empty concourse. Only a robotic mop-and-bucket occupied the space. Its mop slid back and forth over the concrete floor. Chalo turned to the right, heading for a glass door leading to the pedestrian mall. His black sneakers squeaked from the mop's damp residue.

From a large cargo booth behind him came the thudding sounds of its door locking and unlocking. Chalo glanced over his shoulder to see who, or what, had flicked in. From the booth rolled a robotic flatbed cart with a structure at the front for its batteries and its computer brain. Its cargo-handling arms were folded against the structure. On quiet tires, it went the other direction down the concourse, bound for the rear entrance of some boutique, bearing a stack of recycled cardboard boxes marked *Fabrique en France*.

The glass door opened for Chalo. The sky overhead was blue, but the pedestrian mall remained in shadow. Even so, the air was hotter and drier than home and would only grow more so during the day. Chalo began to sweat in his jacket as he followed the winding mall. Most of the shops he passed were closed, their dim interior lights and the dawn glow combining to illuminate window displays of men's suits, ornate jewelry, lingerie, golf clubs. Hidden loudspeakers played orchestral music and water splashed down statues of nudes in the fountains. In front of a perfume store, a sweet floral scent filled his nose.

A glow of lights spilled from a store's front windows onto pavers still in shadow. The sign overhead read *Riviera Maya Coffee & Chocolate Co.* Chalo went in.

A few customers, older men in polo shirts, sat scattered among the tables. They glanced up as Chalo passed, then returned their attention to their tablets. The door from the kitchen swung open, and Hernán approached with a black lacquered tray bearing a cappuccino and a chocolate croissant. He wore a black bowtie, a white jacket, and an imperious look. "You're late," he muttered in Spanish.

Alarmed, Chalo looked at the clock. "It's not yet six."

"That thing does not synchronize properly with the atomic clock. Señor Kaufmann is waiting." Hernán lifted his chin and went to one of the customers.

Through the kitchen, in the break room, Chalo quickly signed in on a touchscreen, moved his wallet to his back pocket, and hung his jacket. He found Kaufmann in his small, windowless office. "I'm sorry I am late, sir."

Kaufmann blinked over his reading glasses, then checked the time display on his tablet. "A few minutes until six. You have the proper attitude. Less than a week and you already understand how the better sort of gringos view time." Kaufmann himself looked like a gringo, pink-white skin and grizzled gray-brown hair, yet he spoke Spanish with an accent native to northern Mexico. It was not Chalo's place to ask if Kaufmann had grown up in Phoenix or Monterrey.

"Better to be five minutes early," Kaufmann went on, "than five minutes late. Remember that."

"I will, sir."

Kaufmann glanced at his tablet. "Three complete days, and you've done adequately so far. Your speed and quality metrics at bussing tables and helping in the kitchen are above average for a trainee."

Chalo had not known. Hernán had continually criticized his work. "Sir, thank you."

Kaufmann's face grew more serious, and he waggled a finger. "But you must not rest. You must approach every job with the idea of always improving. There are ten million Mexican men who would be above average trainees. Do you understand me?"

"I do, sir. I will always improve."

"And hang on to your day pass. I don't know why people squander their opportunity by losing it." He nodded toward the swinging doors to the kitchen. "It's time for you to get to work. Señor Halford has probably left for the golf course by now. His table needs bussing."

Chalo's duties gave the day a steady rhythm, and shifting sunlight and the flow and ebb of customers gave it a melody. He listened to the customers as he carried bins of dirty cups and plates to the robotic dishwasher in the kitchen. Though he understood few words, he wanted to learn all he could about the customers. It would help him improve at his job. And just maybe—a dream so close to impossible he could tell no one, not even Adelina; but thanks to the Virgin, it was possible enough—he might learn how to introduce Berto into their world.

First came doctors and nurses in blue scrubs, stopping at the take-away counter before their morning hospital shifts. Chalo heard the names of gringo cities, names just last week as mythic as El Dorado and Cibola, but now spoken by people a flick away from Seattle, Chicago, Los Angeles. Business people made up most of the crowd between seven and nine, men in three-piece suits, women in skirts and heels. They were often distracted, paying attention to conversations going through their earpieces.

"We absolutely cannot compromise any aspect of our handicraft certification," one businessman said, chopping the air with his hand to emphasize his words. *"If we falsely pass something as handmade and word gets out, our competitors will eat our lunch. No, I don't care what the elder told you. You tell him we can get the same goddamn rugs from the next village...."*

By late morning, the crowd had thinned. Most customers now were older women wearing tight faces and pantsuits modeled by mannequins in the windows of nearby boutiques. The women came in accompanied by blasts of dry, bakingly hot air.

"Yes, isn't this place marvelous? Far better than that robotic swill from the Seattle chain. The flour comes from nitrogen-fixing grains, certified fertilizer-free and they preserve so much habitat compared to the genetically unimproved varieties. The coffee and chocolate are fair trade. And all the employees are Maya from the Yucatan."

Maya from the Yucatan? Had she recently vacationed in Cancún? Chalo shrugged and took another bin of dirty plates to the kitchen. He fed the contents to the dishwasher while Hernán picked up a tray of coffees and pastries laid out by articulated robot arms mounted on tracks in the ceiling.

After a swell of customers stopping by on their way from their lunch hours back to their jobs, the crowd thinned again. Chalo ate a quick lunch of two hard-boiled eggs and a whey protein bagel while standing in a corner of the kitchen. Hernán's scowl lashed him into wolfing down his last bites and hurrying out to the dining room with his bin.

The next customer spike came around three: mothers relaxing for fifteen minutes before picking up children from school, groups of teenagers grousing about homework before pulling out their tablets to study together. Among the latter was a table of two boys. One, pure gringo, sported spiky blond hair and a narrow beard. An animated college logo looped on his tee shirt. His demeanor mixed the privilege of high status, guilt at the privilege, and an earnest desire to reconcile the two. The other was a slender mestizo in his early teens, in a school uniform of khakis and a blue polo. He gulped down one of the coffee cakes the older boy ordered, then looked bored. A tablet set down between them showed the logo of an agency or service called *Tutor For America.*

"Alfonso, describe the Thirtieth Amendment to the Constitution," the gringo boy said.

The younger boy frowned at his chocolate smoothie. *"Let's see. That's the one that gave Washington, D.C. two senators and a congressman?"*

The gringo boy's smile froze. *"That was the Twenty-ninth."*

"The Thirtieth. Something about citizenship?"

"That's right.... Citizenship and birthright...."

The younger boy reached for the tablet. *"Can I look it up?"*

"There are things its good to have in your mind and not just electronically."

"I can't remember. I give up."

The older boy sagged with an exhaled breath. *"The Thirtieth Amendment clarified the Citizenship Clause of the Fourteenth. Someone gets citizenship at birth only if both their parents are citizens or legal residents of the United States."*

"Why do I need to know this stuff? It's not on the SAT. My dad doesn't use this crap to run his restaurants. He'll give me a good job when I'm done with school. You're wasting my time."

The gringo boy blinked in confusion for a moment. *"I know it seems like a waste now... but your father worked to get your name in the lottery for tutoree slots and do you want to tell him you don't care?"*

The younger boy looked away and folded his arms. *"Fine...."*

"Now, where were—whoa!"

Chalo turned his head. A large white blur, then the smack of another body colliding with his. The bin slipped from his grip as he fell on his rear end. Cups and plates clattered on the floor, spilling dregs of coffee and crumbs of pastries. A cappuccino flowed around shards of porcelain. It had left tan drops on Hernán's pants when it fell.

The waiter glared down at Chalo. "You stupid fucking Indian!" His voice carried through the now-silent café.

Chalo's cheeks felt hot. "I'm sorry." He scrambled onto his knees and groped for broken cups and plates.

Motion in the corner of his eye resolved into Señor Kaufmann. "What's going on here?"

"This inept Indian didn't watch where he was going," Hernán said.

Chalo's face felt even hotter. What would this do to his numbers? Would Kaufmann fire him on the spot? He flung porcelain fragments into his plastic bin. Sharp slivers scratched his fingertips.

"That is not the full story," the gringo boy said in slow but correct Spanish. "Both men were looking the other way when they ran into each other."

Hernán clamped his lips together. He glowered at the gringo boy for a moment before it seemed he decided better of it. With a milder expression, he said, "I recall looking straight ahead, and even if I didn't, Chalo should watch for me, not I for him."

Kaufmann looked frustrated. "First we fix the problem. Later we find what went wrong and keep it from happening again. You lost an order, Hernán? Replace it and comp the customer. Then help Chalo clean up if he isn't done by then."

Hernán looked sullen, then stalked off to the kitchen. Chalo picked up more shards of cups and plates and mopped up spilled coffee with a tea towel.

"What did you say?" the younger boy asked the gringo.

"That it wasn't the busboy's fault." His eyes narrowed and his lips parted, as if he wanted to ask a question.

"What's that look? You think I'm supposed to speak Spanish?"

In the gringo boy's face, guilt overwhelmed privilege. *"No, no, of course not. Let's get back to work. Where were we, Alfonso?"*

"You know I want to be called Al...."

Chalo hurried to the kitchen with a full bin. Hernán passed him and gave a cold stare. Chalo hustled to the trashcan and shook the broken pieces out of the bin. A cold feeling washed through him. He had lost his job. He had failed Berto. He–

He would do his best, even if today was his last day here. Chalo stood a little straighter and returned to the dining room.

Walking near the table with the two boys, someone said, "Señor."

Was Kaufmann still about? Chalo hurried on.

"Señor!" It was the gringo boy, and he called for him. Chalo stopped and faced him, but, uncertain how he could respond, said nothing.

"Your wallet." The gringo boy pointed to the floor near the collision site. It must have fallen from Chalo's pocket when he'd landed on his rear end. Minutes ago and he hadn't noticed!

Chalo hesitated, then set down his bin and picked up the wallet. Still barely intact, but it seemed to be in one piece. Wobbly with relief, he shoved it into his hip pocket and bobbed his head at the gringo boy. "Gracias." He tried his English. "Thank. You."

"You're welcome." The gringo boy looked pleased with himself. Chalo picked up the bin and hurried to the nearest unbussed table. A few words from the younger boy reached him when he was still close enough. *"Five billion third worlders want jobs in America, and the owner can't find one who speaks English?"*

Five o'clock brought the last burst of customers, as the after-work crowd filled the tables around the two boys. Chalo eyed the clock. He would have about twenty minutes from the end of his shift until his day pass would expire. Enough time, but he couldn't dawdle.

At five-thirty, Chalo tossed his last load of dirty plates to the dishwashing robot, then went into the break room. Hernán listened sullenly to Kaufmann. "…That's all, Hernán."

"I'm going to take my break now." Hernán turned and scowled at Chalo, then went into the kitchen and turned for the service doors leading to the rear concourse.

Chalo shuffled closer to the office. "My shift is over, Señor Kaufmann. I must return home while my daypass is good. If you want me to return tomorrow."

Kaufmann frowned. "Why would I not? The spilled plates? Accidents happen and you're within tolerances." He tapped his fingers on his tablet. "Let's keep it that way. Until tomorrow." He chopped the air with his hand as a businesslike wave. Chalo tapped his code on the wall-mounted touchscreen to clock out for the day, then hurried toward the displacement booth.

Heat baked him less than two meters from the front doors. He walked a few minutes toward the late afternoon sun, passing the two boys in the window of a teen clothing store. Chalo squinted, and moved his jacket from arm to shoulder in hopes of finding a spot where it would trap less heat against him. Opening the door to the service concourse gave him a relief. The service concourse lacked air conditioning, but being windowless, was slightly cooler than the outside.

He went in the displacement booth and dug his wallet from his pocket. Open it up and—where was his daypass?

Chalo rifled through his debit card and his family photos, then again. If it wasn't there…. He must have put it in the wrong slot after flicking in that morning. He checked the currency slot and found only his few, worn dollars and pesos. In one of his pants pockets? His jacket pocket? He plunged his hands into all in turn. No daypass.

Panic climbed up the inside of his chest. If he'd lost his daypass, he would have to flick to the U.S. border guards. They would send him home, but he would lose any chance for another daypass. A billion men could be above-average trainees, but his son would languish another year in the government school, and that year might be enough to smother Berto's intelligence forever–

Breath deeply. Retrace your steps. Your wallet never left your pocket, except when you collided with Hernán.

He checked the time on his phone. About fifteen minutes until his daypass expired. He ran out of the concourse. His feet pounded down the sun-baked mall. Chalo veered to avoid a pair of tall gringas peering down their narrow noses at him, which brought into his view the gringo boy and the one being tutored.

A sudden idea made him stumble to a stop. A mix of English and Spanish spilled from his mouth. "Señor, favor, please, mi wallet, mi daypass, pase de un día, is fall out–"

The gringo boy took a moment to recognize him. "Oh, you're the busboy," he replied in Spanish. "You lost your daypass? It was in your wallet when you collided with the waiter? It looks like a credit card, yes?" His wince showed sympathy. "I'm afraid I didn't see it anywhere on the floor in the café."

Chalo's face slumped. Frustration tightened his mouth and lowered his brows. He glanced at the mestizo boy. Had this one seen something? He would have to tell. By the Virgin, Chalo would make it clear he had to tell. Chalo stood as tall as he could and drew up to eye level on the boy. Unease panged him as he looked the boy straight in the face. "Did you see it?" Chalo asked in Spanish.

"What?" came the reply, in English. The boy grew surly. "No hablo español."

"Did you see his daypass fall out of his wallet?" the gringo boy said.

"Why would I care enough to look? No, I didn't see it."

The gringo boy winced in more sympathy. "Neither of us saw it." He looked thoughtful for a moment. "But the waiter passed by the spot soon after everything happened. He might have noticed something."

"Thank you," Chalo said in Spanish. Time was too tight to bother with English. He ran down the mall. Sweat stuck his shirt to his back. The air conditioning inside the café made him shiver.

He went to the tables near where he'd fallen. Customers frowned and he barely noticed as he peered around chair and table legs for a glimpse of white with red and blue accents. Nothing. Frantic, he called to another busboy, "Have you seen Hernán?"

"No." The other busboy kept filling his bin.

"He's on break," said Kaufmann. Chalo's eyes widened in alarm. Kaufmann would not want to be bothered with his problem. "Why do you need him? You should be on your way home."

Again, the Virgin helped Chalo stand straight. "I lost my daypass. Sir, it was in my wallet, I swear to you it was, I wouldn't lose it for a stupid reason, but it must have fallen out when I fell down after running into Hernán and I want to ask if he saw it."

Kaufmann frowned, but Chalo soon realized, not at him. "He should be back from break by now. Come with me." Kaufmann went to the kitchen without a glance behind him. Chalo hurried after. The service doors slid apart and Kaufmann led the way onto the concourse.

"That fucking thing's got five minutes till expiration," said a high male voice in Spanish. "I'd be super lucky to find a hoodlum who needs it to make a getaway. Twenty dollars."

"Alright, I'll take–" Hernán broke off. The other, a slender barrio boy, froze wide-eyed. The barrio boy recovered first; he snatched Chalo's daypass from Hernán's hand and ran down the concourse toward the service booths. His boots thudded on the concrete and his pants slipped down his backside.

"Thieving son of a whore!" Kaufmann shouted as he ran after him. Chalo ran too, but with his shorter legs, fell further behind with each step. The barrio boy looked over his shoulder. The white of his eye stood stark against his skin and black hair. As he looked back at them, he lost his footing and stumbled. Kaufmann tackled him. The barrio boy thudded to the floor, breath whoofing out and the daypass skittering from his hand.

"Take your daypass and go, Chalo," Kaufmann said. "I'll deal with the police."

"Yes, sir." Chalo reached for the card, then gave a look back at Kaufmann and the barrio boy. In the distance, near the service entrance to the café, Hernán was out of sight.

"Go! I need you back here in the morning. It will be a busier day than usual, with one less waiter on staff."

Chalo nodded and ran down the concourse to the displacement booth, muttering an Ave Maria as the daypass dug into his palm.

THERE'S NO 'I' IN TEAMOSALYNOL

St. Louis County, Missouri
September 15

The doors from the locker room to the court slid open. The players stopped jawing and joking, leaving the only sound the echo of a solitary basketball dribbled on the hardwood, the squeak of sneaker soles, and then a silence followed by the rip of a ball hitting nothing but twine. They stepped onto the court and Coach Huffman stopped short.

Not at seeing Nikos Moriatis—he'd met Nik five times since the tycoon bought the Spiders at the end of last season. Not at the practice court with its herringbone parquet and the wheeled robots waiting like a line of butlers with balls, towels, sport drinks—Nik had given him a tour a few weeks ago, both of the facility and the rest of his estate. But since that earlier visit, Nik must have ordered the walls painted. A mural of great moments in St. Louis Spiders history towered above the court, and Huffman's focus landed on an image of his younger self, hair thicker, eyes less baggy, hand outstretched and gaze on the ball arcing home to win the first, and last, championship in Spiders history.

Nik was certain he had the key to winning the second. He dribbled, practiced a juke, and shot a fadeaway jumper. Huffman had his doubts, but Nik had three of the top-five-selling neuropharmaceuticals of all time. Nik's shot rattled the front of the rim, kicked off the back, and then fell. He picked up the ball, tucked it under his arm, and turned to the team, his cheeks flushed and his grin toothy. "How do you like the new facility?" he asked.

J.S. scratched his beard and nodded. LeDwayne grinned back. "Man, this shit is *cubed*," he said, and some of the others spoke in agreement.

If Nik didn't know the slang he didn't show it. "Aidan?"

The center looked around and shrugged. "You spent a lot of money, at least."

"Shit, Aid," LeDwayne said. "If you got it, promulgate it."

Aidan scowled back. Huffman knew what LeDwayne was trying to do. *Please, not the first day of training camp. Save the ego until we're eliminated from playoff contention.* "It shows Nik's commitment to this team."

"That's right, Carl," Nik said, and then he spoke to the players, making eye contact with each. "I grew up in south county, about ten miles from here, and I've been a Spiders fan since before I can remember. I mowed every lawn in the neighborhood to scrape up the money for one ticket to one playoff game, and it was that one." He pointed at the painting of Carl's winning shot. "I wanted to play for this team, but I realized in high school I would never be good enough. But I knew I wanted to give back, to the team, to the fans. When I got the chance to buy this team, I didn't hesitate." He glanced at LeDwayne and Aidan. "We have as much raw talent as any team in the North American Basketball League. We have one of the best coaches—"

To never win a championship, Carl added in his mind, completing the phrase he'd read on a hundred basketball websites.

"—but for some reason we've never gelled. We've never gotten the chemistry. But I can give that to us. Literally." He touched the face of his watch. The lights dimmed and a glow behind Carl and the players made them turn. On a giant screen, an NMNeuropharma logo appeared, then shrank and spiraled into the corner. In its place spun a ball-and-stick figure that reminded Carl of a child's toy. "Gentlemen, I give you teamosalynol."

"T-what?" Aidan asked.

"Teamosalynol. My team at NMNeuropharma has developed a compound that can induce changes in neurochemistry and synaptic weighting comparable to those seen in the brains of Tibetan monks and soldiers in elite combat units. It can promote selflessness and complementary cooperation in social units. It can make us a team."

For a moment, the only sound was the whirr of the air conditioning high overhead. J.S. was the first to speak. "You want to drug us."

Nik had a lopsided smile. "*Drug* is such an ugly word."

"Aight, say *medicate*," said LeDwayne.

"I want to help you succeed as a team. I've built this facility, I've recruited the best sports medicine team between Kansas City and Chicago, all of it, to help you succeed. This is part of it."

"I've never heard of this—compound," J.S. said.

"It's brand new."

"Then how do you know it works?"

"Krish and Rajeev in R&D have run hundreds of sims and tested in model animals. We'll unveil it early next year for the marriage counseling market and make billions."

"Is it safe?"

Nik smiled, confident in his product. "It's been tested for safety on dozens of college students."

J.S. didn't reply. Carl, prompted by that, stole a glance. It was easy to forget J.S. had been the first Sikh in the league—his sport turban was as much a part of him as the hair it hid, and his *kirpan* was sheathed and hidden on a pendant under his jersey. Carl hoped they hadn't stumbled into a religious taboo. But J.S. was also a sixth man with aging knees who had never won it all. "I will do it."

"Not me," LeDwayne said, and he paused while heads turned. "I ain't being enfettered like that."

Nik must have prepared for that. "No one's being singled out. I'll be taking it too. So will Carl."

I will? Carl thought. He frowned at the mural on the far wall while subconscious thoughts slid into place. *Yes, I will.*

LeDwayne shook his head, whipping the diamonds on his cornrow extensions against his neck. "I can carry this team. I don't need no chains to make me."

Nik chuckled. "LeDwayne, you're one of our best players, but carry this team? I haven't seen it yet. Carl?"

"Me neither."

"So it's either do this with the team or ride the pine," Nik said.

A look of shock and comedic disbelief appeared on LeDwayne's face. "Bench me? Damn, that's almost risible if it weren't so crazy. I'm the highest paid player on the team. Eight-point-four extra large." Carl glanced at Aidan out of ingrained habit; the center's eyes narrowed briefly. LeDwayne was too focused on the owner to notice. "You be a fool to bench me."

"Eight-point-four? That's point-one percent of my net worth," Nik said, and he nonchalantly tossed the basketball to his other hand.

"You serious." LeDwayne peered down at Nik, but the owner returned the look, betraying no weakness. The player shrugged and nodded. "Aight, if that's how it be, I'll collaborate." A ripple ran through the crowd.

"Thank you," Nik said to LeDwayne, then raised his head. "Everyone's agreed?"

Nods and assenting murmurs erupted, then ground to a halt when Aidan said, "No."

"No?"

"No." Aidan looked calmly defiant.

Nik shrugged. "Your choice. Enjoy the bench. Everyone else, the first dose will be ready in the locker room after practice. I'll see you then. Carl, they're all yours."

Carl nodded. "Gentlemen, ten minutes to warm up and then it's layup drills. Let's go."

Austin, Texas
October 18

Two o'clock chimed, and Laszlo Horvath swept all but one work-related windows off his monitor. Transcraniallaxy Inc. could run its affairs without him for an hour. The one window he kept open tied in with his duties for the next hour as CEO of the NABL's Austin Netrunners: Project TeamWorx. Electromagnets placed strategically around someone's brain could induce feelings of cooperation and hierarchical comfort; could make a great team one for the ages. The theory was sound—his researchers had found the brain regions involved in social behavior. The only hurdles were engineering ones. A prototype should be ready by the middle of the season, and his team should be using it on a regular basis by the start of the playoffs next April.

Enough daydreaming. He had a team to run in preparation for the start of the regular season on November 1. Reports to read, directions to give, calls to field—

His virtual secretary appeared on his monitor. "Sorry to disturb you, Laz, but there's a call I think you should take."

The social-analysis software that drove her smooth, fair face was usually very good. "Who?"

"Sumner Wieselmann. He's the agent representing—"

"Aidan Beckett of St. Louis." He'd read a competitive intel report. Beckett hadn't played in either of the Spiders' preseason games so far, and his staff didn't know why. Everyone knew the Netrunner's biggest weakness was at center, and everyone also knew Beckett would be a free agent after this season. "I'll take it."

Wieselmann had thin, grizzled hair and eyes owlish behind round glasses. Laz read custom tailoring in the bespoke lines of Wieselmann's lapel, collar, and tie. "Sumner, greetings."

"Thanks, Laz, for talking to me. I know you're busy. You've noticed Aidan hasn't played so far this preseason and I wanted to talk to you about that. I tell him Austin would be a great place for him to take his career to the next level as a free agent."

"You don't have to butter me up. What is it?"

"Moriatis ordered Coach Huffman to bench him. Moriatis has a vile scheme that Aidan won't buy into. It involves a new drug Moriatis' company has invented."

"What sort of drug?"

"The name is—" Wieselmann squinted myopically at notes outside of camera range. "Teamosalynol. It turns people into cooperative members of a team."

Laz said nothing. His gaze slid involuntarily to the Project Team-Worx window. Apparently Sumner assumed the worst from his silence. "I mean, Aidan's already a team player, it's that he can't work with LeDwayne Jones. You know that."

He couldn't believe it. Not only had Moriatis pursued the same research project, he'd beaten Transcraniallaxy to the punch. Laz blinked a few times and fumbled over his words. "Why are you telling me this?"

Wieselmann smiled. "Like I said, I tell Aidan he'd be wise to consider Austin for his next move. If you arranged a trade for him—"

"We've tried. Moriatis isn't interested." Laz had offered one of his best deals ever, but the Spiders' owner had rebuffed him. Johnny-come-lately. He needed to learn how the NABL operated.

"Maybe that will change." Wieselmann's tone showed he didn't expect it. "Moriatis is stubborn, I have to admit."

"So there's no trade and I'm competing with the other owners for one of the best free agents next summer. What good does that do me?"

"Let's say Aidan doesn't play for months. Or at all. They'll assume the worst: he's injured, he's a junkie, he's in the doghouse for being a prima donna. It'll hurt his marketability when he negotiates a new contract."

And your fees for doing so. "You expect me to not hold this against him at the negotiating table next summer."

"He refuses to poison his brain. That's a statement of principle. You know the dangers of brain drugs."

Laz ignored the flattery. Beckett would raise the Netrunners another notch. He'd be worth any price. And if Moriatis could be taught a lesson, even better. "I certainly do." He hesitated a moment to weigh words and dodge any charge of tampering with Beckett's contract. "You didn't hear this from me, but if Beckett doesn't play at all this season, and goes public with his principles against drugging his brain, I'd give him a five million signing bonus."

Wieselmann shook his head. "Five meg to not play this year?"

"That's exactly right."

"He'll welcome the support for his principles."

"Anything else?" Laz asked. "No? Then go talk to your client. Thanks again."

Laz cut the call and spastically waved his fists in the air, a grin splitting his face. If St. Louis didn't gel this year, Austin would win the otherwise weak division. If the Netrunners clinched early enough, they could selectively rest players late in the season and be fresh going into the playoffs. And as soon as St. Louis was eliminated from contention, he'd call Moriatis, or hunt him down at the spring owners' meeting, and rub it in. *Winning the brain activity race got you soooo far, didn't it, punk? Any guesses how many times Beckett will slam on the Spiders next year?*

St. Louis County, Missouri
November 22

LeDwayne's electric autocar, a Lorelei sedan with stretch massaging seats, hummed into the parking lot and stopped in its spot outside the practice facility. The only other car in the lot was Coach's old Keyser. As he crossed to the entrance, LeDwayne hunched his shoulders against the cold, foggy morning. He didn't have to be here; the team's flight from Edmonton, at the end of a grueling and disastrous road trip, had landed at three a.m., and Coach had given the team the day off. But he chose to be here, to hit the strength room and the practice floor. He was irascible.

1-5 on the road trip, 3-7 overall. A bad start, just like last year and the year before. But the Spiders were playing better than their record. LeDwayne didn't need Nik's spreadsheet jockeys with their fancy statistics to know that. He could shut his lids and see it in his mind's eye, memories of men being open, crisp passes, pick-and-rolls. They'd run into bad luck and foul trouble, but above all had been over-matched in the paint. Davis, their backup center, was no Aidan.

LeDwayne hesitated. Was he T'd up? Couldn't be it. He hadn't felt any different from taking Nik's drug. He wasn't here on an off-day because T was modulating his mind. He was here because the harder you worked the lucker you got. *See, Coach, I heard you every time you enunciated it*. And he didn't like Aidan with his whitebread good looks and his suburban-dad endorsement contracts; but he was much better under the basket now than Davis had been in his prime.

The door slid open for LeDwayne and he turned right toward the locker room, but paused after a step. To the left, Coach's office door was open. From the sound of voices, he wasn't alone. No other car in the lot? Wait, Nik's mansion was a two-minute walk.

"We're better than our record," Nik said in his pinched baritone. "The guys in the front office have run their analyses. Everyone's expected-points-per-decision is up. Jesus, LeDwayne's EPD is number three for all guards in the league. He's passing like a quarterback. Who'd have thought that a month ago? Our luck will run warmer."

After a pause, Coach said, "You know I think EPD's a flawed stat. Not because it's newfangled. It's dependent on who's on the floor."

"You mean Aidan."

"Yeah, I mean Aidan. Doc's shooting chondroitin and MSM into Davis' knees every day, but he may still need to get scoped before the end of the season. But even if he were healthy he wouldn't be able to get it done. We need a dominating center."

Nik sounded stubborn. "Aidan knows what he has to do."

Coach cleared his throat. "Have you thought about a trade?"

"Aidan's a top five center. We wouldn't get someone half as good."

"Half as good but playing is better than top five on the bench." Coach sounded dignified, but LeDwayne heard a tone of desperation in his voice.

After a while, Nik said, "Let's give him a couple of weeks. Could we make the playoffs from a 5-10 start?"

"What a question. With a healthier and younger center than Davis, maybe."

"But with Aidan on the bench and nothing in return, no?"

Coach sighed. "No."

LeDwayne felt suddenly embarrassed at hearing things not meant for his ears. He eased down the hall to the locker room. But throughout the morning, while he did physioball squats and kettlebell swings, and practiced his jumper alone on the court, he replayed the overheard conversation. He shot out of habit, the ball clanging the rim, while past glories stared down at him. After showering and dressing, he told his car to drive to Aidan's house.

A jeeves appeared in the monitor embedded in Aidan's front door. "May I ask who's calling?"

"LeDwayne. I'm here to see Aidan."

The jeeves' image froze on screen for a few seconds and LeDwayne worried Aidan had declined to see him; but then the door swung open and the jeeves said, "He's in the kitchen."

The kitchen could hold a team of chefs preparing a four-course meal. Synthesized marble, vat-grown wooden accents, gleaming stainless steel. A woman with thin lips and black hair stood at a bar and spooned orange goop into the mouths of two babies strapped into high chairs. She glanced up nervously at LeDwayne, then her husband. Aidan didn't notice. "We're eating lunch," he said.

"I ain't here to discombobulate your family's routine, but I do need to talk to you."

Aidan scowled. His wife said, "Honey, go." The center sighed and nodded. As he led LeDwayne out of the room, his wife said to the babies, "Daddy's going to talk to Mr. Jones about work."

The men stopped in a home theater with extra long red leather chairs and a monitor the size of a small European country. "What do you want?" Aidan asked.

"I'm here to ask you to collaborate with us and T yourself up." After no reply came, LeDwayne went on. "The team needs you. We won't make the playoffs without you. You know that as well as I do."

"Nik doesn't."

"No, Nik do know it, intensely."

Aidan dropped into one of the chairs. "Then he can tell Coach to play me without me T-ing up."

LeDwayne shook his head. "Nik's a stubborn man."

Aidan laughed. "He put you up to this. Goddam, he's not thinking straight. If I wouldn't listen to him I surely wouldn't listen to you carrying water for him."

LeDwayne's fists clenched, but he exhaled slowly and let them relax. *Don't let the other guy diss you into a fight.* "He didn't talk to me. He doesn't even know I overheard."

"Overheard?" Aidan's eyebrow rose and he hitched up in his seat.

"If you don't T yourself up within two weeks, he'll trade you."

"Please. No one of my caliber will be available on the trade block."

LeDwayne sharply shook his head. "That don't matter. He'd take a second-stringer with one good knee. You be outta here instantaneously. You in a hotel, your wife alone with those babies till April?"

Aidan blinked, unseeing. "He thinks I'm not good?"

"Ain't you been listening? He does, but he don't care. He wants someone who'd collaborate with the team."

Aidan rested his chin in his hand. He looked thoughtful for a moment, then shook his head. "I'll pay the price. Anita will understand."

"She will?" Anita said from the doorway, one hand on the jamb and her face tight with concern.

"You heard Nik will trade me if I don't dope myself?"

She nodded. "Don't let that stop you. I could get by with the twins. I could hire au pairs for each with the money Austin offered."

"Honey—"

LeDwayne perked up and asked, "Austin?"

"The Netrunners owner told Aidan's agent he'd get a five million dollar bonus if he doesn't play for the Spiders this year."

LeDwayne's mouth hung open. "Oh shee-it. Five million? That feed your family a long time."

Anita shrugged. "We don't need it. I'm investing his money, we'd be set for life if he never got paid again. All that he's got to play for is a championship." Elsewhere in the house, a baby cried. "Excuse me."

LeDwayne stared at the vacated doorway for a few seconds. How do you argue with five extra large? "I'll take a paycut. A salary equal to yours."

"That's the T talking."

"Is it?" LeDwayne thought and pursed his lips. "No, it's me. The T just helped me see the veracity. If we work together, we can carry this team. We can make the playoffs. We can win a championship." He inhaled strongly. "I ain't saying we gonna be friends or we gonna be smooth as Astroglide. But I am fully solemn when I say I will do what I can to make this work if you meet me halfway."

Aidan rested his chin in his hand again and the only sound was their breathing and the clink of LeDwayne's chains under his shirt. Abruptly, Aidan stood and extended his hand, his gaze locked on LeDwayne's eyes. "Deal."

Norfolk, Virginia
January 30

Nik walked through the VIP party section of the arena with a giddy smile. His first All-Star Game and he had two of his players starting, Aidan and LeDwayne. After their poor November, the Spiders were 20-16 and thick in playoff contention. They were six games behind the Netrunners for the division lead, but in their most recent game they had beaten them at the buzzer in Austin. St. Louis had almost half the season left and was still improving.

The game was two hours away, with only a few hundred fans in the lower bowl of seats, yet already dozens of VIPs filled the luxury suite. Nik turned and raised his arm to catch a serving robot's attention and bumped into a tall man with disheveled gray hair and eyebrows like inchworms. Speak of the Austin devil. "Laz, good to see you!"

Laz Horvath stared for a moment and rattled ice in his glass. " Greetings."

"Should be a fun game tonight. I'll be rooting for Cabrera and Nkrumah, enjoy it will you can." Of course Austin's two best were here, though Nkrumah was a backup to Aidan.

"You seem cocky."

"I don't mean to be immodest." Nik shrugged with a nonchalant grin. "I like how we played on your court the other night. I like our chances the rest of the way."

Laz raised his glass halfway to his lips, then paused. "I'd like our chances too if I forced my team to take a performance-enhancing drug." He lifted the drink and slowly finished it.

Nik felt as cold as the ice rattling the other's glass, but masked it with a bluff front. "What are you talking about? None of my guys are using steroids."

"Teamosalynol. I know the truth."

"It's not a performance-enhancing drug. A neuropharmaceutical to enhance mental acuity. Within the ambit of the collective bargaining agreement with the players' union and perfectly legit according to the owners' competition committee."

Laz handed his glass to a trundling robot. "It's not like ginseng and you know it. It's a medical attempt to construct team chemistry where there wasn't any. It's a cheat."

Time to get aggressive. Nik leaned forward, lowered his eyebrows, flattened his voice. "Call it what you want. I don't care."

The other didn't flinch. "If the competition committee calls it a cheat, will you care then?"

When in doubt, keep bluffing. "Bring it."

Laz smirked and clapped Nik on the shoulder. "Enjoy the game. See you in St. Louis. And New York." The NABL's home office was in Manhattan at First and 45th, on the site of the former UN headquarters. Laz hailed a serving robot and followed it away while Nik stared daggers at his back.

Sportsnews.com/stl/today.home.html
February 10

Last night, the Spiders showed the Southcentral Division title is still up for grabs by dismantling the Austin Netrunners 121-87 before an SRO crowd at the Löwenbrau Center. LeDwayne Jones had 21 points and 22 assists, the best in the league this year, Aidan Beckett dominated in the middle with 29 points, 12 rebounds, and 11 assists, and J.S. Grewal came off the bench to make five steals....

Records: St. Louis 24-16, Austin 27-14.

Sportsnews.com/forums/nabl/stl/home.html

brad_lee_cap_tx commented on "Spiders dismantle Austin"

Not bad show for your pack of cowtown zombies. Everyone knows teamosalynol is fueling them. Without Nikki's drug, AIDS and

LaDyawne would be ballhogs and the Sliders would be 14-26 as usual....

Austin, Texas
April 8

Being a coach was like being the parent of a small child, Carl thought while he stood up behind the desk of the coach's office in the visitors' locker room of Transcraniallaxy Arena. *You have to shield them from the truth so they don't psych themselves out.* Not the truth of a hostile crowd waiting for them; the crowd's pregame chants and *rai*-metal thundering from the PA system echoed down into the basement. Besides, this team could tune that out.

But how would they respond when they discovered why the competition committee had called a closed-door meeting of all owners in New York tomorrow?

Carl shook his head and walked toward the locker room. That was tomorrow. Tonight was the final game of the regular season. Tonight was the most important game the Spiders had played in years. Maybe decades. Around the corner the players jawed and joked. He strode out and they cheered.

Cheer yourselves, he thought, and smiled and raised his hands. Nik stood to the side, next to a small chest, and smiled. If the players didn't quiet down soon Carl knew he'd have to impose it on them, but they sensed he was ready to speak and grew silent on their own.

"Guys, I'll be brief. You can read the standings table as well as I can. You know we're in the playoffs."

"Yeah Spiders!" Nik yelled and clapped, and the players cheered briefly.

"But is that all you want? Austin's a game ahead of us. If we win tonight, we'll be tied for the best record in the West, and we'll have the tiebreaker. We'll have home court throughout the playoffs. Do you want that?"

"Yeah!" shouted the players.

"But there's even more." He slid his pda from the inside pocket of his suit jacket. "Anyone read this in sportsnews.com/centex the other day? 'Though the Spiders have shown a newfound ability to consistently defeat weak teams on forgettable Tuesday nights, not once this season have they shown the killer instinct needed to beat strong teams like the Netrunners in pivotal games.' Do you want to show up this motherfucker?"

"Hell yeah!" yelled LeDwayne, and others followed in a stampede of sound echoing off the concrete-block walls.

"Guys! Guys!" Nik shouted until they quieted. "One last thing." He pressed a button on the chest and its lid clamshelled open to reveal ice cubes. He dug in and pulled out two large bottles by their necks. "I've got Dom P and Cristal for my division champions after the game."

The players shouted again and Carl led them onto the court.

They were a joy, that game. Crisp passes, sharp cuts, running the court, weakside help on defense. LeDwayne and Aidan played the pick-and-roll and hunted for teammates with open looks. There were glitches—during a timeout early in the second quarter, the two stars argued about positioning on the pick, but before Carl felt the need to intervene they resolved it, Aidan nodding briskly and LeDwayne's eyes going wide in recognition. J.S. came off the bench and rode Cabrera, Austin's shooting guard, like a tight shirt. The only negative moment came early in the fourth with Aidan on the bench, when Davis crashed into a crowd in the paint and came out limping badly. Within a minute his knee looked like a cantaloupe. But the sour taste was washed away five minutes later when Aidan, low in the post with his back to the basket, lightly tossed a no-look alley-oop to LeDwayne cutting untouched through the lane. The guard rattled home a dunk and the only sound in the arena was cheering from the Spiders' bench.

It wasn't until after the final buzzer, St. Louis 114, Austin 103, that Carl remembered the owners' meeting the next day would ban teamosalynol and all other neurostimulatory chemicals.

Edmonton, Alberta
April 21

The visitors' locker room at CoshMedia Centre wasn't as fancy as the one in Austin, but LeDwayne didn't care. Walking in from the court, he felt like a king and his mood lifted even higher when he saw Nik standing in the middle of the locker room next to a folding table. On top of the table lay a dozen brooms. "How 'bout them Spiders?" he shouted.

LeDwayne put on a cartoon voice and said, "Sweeeeep."

Laughter and joking surrounded him. LeDwayne grabbed a broom and leaned it against his locker while he removed his jersey. The broom's balance was precarious and it clattered to the floor a couple of times. No matter. They hadn't just won, they'd dominated the Trappers, 4-0. Okay, the Trappers had the worst record of any playoff team, but the sweep was still an accomplishment. Strong teams. Pivotal games. Right? He leaned the broom back up and meandered into the shower.

Aidan was already there, lathering shampoo and looking pensive. "Yo Aid," LeDwayne said.

The center lifted his chin in greeting. "Who do you think we'll get in the conference finals?"

"If it ain't Austin I be flummoxed."

"They obliterated the Aces last night."

The whole team had watched in the smoothie bar at the Princess Patricia Hotel. LeDwayne nodded. "Vegas looked hung over."

"The Netrunners are hungry."

Sweat ran down LeDwayne's face as he squinted at the other. "We ain't?"

"No, I am. I know you are too. And I know we beat them consistently during the regular season."

When we was T'd up. He knew that's what the center meant. "You think we can't beat them now?"

"Things are different."

LeDwayne shook his head firmly enough to clack the diamonds on his extensions. "They ain't no different. You saw how T works. It don't make you any more collaborative than you was already. It just bring it out. It out now. I know for me it is." The center scowled and LeDwayne hurriedly added, "I'm sure it is for you too."

Aidan leaned his head back into the showerhead stream and stared at the ceiling. "Even if we're the same team, they're different."

LeDwayne forced himself to laugh. "Even if the Netrunners be half the bitches they was, they still gonna get they asses pimped out by they daddy." He squirted soap on his hands and suddenly hoped he was right.

St. Louis County, Missouri
April 30

Carl arrived at the practice facility around seven, the sun barely up and dew glistening on the grass. He rubbed his eyes and hoped his car had emailed the office snackeria to get a pot of coffee brewing.

The Spiders had been flat in game one of the conference finals the night before. Austin had only won by seven points, but it never felt that close. Had he mismanaged the team in practices during the week between their sweep of Edmonton and yesterday's game? Had the sweep made them overconfident? A little adversity might be good for them. They had six games and two losses to give. No need to panic. They could dig it out.

Without teamosalynol?

They had to.

Inside, approaching his office, he saw a steaming mug on his desk. Nik, inside the office, poked his head into view. The owner's hair was disarrayed and his eyes bloodshot. "Carl, you have to see this."

"See what?"

While Carl sat, Nik cleared his throat and pointed at a monitor on the far wall. "The custodial staff at the Löwenbrau Center shoots surveillance video of the locker rooms. Look at what Austin did before last night's game." He sat in front of Carl's desk.

The video came to life and showed a Netrunners' equipment manager setting down dark plastic bowls with retractable power cords at each locker. Without a sip of coffee Carl bolted upright. "Those are transcranial magnetic stimulation helmets."

Nik nodded grimly and tapped his watchface. The video jumped.

Players now sat at each locker, helmets on their heads. The timestamp showed an hour before last night's tipoff. The accompanying audio played the voice of Austin's coach urging his players to look for the open man, make the proper cut, use their knowledge of each other to know where their teammates were going. "Constructing team chemistry where there isn't any. Laz, you cockbiter."

Carl realized what had happened. "The owners' meeting banned administered chemical compounds, not transcranial stim."

"Lot of those old bastards don't know transcranial stim exists." Nik cradled his head in his hands and leaned back. "There's nothing we can do. It's against league rules for us to see this video. We'll need producible evidence to do anything, which would take a few days to get, and Laz can stall me from convening the competition committee until the series is over. If Austin can beat us, they won't need electromagnetic teamosalynol to beat Montreal or Cincinnati in the league finals, both teams are weaker."

Carl crossed his arms in front of him while Nik's words rattled around his mind. He stared at the monitor, but he realized he wasn't seeing the video; in his mind's eye he saw his larger-than-life younger self on the wall a few dozen yards away. "Then we can't let Austin beat us," he said.

St. Louis, Missouri
May 13

Carl and LeDwayne happened to arrive at the player/staff parking garage underneath the Löwenbrau Center at the same time. Hype descended on them as soon as they climbed out of their cars, in the form of klieg lights, videobloggers, and, further away, fans screaming from behind portable, orange barricades. Game seven of the conference finals. Win or go home.

The game of their lives, Carl thought, but he kept calm. "How you feeling?" he asked LeDwayne as they strode up the tunnel. Nearby, an air conditioning condenser the size of a bus whirred, and a siren dopplered amid the concrete canyons of downtown.

"I've accreted. Let the extraneous stuff go, pulled in the stuff I need." LeDwayne took a couple of steps, then, in stride, said, "I hear tell Nik has a demonstration for us."

"That's right."

"What is it?"

"It's better if he shows you."

Nik was in the locker room already, gothrap audible in his earbuds and a distant look on his face. He sat next to a table with a cloaked bundle. Carl knew what lay under the cloak: a Transcraniallaxy helmet, acquired and its software decoded by Nik's employees. Electromagnetic teamosalynol. But Carl kept his routine up, and as the players arrived he could tell his doing so kept them focused.

An hour before tipoff, with crowd noise filtering down to them, he called Nik's mobile. "It's time," he said, and moved closer. Nik pulled the earbuds out and stopped the music.

"Guys, you've heard I have something to show you. I'll get to that in a minute. First, I want to say I'm really proud of how you guys have played, both in the Edmonton series and especially against Austin. They're the second best team in the league and you've played them to a 3-3 tie.

"Despite this, I've sensed some doubts. Thanks to a bad decision by the league, we've been off T for a month. But you've played well without it. 7-3 against two tough teams. Maybe I shouldn't say this as the holder of twenty million shares of NMNeuropharma stock, but you don't need it. But do you know who does?"

Nik pulled the cloak off the Transcraniallaxy helmet. "The Netrunners."

Carl looked at his players. Aidan's eyes widened with realization. LeDwayne idly shook his head and Carl read *Shee-it* on his lips. Nik held the moment just long enough. "Guys, it's your game to win."

The players were a joy, that game. Crisp passes, sharp cuts, running the court, weakside help on defense. LeDwayne and Aidan played the pick-and-roll like a machine. There were glitches—Aidan picked up two fouls early and spent long minutes on the bench while Nkrumah dominated the paint. J.S. came off the bench and shadowed Cabrera, but the Austin guard didn't look for the ball and spent the next minutes setting picks and playing tight defense. Carl's stomach felt sour, but he couldn't fault his players, and the fans were getting their money's worth. The third quarter ended with the score tied, 81-81.

Late in the fourth, the Spiders put together a run to go up by five with three minutes to play. On their next possession, Aidan took the ball in the lane and slammed it home over Nkrumah. The crowd erupted in cheers; Carl couldn't remember so loud a moment on their home court. But the cheers rapidly turned to boos. It had been so loud he hadn't heard the whistle, but he saw a referee wave off the basket and call charging. Aidan had fouled out.

"Jesus fucking Christ!" Carl shouted as he stepped onto the court. "You goddam need lasik!" One of his assistants put a hand on his upper arm, but Carl shrugged him off. "Nkrumah was fucking tap dancing!"

"Enough f-bombs!" the ref yelled back, and made the T symbol for a technical foul. Carl let his assistant pull him back to the bench.

Cabrera made both technical free throws. St. Louis by three. But the next St. Louis possession, LeDwayne made an ugly pass the Netrunners stole. Austin layup, and St. Louis by one.

Carl called timeout. "Play smart, guys. Smart." He called a play and sent them back out.

The game seesawed for the final minute and a half. LeDwayne to J.S., wide open for a rare shot, two points. Cabrera answered with a three-pointer to tie. St. Louis answered with a two-pointer. Thirty seconds left. "Tight D!" Carl yelled to his players. But somehow, with the shot clock expiring, Cabrera launched a three that rattled around the rim but fell home.

"Time out!" Carl called. Down by one, six seconds left. The players gathered round. "Inbound to LeDwayne. Shoot if you have it, pass if you don't."

"Aight. I'll execute." The horn sounded and they stepped back out.

They did everything right. LeDwayne cut to the inbound, dribbled, looked for an open man—everyone was covered—juked his defender, put up a twenty footer with a second left—

It clanked, short and right, and Nkrumah swatted the ball into the stands as time ran out. Netrunners players ran off the bench and jumped around while the fans streamed up the aisles. Carl stood for a moment, unable to move.

An hour later, the Spiders all back in street clothes, they opened the locker room to wives and children. The mood was somber but not despairing. Carl observed, barely speaking. Nik went to each player, thanking them for a great season, thanking their families.

"I'm going to retire," J.S. said.

"I won't hold you to that," Nik said. "Take the time to think about it."

"I have. I want you to know now so you can find someone to fill my role right away."

Nik shook his hand and stepped closer to LeDwayne and Aidan. Anita held a baby in each arm. "Say good-night to LeDwayne uncle." One was already asleep, and the other looked close to it. LeDwayne pressed his fingertip to his lips, then touched his fingertip to each baby's forehead.

"Guys," Nik said, "thanks. Both of you. I knew we could get at least this far."

"You knew when we didn't," Aidan said.

Nik cleared his throat. "You guys are both free agents now. What will it take to keep you?"

"That's simple," LeDwayne said. "Average our salaries."

Nik blinked. "Cut yours, raise his, make them the same?"

LeDwayne reached up for Aidan's shoulder. "Well, offer a ten percent raise and we won't turn it down."

TED WILLIAMS EYES

ooper jogged out of the Astros clubhouse and up the dugout steps toward the batting cage. Echoing around nearly-empty TeXolar Power Park, cameras whirred and reporters shouted questions. Magazines, websites, and TV from around the world, all here to see him take batting practice before the final game of the season.

Back in the stands, a hundred fans in team colors cheered. Cooper lifted his batting helmet. Just like the reporters, they didn't come to find out if Astros would finish four games out of playoff contention, or five. They didn't even come to see if tonight's opponent, the in-state rival Rangers, would make the wild card with a win. They came to see Cooper make history.

No matter what happened tonight, Cooper would have the highest single season batting average since Gwynn way back in '94. With a couple of hits, he would be the first ballplayer in almost a century to reach—

"Four-oh-oh! Four-oh-oh!" Twelve rows back, a pudgy fan in a retro '70s-style Astros jersey, with a flat-brimmed cap and a dime-sized beard patch between his mouth and chin, chanted. Others joined in.

Playfully, Cooper shook his head, then put on his helmet and went to the warm-up circle. He slid donut weights onto his bat handle.

A reporter in the front row called out, "Even if you miss .400, you've gained a hundred points in batting average over last season! Is it true performance-enhancing drugs explain it?"

Cooper checked his warm-up swing and peered at the reporter. Bob Jackson, from purebaseball.com. Jackson needed to trim the hair in his nose and do a better job concealing the pimples on his neck. "You know how many times I've peed in a cup this year." He looked at the other clustered reporters. "Anyone have a real question?"

A reporter from Japan asked, "How else can you explain your great improvement in all offensive statistics?"

Despite his long-sleeved uniform and the slice of blue, cloud-puffed Texas sky through the open roof, Cooper shivered. Could anyone have found out? His childhood friend, Derek Liu, now a biotech entrepreneur in Singapore, had paid all of his travel expenses to Derek's new CRISPR/Cas9 clinic. He'd checked into the hotel under an assumed name....

He rested the bat across his shoulders. No one would ever know. "I'm seeing the ball better. That's all." He lowered the bat and tapped the handle on the ground. The donut weights clattered to the grass. "Time for me to get to work."

Cooper strode to the batting cage, waggling his bat. Among the group waiting their turns stood the team's three next best batters. Odysseus Skelton, the stocky first baseman, rolling his lips while undoing and redoing the hook-and-loop fasteners on his batting gloves. Chalo Dominguez, the rookie left fielder, his hand on the crucifix hanging around his neck and his eyes squeezed in prayer. For a 22-year-old, Dominguez had a broad tracery of crow's-feet at the corners of his eyes. Jordan Himmelblau, the shortstop, facial muscles bunched and jaw working like a piston on his chewing gum.

Sometimes, your teammates became friends. Others, they were just guys you worked with.

Himmelblau spoke. "Here comes Mr. Ted Williams eyes."

The Hall of Famer, last man to bat .400, but—"What about his eyes?" Cooper asked.

"Legend has it Williams had 20/3 vision. Talk about seeing the ball better."

Cooper shivered again. Did Himmelblau somehow know?

No. He wanted to know his secret, of course, no less than the reporters. But the reporters just wanted click bait. His teammates wanted the magic to rub off on them so they too could become rich free agents after their contracts expired.

Cooper returned a flat stare. Only one player could become baseball's first half-billion dollar man.

"Next group, your turn," the BP coach called. "Coop, get in here."

Cooper gave Himmelblau, Skelton, and Dominguez one last look. "Watch and learn, boys."

Inside the cage, he stopped outside the right-handed batter's box and raised his bat in front of his eyes. Fine details in the wood grain and minute scorched curlicues in the manufacturer's brand seemingly jumped to his eye. Used to it now, but the first time he'd studied a bat after Derek Liu's gene therapy, newly-visible details had stunned him.

He shut his eyes, drew in a breath. An early summer day came to him, cloudless sky, field greened by dozens of child-league fathers. Eight years old, coming up to bat against a kid from the opposing team for the first time.

The other boy put the ball over the middle of the plate. A smooth swing. The ping of the ball against the aluminum bat. The white dot shrinking as the ball flew up and away. His lips parted, his gaze rapt, his heart soaring with the ball.

He'd liked baseball before then. From that moment, he'd loved it.

Cooper opened his eyes and stepped into the batter's box.

The coach swiped and tapped his phone. The pitching machine light glowed green, ready to fling balls in the style of Huerta, tonight's opposing starting pitcher.

The machine whipped forward its arm and released the ball. It looked as big as a full moon. Cooper read the seams pulsing across the visible face as if he watched slow motion video. He swung, arms whipping the bat head through the zone.

The ball sliced to right-center, higher than a second baseman could catch, low enough to fall in front of the outfielders.

Slider, thigh-high, outer half. He nodded to himself, then dug in his cleats for the next pitch.

A different pulse of seams, a different trajectory leaving the mechanical hand. He swung.

Line drive. The ball clattered against the pitching screen. The coach jumped, then nodded and gave a thumbs-up. "Do that in the game and he won't try his curve."

Cooper set his feet, cocked his bat. Dust motes drifted in air near the machine's arm. "Ready."

Fastballs, cutters, changeups, curves, sliders. He read them all an instant after the machine released them. He pulled some, went the opposite way on others, lining most for what would be singles or doubles. He sent one ball to Tal's hill, the flagpole mound inside the fence in dead center, another into the boxes behind the short fence in left field.

He nodded to himself. He'd found his groove. "I'm ready to play, coach."

In the locker room, every player prepped for the game in his own way. Cooper imbibed sports drink. Dominguez listened to bachata music loudly leaking from his earbuds. Ode Skelton played dominoes with two guys from the bullpen.

Himmelblau unrolled his tablet and read baseball news. He quickly swiped past stories about Cooper's chase of .400, then lingered over an article, raking his fingers through his wiry hair as he read. "Huh."

Cooper capped his bottle of sports drink. "Don't leave us hanging."

"A local sabermetrics blogger speculating about next year. He says if you stay at your new level, and three other guys on the team matched your same spike in offensive statistics, we'd win a hundred games."

Cooper's eyes widened. A hundred wins. Five teams a decade reached that mark. Division champions for sure, probable home-field advantage through the league playoffs. The best chance of any team of winning the World Series.

He leaned back in his chair and folded his arms. Year after next, he could get as good a chance of winning the World Series as a free agent signed with a perennial power, like St. Louis or Kansas City. He opened his mouth, but Skelton spoke before he could.

"Man, that stathead stuff is flim-flam."

Himmelblau lightly smacked his palm against his high forehead. "I keep telling you, Ode, advanced statistics have value. Coop's OPS has gone up 343 points this year."

"What's that OSP business again?"

"OPS." Himmelblau scowled. "On base percentage plus slugging percentage. The sabermetricians have correlations between OPS and runs created, and from runs created to the Pythagorean win projection. Our Pythagorean win projection this year is spot on—"

Ode Skelton shook his head. "Come on, man, formulas don't play the game. We do. Ain't that right, Cha-lllooowww?"

Dominguez blinked a few times. "I just want to play. Give 110%. Every game."

"You see?" Skelton said to Himmelblau. "You with me too, Coop?"

He shrugged. "Most GMs these days pay attention to the statheads." Cooper stood, sports drink bulging his bladder. "Time to hit the head."

After taking a leak, Cooper went to the sinks under the broad, paneled mirror. He washed his hands by feel. His gaze landed on his reflection's crow's-feet and wisps of graying hair. Even a long career would end in another dozen years.

Would you rather have half a billion dollars, or a World Series ring?

He shook his head, flicked water off his fingertips. His secret trip to Derek Liu's gene therapy lab meant he would get both.

From the main part of the locker room came manager Gray Wade's hand claps. "Saddle up, men! Time to win a ball game!"

A minute later, the team filed out of the clubhouse. Music from the stadium PA and the noise of thirty thousand spectators funneled down. Amazingly large crowd for a home team already eliminated from playoff contention.

Cooper jogged up the dugout steps. A cheer erupted from the crowd, echoing from the upper decks and the closed parts of the retractable roof. The chant began. "Four-oh-oh! Four-oh-oh!"

He lifted his cap. Half a billion dollars and a World Series ring? He was on track for both.

For his first plate appearance, Cooper came up with bases empty and two outs in the bottom of the first. The colossal video screen behind center showed his picture and, in giant alphanumerics, *AB 591. H 236. BA .399.* The crowd shouted and clapped. Cooper stepped into the box like he walked on air.

The opposing pitcher, Huerta, pulled his cap low over his eyes and peered at the catcher's signals. He nodded, then started his windup.

The ball left Huerta's glove. Cooper read it instantly, kept his bat over his shoulder. Curveball, going low.

The pitch skipped off the dirt in front of the plate, then into the catcher's glove. Ball one.

Cooper grinned. "All he's got tonight?"

"He's got enough," the catcher replied, "to keep you below .400."

Huerta looked for the next signal. Nod, windup. A fastball low and heading outside. Cooper's bat stayed on his shoulder.

"Stee-rike!" the umpire called.

Cooper looked back. The umpire's lowered eyebrows dared him to argue. Cooper blew out a breath. The fine detail of the batmaker's label caught his gaze for a moment, returned part of him to that little league field decades ago.

Huerta's next pitches nibbled the edges of the umpire's generous strike zone. The count reached 2-2. A fastball left the pitcher's hand on a trajectory low and inside.

Cooper swung. The ball skipped hard off the infield grass and dirt, on a line to thread the needle between the shortstop and third base-man. The crowd shouted with excitement. A hard grounder dribbling into the outfield would give him that one more hit.

He raced toward first base. The crowd noise suddenly gained a nervous edge. Cooper stretched his leg, his foot descending, inches from the bag—

The ball smacked into the first baseman's glove. Cooper's foot struck the base. He ran through and turned his head, face tight, watching the first base umpire. *Come on, they haven't replaced you with robots yet, make this your one blown call all season.*

The first base umpire raised his right fist.

Cooper walked back to the dugout, head turned to the video screen for the replay. The shortstop got a great jump on the ball, extended his glove at the last moment, and quickly planted his foot to make a perfect throw.

Nothing you can do. Cooper trotted down the dugout steps.

His second plate appearance came in the fourth. Nobody on, one out. Direct rays of the setting sun partially washed out the video display, but the key numbers remained readable. *AB 592. H 236. BA .399.*

Cooper took the first pitch, a four-seamer outside, and soon worked the count to 3-1.

Huerta looked at the catcher's signs, and his black eyebrows crinkled. The expression faded and he came set.

Cooper guessed at the next pitch even before it left Huerta's palm. Change-up. Cooper shifted his weight into his swing.

The crack of the bat rang for a moment, then the crowd roared. Cooper watched as he ran into foul territory to round first. High enough, hard enough, it could clear the wall in left-center. On the balcony jutting over the wall, fans holding half-full cups of beer next to the solar-powered home run tally board reached out one-handed.

The center fielder's cleats dug dirt from the warning track. Directly under the balcony, he leaped, right arm mashing the wall. His glove plucked the ball from the air inches above and beyond the bright yellow stripe.

Thirty thousand voices groaned. Cooper jogged back to the dugout.

His third plate appearance came in the sixth inning, Himmelblau on first, two out, score tied 0-0. The scoreboard blazed *AB 593. H 236. BA .398.*

Lips pressed together, Huerta shook off signs throughout. He stayed away from his curve, throwing his other pitches—slider, two-seam fastball, Vulcan changeup. 3-2 count.

Huerta threw a slider. Cooper swung. A line drive, slicing well above the second baseman's reach. The ball landed deep in the right-center gap and motored toward the wall. The crowd sounded like a rock concert or an airplane runway.

The two nearest outfielders sprinted after the ball. Cooper sprinted too. Nearing second, he looked ahead to the third-base coach. Coach waved him through, then made the stop sign.

Cooper slid into third, well ahead of the relayed throw. He called time and brushed dirt off his knee, looking at the team's dugout.

At home, players high-fived Himmelblau. He returned the gesture, then glanced toward Cooper. A crisp nod, then he trotted to the dugout steps.

The Astros led 1-0. Cooper on third. Two out, but time for more. He shouted toward the plate. "Come on, Ode!"

Skelton, a left-handed batter, spat tobacco juice and stepped in. He held his bat straight up, rocking the barrel back and forth more forcefully than usual. With narrow eyes he watched the pitcher.

Don't swing for the fences, Ode. A single to the outfield scores the run.

Huerta threw a fastball, low and away. Ode lifted his right foot but held back his bat.

"Steee-rike," called the umpire. Some fans booed. Ode gave the umpire a mean look, then shook his head and stepped back in for the next pitch.

Next pitch, a changeup. *Be patient—*

Ode swung too early. The ball chopped foul past the home dugout. The ballboy tossed it to a small child on the fourth row.

Now an 0-2 count. Huerta smirked. The next pitch, a curveball. Cooper's heart hung, ready to drop with the breaking ball. Ode swung, waist high. The pitch crossed the plate at his knees.

"Steee-rike three. You're out!"

Ode flipped his bat end-over-end to the grass as he trudged back to the dugout.

The seventh and eighth innings went quickly, with the Astros going three-up-three-down in both frames. The crowd grew restless. A fan in the front row behind the dugout told someone that Cooper's triple had only gotten him back to .399. Cooper would come up second in the bottom of the ninth—if the Astros batted.

Top of the ninth, the Astros still led 1-0.

The Astros' closer stalked around the mound as the PA blared *Flight of the Valkyries*. He took the mound, his brows lowered, the image of focus on getting the save regardless of Cooper's pursuit of .400. But the closer's first pitches missed the plate and he gave up a leadoff single to a speedy runner. A pickoff throw went wide and the runner slid into second.

Tying run in scoring position, a right-handed pull hitter at bat, the second baseman shifted to join Cooper and Himmelblau on the third-base side of the infield. Cooper took position with his right foot almost touching the foul line.

If the batter lines one you can't handle, tie game and you get one more chance in the bottom of the ninth.

Cooper blinked. He slammed his right hand into his glove and watched the batter.

The batter fouled the first pitch back off the screen, then took the second low and in. Third pitch, fastball on the inside half of the plate. Swing, crack.

Cooper's feet shifted to his left. His glove hand rose. He looked back the runner on second, then rifled a one-hop throw to Skelton at first. One out.

He paced across the dirt to his usual fielding spot. On his way, he nodded to himself. He'd done the right thing without thinking, from habit born on that distant sunny field of his youth.

Warmth filled his chest. Your line in the box score didn't matter. Winning a ball game mattered.

The next batter came up. He fouled off four pitches before the closer left a curveball hanging. Well hit to left. Cooper's shoulders sagged as the ball sailed over his head. It landed in the seats, five rows back and five feet inside the foul pole.

The Astros now trailed 2-1. He would get that one more chance.

To start the bottom of the ninth, a pitch struck Himmelblau in the thigh. The closer, Ryerson, had a nasty curve and slider, when in the groove. The scoreboard blazed *AB 594. H 237. BA .399.* The crowd came to its feet, chanting "Four-oh-oh! Four-oh-oh!"

Energy jittered into Cooper's arms and legs. He raised his bat and that memory from his childhood returned, grounding the energy. Calm, focused, he stepped in.

Ryerson came set and Cooper decided to take the first pitch. The ball left the pitcher's hand. A slider, low and outside, but it would probably catch the corner of the umpire's generous strike zone.

"Ball."

The catcher tossed the ball back to the pitcher, then looked over his shoulder. "Low or outside?" he asked the umpire.

"Outside," the umpire replied in a firm tone.

Cooper smiled to himself. This plate appearance just got easier.

Next pitch, curveball, breaking too hard. It hit the dirt in front of the plate and skipped under the catcher's glove. Cooper jumped back and waved Himmelblau forward. The ball rolled to the backstop, catcher chasing it. Himmelblau slid headfirst into second. The catcher didn't even throw.

2-0 count, and no chance of hitting into a double play. A base hit would score the tying run.

The next pitch. Another curveball, this one would barely break. Cooper shifted his weight and lashed out with his hands.

It broke even less than Cooper expected. He caught it low and it sliced foul, landing in the second deck behind the home dugout. The crowd noise lulled, then picked back up as Ryerson readied his next pitch.

Fastball, sailing high. Cooper leaned back. The catcher rose from his crouch and extended his mitt. The pitch smacked leather. The catcher tossed the ball back to Ryerson, then made a settle-down gesture with his hands.

3-1. Thousands of voices took up the chant. "Four-oh-oh! Four-oh-oh!"

If Ryerson missed the zone again, foul it off or take ball four?

Cooper readied the bat and turned his augmented eyes to the pitcher. The wrist snap, the roll off the fingers, the spinning seams, a slider, inside, he could foul it off—

The bat stayed over Cooper's shoulder. "Ball four!"

Boos drizzled down on Ryerson from the first fans to realize the walk would not get Cooper back up to .400. The boos rained down as

Cooper dropped the bat and jogged to first base. Then the boos broke up, giving way to applause and cheers. A new chant sprung up. "MVP! MVP!"

Cooper stopped at first and doffed his batting helmet to the crowd. He turned, taking in the fans all around the park. A glow filled his chest.

Then his gaze met Himmelblau's. His teammate gave one curt nod.

The glow remained. Cooper nodded back.

Nearby, the first base umpire stepped back to position. Still three outs left in the game. Cooper reseated his helmet, stuffed his batting gloves into his back pocket, and looked to the plate. "Come on, Ode!"

Skelton squirted tobacco juice from his mouth and stepped into the box. He worked the barrel of the bat forward and back, as usual, but from the fraction of his face visible to Cooper, Skelton seemed more relaxed than he had in the sixth.

Ode took a pitch outside, dribbled foul a strike on his hands. 1-1. Next, Ryerson flung a fastball on a chest-high trajectory.

Cooper sucked in a breath. Skelton's arms tensed, but he didn't swing. "Ball!" called the umpire.

The catcher tossed the ball back to Ryerson. 2-1. Ryerson stepped to the rubber, came set. The pitch. A slider, running in, not far enough.

Skelton lined the ball to right-center. Cheers thundered from the crowd. Cooper ran the instant he saw the ball would hit the ground. The third base coach waved him all the way through.

Cooper's foot jabbed third and he headed home. He looked over his shoulder. On the warning track, the right fielder bent down for the ball.

A grin split Cooper's mouth. Himmelblau stood behind home plate, hands high, waving him in standing up. Near the on-deck circle, Dominguez lifted his bat into the air. In front of the plate, the catcher stood with face mask up and a dejected set to his shoulders. Cooper ran hard, as hard as that eight-year-old in his memory. Another glance toward right-center showed the ball arching slowly toward the cut-off man.

Cooper ran across the plate. Himmelblau wrapped an arm around him. Dominguez jumped in. Players and coaches streamed from the dugout and joined the pile. Skelton high-fived teammates and shouted, "That's what I'm talking 'bout!"

The crowd roared. Fireworks burst above the open roof. The scoreboard behind center showed graphics and numbers and a snorting 8-bit bull. Cooper could only make out the final score, 3-2.

Slowly, the cluster of coaches and players drifted toward the dugout. Fans on the front row chanted "MVP! MVP!"

Cooper lifted his batting helmet. Something deep in his mind clicked, and he extended his arms, taking in Skelton, Dominguez, Himmelblau, and the rest of the team.

The chant died away. The cheers mounted, echoing around the stadium, pouring out the open roof toward the city, flowing with the team down the dugout steps and the tunnel to the clubhouse.

An hour later, the clubhouse was nearly empty. Only four players remained, dressed in tailored suits, hair slick from showers, styling products, and Dominguez' black hair dye. Cooper stood in front of his locker, facing the others.

"Alright, we're alone," Skelton said. "What you got to say?"

Himmelblau nodded. "We're all curious."

"Yes, yes," added Dominguez.

Cooper took a deep breath. "I've been thinking about what Himmelblau said before the game." He twisted his upper body, pulled a tablet from the top shelf of his locker. From the end of the rolled-up tablet came the glow of the private, password-protected, encrypted website he'd already loaded.

Himmelblau's forehead creased. "You have a way for us each to gain three hundred points of OPS?"

"Yes." A grin tightened Cooper's cheeks. He unfurled the tablet and snapped it rigid. On the display, Dr. Derek Liu looked authoritative in lab coat and eyeglasses, under the caption *Singapore Clinic for Personal Improvement.*

Cooper said, "I'll show all three of you where to get Ted Williams eyes."

THE EVERPINK SLAUGHTER

The farmer's dogs trotted alongside as the sheriff department cruiser rolled down the asphalt driveway between the house and the barn. When the car slowed and stopped, the dogs barked sporadically, watching one another from the corners of their eyes. After the gasoline engine chuttered to silence, their barking was the only sound for what seemed to be miles of the cold morning.

Deputy Matt Schaffer climbed out. "Hush," he told the dogs. His breath steamed in the dry air. The dogs grew quieter. Matt held out the back of his gloved hand to the nearest one, a neutered yellow mutt. The dog leaned forward, eyes wide, nostrils snuffling, until something near the barn caught his attention and he trotted toward it.

"Morning, Matt. Thanks for coming out so soon after I called."

Matt remembered Jake Helland from high school. The intervening fifteen years had worn his face with Iowa winters and the financial stresses of farming life, and what had those same years done to Matt? "Good to see you, Jake, though I wish it wasn't like this."

Jake nodded, face impassive. Whatever he felt only leaked out with a few blinks.

"They're in the barn?" Matt added. "Could you show me the way?"

Not that Matt needed a guide, but having a task might keep Jake from feeling overwhelmed by his emotions. Against the red, corrugated steel walls stood out a large sign with pink letters against a white background:

Everpink Transgenic Pigs

and at the bottom, in smaller red letters flanked by icons of a pig and the Earth:

Fresher Ham, Less Waste, Better for All

The line of Jake's jaw hardened as he started that way. Grass crackled under his steps. Matt and the dogs followed him, but the dogs soon whimpered and held back from the barn. The two men approached a plain white door with a single small window at eye level. The window had fogged over.

Jake reached a gloved hand toward the doorknob, then drew in a breath. "This will be the second time I've touched the knob this morning. Gloves both times. Is that a problem?"

The perpetrator would have worn gloves, if he'd come through that same door during the frigid night, so the knob probably lacked useful evidence. "No. But leave the door slightly open and don't touch the knob again until I lift prints."

Jake opened the door, then gripped its edge. The door trembled slightly. "Do you need me to go in?"

"Go back into the house. Get warm. I'll talk to you when I'm done here."

Though he nodded, Jake didn't move. "It isn't right. The Everpink people offered us a big discount for buying their piglets, on top of the price premium we can get for them at market. We were just trying to get ahead, the American way, following the rules." His voice faltered. " Twenty head...."

Part of Matt's job was to listen. "Insurance?"

Jake shook his head. "Costs are high and money's tight. The animal rights nutjobs don't want to leave their lattes in Minneapolis to come out to the country and ruin a man's livelihood." Moisture glistened in his eyes. "I told the missus that and she believed me."

Matt winced in sympathy. "Livestock abuse is two years per count. We'll talk to the DA, maybe he can string the jail time out consecutively. The perp might be looking at forty years." Small condolence—

justice wouldn't help Jake's financial situation—but the only one Matt could offer.

Without another word, Jake walked toward his house. Matt went into the barn.

The stench hit him right away. The musty smell of grain pellets, and a whiff of pig shit from a manure treatment bioreactor, a tall tank at one end of the barn. But with those smells came one he'd encountered a few times during his decade on the police force in Des Moines. The thick odor of blood.

Triangular windows where the end walls met the peaked ceiling let in gray light. The barn held a large pen defined by a concrete slab and tubular steel fencing. The side nearest the door held food and water troughs. The slab sloped slightly away, toward sewage drains at the far side of the pen.

Matt climbed over the tubular steel fence and into the pen. Dead pigs lay around him, with pallid skin and glassy eyes. The perpetrator had slashed the side of each pig's neck. Blood had poured down the slope and clung to the covers of the sewage drains.

Most of the pigs lay near the troughs. Three had made it a few steps downslope. Otherwise, Matt saw no sign of struggle. A result of the Everpink transgene, he assumed. A protein in their muscles bound oxygen so tightly their muscles as a whole were starved for it. The pigs could barely move before they got winded. Somehow that led to cured ham that stayed fresh longer.

Matt pulled his phone from an inner pocket of his jacket and methodically photographed the dead pigs. He gritted his teeth as he worked. The pigs had been domesticated to serve man's will, with lives that shouldn't matter save for the financial losses inflicted on their owner; but creatures too, capable of suffering, with enough in common with man to elicit pity. He set the thoughts aside and refocused on his work. The only sound was the atavistic shutter effect from his phone's speaker, fluttering off the barn's corrugated steel walls.

Once he finished, he straightened up. More evidence showed in red spray paint on the wall next to the door. It explained Jake's comment about animal rights terrorists. *GMO = SIN*, spelled out in narrow, splotchy letters and punctuated with streaks of running paint. Matt took more photos. From the height and line quality of the tops of the letters, the graffiti artist was six feet even or a little taller.

He spent an hour hunting for physical evidence. The perpetrator had been careful. No fingerprints on the doorknob, no knife or spray paint can in the trash, no footprints in pig blood.

Outside was no different. Matt walked around the barn. The ground was too cold to show footprints. One of the dogs, the neutered yellow mutt, followed him at a cautious distance.

He went up the steps to the front door of the house and scraped his feet on the doormat. The yellow mutt sprinted into the carport and a dog door into the house flapped. Over a sudden eruption of barks from the living room, Jake's wife Emily let Matt in. She hushed the dogs and guided him to an armchair angled to Jake's recliner, and turned off the old sitcom blaring on the 3D. Though the furnace ran constantly, after Matt's time in the barn and outside, it couldn't dispel a cold feeling that clung to him. When Emily offered him coffee, Matt demurred, but she brought him a cappuccino anyway and sat next to her husband for Matt to take their statements.

They'd seen nothing, heard nothing. The pigs had been fine when Jake had fed them the evening before. Matt asked again about insurance, watching both their faces for a tell, then pretended he'd forgotten he'd asked before. Jake and Emily seemed decent, but financial troubles could drive even decent folks to attempt an insurance fraud. But their reactions to his question were innocent. He kept talking to them. No enemies, no squabbles. The Everpink reps were good people who wanted them to succeed.

When Matt left, he told his cruiser to drive back to the sheriff's department in Putnam City. At the end of Jake's driveway, the car waited for a pickup to drive past on the state highway. A white extended cab with dually rear wheels, its diesel engine roared as it approached the posted speed limit. Just as it passed Jake's driveway, the electric engine kicked in and the diesel fell silent.

Matt's cruiser turned onto the state highway and slowly closed the quarter-mile gap on the white pickup. Soon his cruiser drew close enough to make out the badges of new features on the tailgate, CO_{sink}™ Climate Change Abatement Service, ODEL™ On Demand

Electric Only mode, Cowfree™ Bioscaffolded Leather, AutoPilot™ v3.1. Matt looked in the pickup's cab as his cruiser passed. The eldest son of the Grangers, farmers with several hundred pigs, napped while the pickup drove itself to the high school.

On the far side of town, the Sheriff's Department occupied a one-story structure of glass and honey-colored brick. Matt hurried into the warm building and settled into his cubicle.

Sheriff Carlson came by as Matt synced photos to the department's server. About sixty years old, with thin gray hair and a paunch. Behind Carlson's broad face worked a mind shrewd enough to keep his office since Matt's childhood.

Carlson lifted his gaze over his coffee to the monitor showing photos of the dead pigs. "Hell of a thing, Matt. At least for around here. Is Jake Helland working an insurance scam?"

"I don't think so." Matt gave his reasons. "But I'll call the Everpink people. Maybe they indemnify their piglet buyers for this sort of loss."

Carlson sipped coffee, then winced and wiped milk froth from his upper lip with the back of his hand. "Damn big city coffee drinks. Wait, what did that one say?"

Matt sent the sync to the background and opened the photo with the spray painted graffiti. *GMO = SIN* stood out against the white steel in the photo and the monitor's black bezel.

"An animal rights wacko?" Carlson squinted at the photo. "Talk to Brad Fleischer."

Matt had to think for a moment. "The Fleischers have a kid? Why him?"

Carlson looked down his nose at Matt. "You ought to read putnamcitypost.com. Might learn something about what's going on around the county. The kid wrote a letter to the editor last week condemning local farmers for cruelty in their transgenic cattle and pig operations."

"And then he was stupid enough to kill twenty pigs when he would be the prime suspect?"

"He's seventeen. He easily could be stupid enough. All it takes is a girl with purple hair promising to show him the piercings in her hoohah if he did."

Matt leaned back in his chair. His first look at the evidence had failed to give him any other lead. "I'll take a look at him."

Thirty minutes later, after reading the kid's letter to the editor, Matt reached the high school. He arrived just before a class hour ended, and waited in the principal's secretary's office for Brad Fleischer to answer the principal's summons. From his vantage point, Matt could see through floor-to-ceiling windows down two perpendicular halls. Kids flowed through in cliquish clumps. A number of girls had hair dyed artificial colors, and one of them met his gaze through the glass.

Sheriff Olson's further speculation about those girls jumped to mind, and Matt pushed it out of his thoughts. He pulled out his tablet and reviewed the letter to the editor, looking for more angles to question the boy. *Everpink pigs can't walk three steps without running out of breath. With new, protein-enriched soybean strains on the market now, and meat products from cultured animal muscle cells only a few years from store shelves, the time has come to stop mutating and inhumanely treating animals for the sake of big business.*

The boy came in the door. Tall, skinny, with an air of superiority and boredom. To the secretary, he said, "Why does Principal...." He frowned at Matt, and flicked his gaze over Matt's belt-mounted radio and sidearm.

"Brad Fleischer?"

"Bradford."

"Okay, Bradford. I'd like to speak with you. Principal Dickmann, do you have a spare office we could use?"

The principal, pudgy as his name, said, "Use mine." Some passing boys mockingly shouted *Brad-fooooorrrrrdddd* through the glass. The principal glared at them as Matt and the kid went in.

Once the door was closed behind them, Bradford sat in one of the visitor chairs in front of the desk. He pushed his back against the rest and crossed his legs. Matt took the other visitor chair and pivoted it on the thin, rough carpet. A poster of Minnesota Wild players hoisting the Stanley Cup looked down from the wall.

"Bradford, what happened at the Hellands' farm last night?"

"The who?"

"The Hellands. They live on the state highway east of town. They have a small herd of Everpink pigs."

The kid squirmed. "I never heard of the Hellands."

"Really? I thought you might have."

Arms folded, and scowling, the kid said, "You have a problem with me exercising my right to free speech? Is that what this is about? Your masters in the agribusiness industry are scared of the truth and they ordered you to suppress dissent?"

Had Matt been as full of idealistic piss and vinegar as a high school boy? He couldn't remember. But he never would have been so confrontational with a law enforcement officer. Matt lowered his brows and deepened his voice. "'Free speech rights?' 'Dissent?' Is that what you call what happened?"

"Why do you keep saying, 'what happened?' How should I know what goes on on some farm at night?"

Matt kept his gaze on the kid. "Twenty Everpink pigs were killed. Someone slit their throats and bled them out."

Disbelief filled the kid's face. "Killed? Everpink?" He shook his head. "Let them bleed to death? That's depraved. Monstrous."

Matt put on his good-cop face. "Even though those pigs were an abomination against God?"

Bradford rolled his eyes. "You small towners think the universe revolves around you. Even if God existed, why do you think He would care what happens on Earth?"

Anxious disgust hardened Matt's face. Sure, he hadn't been to church since Easter, but this self-absorbed brat, too smart for his own good, rejecting a couple thousand years of tradition because he couldn't live with the contradiction between religious ideals and the reality of the world?

Complaining about kids these days wouldn't get this boy to confess. Matt fortified his good-cop expression. "But the genetic engineers are mutating animals against nature. Isn't that—"

"Evil? Not necessarily. There's a lot of genetic engineering used for good. Like those fast-growing bamboo trees they dump in anoxic deep ocean for climate change abatement. Engineering pigs isn't wrong in itself. Making those Everpink pigs unable to live a normal life is what's wrong."

Matt folded his arms and narrowed his eyes. "So where were you last night?"

The boy put on a challenging face. "Home. I finished my homework around 8, hung out on the NowheresvilleMisfits forum till about midnight, then went to bed."

"Your parents would agree with that?"

"Yes." Mockery tinged his tone.

When did his parents go to bed? The boy could have sneaked out and driven to the Hellands' farm. But if the boy was guilty, let him think he was in the clear. "That's all I have. You're free to go."

The boy stood to go. "I hope you catch the guy. Those pigs were a crime against nature, but they should've died of old age."

Matt left the high school and stopped at Fleischer Insurance. Mr. Fleischer had the sunken cheeks and skinny limbs of someone who ran marathons. He bristled at the suggestion his son had killed the Everpink pigs. "He has his mind set on Northwestern or the University of Chicago. He wouldn't put that in jeopardy."

"So where was he last night?"

"I checked on him at 10, when I went to bed. He was in his room. I happened to wake up around 2. His car was where he left it when he got home from school yesterday."

"He could have driven somewhere between 10 and 2."

"My wife usually comes to bed around 11."

"11 and 2, then." Matt thought further. "And when did you get up?"

"I left the house to go running at 5. His car looked like it hadn't moved."

"So 2 to 5 is another window in which he could have committed this crime."

Fleischer shook his head. "I still can't believe he would have killed those pigs. He has strong opinions about what he thinks is wrong with Putnam City, but I keep telling him, living well is the best revenge, and I was certain he understood that."

Matt nodded to let Fleischer think Matt believed his self-serving talk. "Does his car have a GPS tracker from your insurance company?"

"No. When I brought it up, he refused, and I didn't push it."

And he got the family discount without it. Kids, thinking Big Brother had nothing better to do than track them, when instead a GPS tracker could have exonerated him. "Thanks for your time."

A few minutes later, a chat with Mrs. Fleischer at her home gave Matt the same information. Unless her husband had contacted her while Matt drove over—or the Fleischers had agreed on a cover story with their son before school—that limited the boy's opportunity to commit the crime to a pair of three-hour windows.

Back at the sheriff's department, Matt turned to his computer. He would need a warrant to get the Fleischer's internet traffic records from the local broadband provider, but not to surf nowheresville-misfits.com. Matt soon found Bradford Fleischer's posts from the night before. Condemning agribusiness cruelty, praising crop plant genetic engineering, posting comments on other threads. He made his last post at 12:02am.

Could he have gotten to the Hellands' farm, killed the pigs, hidden or destroyed any evidence, and returned in two hours? Possibly. Three hours might have been a more comfortable window, but why would he assume his father would wake up in the middle of the night and wait to act till after?

Matt made a phone call to the manager of the local branch of NIowa Bank. The bank had two hundred feet of road frontage on the state highway heading east from town, and security cameras watching the parking lot entrances.

"Come on over, Matt," the manager said. "I'll have last night's roadview camera footage set up when you get here."

Before Matt left the sheriff's department, he pulled the Fleischers' automobile insurance records from the state Motor Vehicle Division. The family drove three Tatas, an uncommon make around town. A late-model sedan and SUV, plus an older, red coupe with an all-gasoline engine and a retrofitted autopilot. A call to the high school confirmed the red coupe was the boy's car.

In the bank's security office, the manager played back the previous night's camera footage at high speed and left Matt alone. A few cars headed out of town in the hours after midnight or after the bar closed, but none were a Tata, red coupe or otherwise. Long stretches of the night passed without any traffic on the road. The kid had not driven out of town.

Unless he knew about the bank's camera and had taken side roads to avoid it?

Matt shook his head. The stream of evidence suggesting Bradford Fleischer was the perpetrator had dried up. But if not him, then who had killed the pigs? Matt rode back to the sheriff's department in frustration.

Sheriff Carlson waited for him. "It's the Fleischer kid?"

"Doesn't look like it. We have a couple of time windows when he could have driven out there, but no sign he did."

"We need to find the perp, Matt."

"Yeah, he's a criminal."

Sheriff Carlson shook his head. "There's more. Everpink corporate called me a few minutes ago."

The boy's accusation, that Matt was an agribusiness puppet, came back to mind. "We don't work for them. We work for the citizens of the county."

"Hundreds of whom want to buy piglets from that company. Everpink pigs are the nearest thing to a fracking boom this county will ever see. Everpink's sow barns are running at maximum capacity. If Everpink is unwilling to provide piglets to farmers in our county because there's a lack of security, who are the local farmers going to blame at election time?"

"Us."

"No, Matt. Me. So get more evidence on this kid or find me a better suspect."

The winter sun had long set by the time Matt went home to his apartment and a frozen dinner. He scraped the dregs of his microwaved tikka masala and chickpea daal into the garbage disposal as his phone's calendar app chimed to remind him to call his son. He threw the cardboard tray into the compost collection bin, then went to the dining room and leaned his phone against its stand before making the call.

Lucas wore a Chicago Cubs cap with a brim ironed flat, turned sideways on his head. The hood of his shirt lay bunched at the back of his neck. Anger at his ex-wife bloomed in Matt's chest—*you let a nine-year-old dress like a shitbird?*—and was soon chased by despair. If a small town kid with two well-off parents could turn into a pig slaughterer, what hope was there for a kid of divorce living in the nearest thing to a big city in the whole state?

Then Lucas spoke, voice innocent. "Dad, it's so good to see you. I can't wait till you come next weekend."

Matt's dark feelings washed away. "I'm glad to see you, kiddo."

"I've been reading that Sherlock Holmes book you gave me for my birthday."

"You have?" Surprise touched Matt's voice. Lucas had responded to the gift with poorly-masked disappointment.

Lucas nodded. "I thought it would be boring, but it's not. How did Holmes figure those things out? Are you as good a detective as he is?"

"Holmes was smarter than me. What stories have you liked so far?"

With a frown, Lucas said, "I can't pick one. They're all good." His eyes widened and his frown evaporated. "I just read 'Silver Blaze.' That's a good one."

"It's been a while," Matt said. "Remind me how it goes?"

"The famous race horse goes missing and his trainer is killed and the dog did nothing in the nighttime and that was the curious incident. Do you remember now?"

A cold feeling washed over Matt's jaw, stippling his five o'clock shadow. "I do. You're right, that is a good story." He reached for his phone and called up the notetaking app over the videocall. He swiped letters with his finger over Lucas' ghosted image.

"Da-ad."

Matt finished and saved. "Just thought of something for work. I'm done now. So what other Holmes stories have you read?"

They talked for a while. Matt still didn't like his son's clothing choices, but he was a good kid underneath it all. The call only ended when Matt's ex hovered behind Lucas' shoulder and muttered a few words in a tone meant for Matt to hear.

"I gotta go, dad. I can't wait to see you Friday night."

"Me neither."

"And remember, 'whatever remains, however improbable, must be the truth.' Love you."

"I love you, son." The call ended. Matt sat for a moment, savoring the connection with his son, before he made another call.

Jake Helland's face, weary beyond his years, appeared on the screen. "Matt? Did you find the man that killed my pigs?"

"Not yet. But I do have a lead," he quickly added in response to Jake's sinking face. "Can you do me a favor? Are your dogs in the house?"

Jake frowned in puzzlement. "They're curled up near the wood stove."

"Keep them indoors for about fifteen minutes, but leave the dog door accessible. Can you do that?"

The frown remained, but its emotional charge turned into fatalism. "Sure."

Fifteen minutes later, Matt's cruiser slowed as it prepared to turn off the state highway onto Jake's driveway. He turned off the headlights and traveled slowly toward Jake's house. The front porch light glowed against the dark plain, and the only sound was the rumble of the cruiser's gasoline engine.

When he was thirty yards from the house, the dogs rushed out into the bright patch cast by the porch light. Their barks subsided after Matt climbed out. He let them sniff the back of his hand while his breaths streamed out.

The front storm door twanged open. "You alright, Matt?"

"I'm fine, Jake. Thanks for helping me. I should have an answer for you by the morning." Matt waved and climbed back into his cruiser.

Once back at the state highway, instead of turning left toward town, Matt turned right. Half a mile away, long banks of lights showed the large barns of the Grangers' pig farm. The entrance to their driveway had brick columns and cast iron gates, and a sign reading *Granger All-Natural Pigs*. Matt used his phone to buzz for entry.

"Who is it?" said a craggy male voice. From one of Sheriff Carlson's reelection fundraisers, Matt knew it belonged to Mr. Granger.

"Deputy Schaffer."

Granger sounded surprised. "What brings you by?"

"I'm looking into the killing of the Hellands' Everpink pigs. You live so close I wanted to ask if you or a family member had seen or heard anything. May I come in?"

After a hesitation, Granger said, "I'll open the gate."

A motor hummed and the gate swung open. The cruiser rolled forward. Rows of elms flanked the Grangers' driveway and framed the view of their house. Two stories with a tower at one corner and a pair of two-car garages on the east side. Apparently the all-natural pig business had been good to the family. When Matt drew closer, he looked at the garages, but the doors were down. The white pickup with on-demand electric-only mode might be inside.

The front entryway of the house held a coat rack and a framed needlepoint homily. Granger, balding and paunchy, wearing trousers and a sweater from the mall in Minneapolis, met him. "Welcome, deputy. How's Sheriff Carlson? He's a good man and a credit to the county. Glad too the department's taking that crime over at the Hellands' seriously, though I heard you got the guy?"

"Where did you hear that?"

"My son saw you talking to Brad Fleischer in the principal's office at school this morning."

"We're investigating every lead."

Granger shrugged and gestured deeper into the house. Matt took a few steps and found himself in a double-height living room. A ceiling fan lazily directed hot air down the walls, and through his feet, Matt felt radiant heating underneath the tile floor.

"Thank you for your time," Matt said. "I won't be long. Did you notice anything out of the ordinary at the Hellands' last night?"

"No. I watched the Wild game on 3D with my kids. We were in the media room in the basement."

"After the game?"

"We all turned in. Around 11."

"Okay, I had to ask. Did your wife watch the game? Did your kids leave the room? I'd like to talk to them, too."

Granger shook his head. "They won't tell you anything different, but I know you have a job to do." Granger lifted his phone and opened an intercom channel to his family.

His oldest son approached the living room first. The kid started at the sight of Matt and warily came all the way into the room. The boy was taller than Matt had guessed from seeing him in his pickup that morning. Six feet at least. "Deputy Schaffer? What's happening?"

"I'm trying to gather all the evidence I can on the thing that happened at the Hellands' last night. Did you see or hear anything?"

"I was watching the Wild game with my dad and younger brothers."

Matt nodded. "After that?"

"I got ready for bed."

"Did you have a late night? I noticed you sleeping in your truck on the way to school this morning."

The kid started again. "Uh, no, uh, I just had trouble sleeping."

"You have a nice truck. That on-demand electric mode seems it could come in handy."

"Uh, what?"

"If you were sneaking out. Or sneaking in. No one would hear you. The dogs wouldn't even bark."

"We don't have dogs. Sir."

Granger leaned forward, gaze piercing. "What are you getting at, Matty?"

"The Hellands' dogs didn't bark while someone went past them to the barn and slit the throats of eighteen pigs—"

"Tw—" the kid started to say, then swallowed and avoided Matt's gaze.

Matt took a half-step closer to the kid. "I didn't catch that. What were you saying?"

"Nothing."

Matt shrugged. "Someone either walked a long way to the Hellands' barn, or drove up in a car, or truck, with its fossil fuel engine off. Given how cold it was last night, I'm going to wager no one walked all that distance—"

"We're done here." Granger's voice was low but carried through the room. "You're going to leave right now or I'm going to have a serious talk with Sheriff Carlson about his staffing decisions."

Get me fired? DMPD would take me back. I can't stand his mother but I'd live a few miles from Lucas.... But willfully losing a pissing contest to Granger wouldn't serve the cause of justice. Matt held his ground. "I don't need to come back, if I subpoena your car insurance company for GPS records from your kid's truck."

The kid blanched. Granger squared his shoulders to Matt and stuck his thumbs in his front belt-loops. "The judge has to sign off on that. You think he's going to listen to you, or me?"

"You want to take that chance? If your son cooperates, we can suggest the DA pursue leniency. Twenty counts, concurrent, probation. Better than forty years in jail."

Behind his father, the kid made a strangled sound. Granger raised his hand to the kid while keeping his gaze on Matt. "This interview is done."

Six months later, the summer sun was still high in the sky when Matt left the sheriff's department one Friday. A cool breeze cut the edge of the hot late afternoon as he walked to his car.

The trial resolving the Hellands' civil suit against the Grangers had ended just before noon. Once evidence the Grangers were losing sales to farmers raising Everpink's pigs had entered the record, alongside their son's plea-bargain of two years probation for livestock abuse, the jury had found for the Hellands. Jake and Emily were owed compensation for the loss of their Everpink pigs, plus interest and punitive damages. Granger might declare bankruptcy to preserve his homestead from judgment, but the assets from his pig operation would be forfeit, and his entire family's reputation in the county had been stained for decades to come. The Hellands had won more justice than this world usually provided.

Matt climbed in, and the cruiser headed south, soon leaving the last houses of the town behind. A dozen signs marking farms raising Ever-pink pigs stood along the roadside between Putnam City and the county line. He saw twenty more before he got on I-35 southbound for Des Moines and his son.

—The author would like to thank Dr. John S. Olson, Rice University, for providing equipment, materials, and guidance in research into the reactions of nitric oxide with myoglobin; and Michael Eich for technical background on pig farming.

THE MALABAR COAST

The boat bobbed on the brackish waters of the tidal lagoon. Across the lagoon, partially obscured by palm trees, the resort's main building showed teak timbers and a steep roof tiled in orange-red laterite. "Come aboard, come aboard," the dock attendant said in his Indian accent.

Liam Kleinschmidt took his wife Courtney by the elbow. They shuffled forward in line with a dozen other American medical tourists. Like Liam and Courtney, most looked middle-aged, with paunches and wrinkles and a few gray hairs. The men wore polo shirts with golf logos or the names of the small businesses they owned. The women wore hats and blouses, capri pants and flat-soled shoes. Everyone — even the swarthy couple, South Asian or Hispanic? — had white dabs of sunscreen on their noses and ears.

The dock attendant helped Courtney over the canal's low stone wall and onto the boat. Liam's heart tapped faster. He took the three steps up the wall in a single leap. He hesitated with one foot on the railing. The apogee of a suborbital flight, the moment where its momentum balanced with the Earth's pull, must feel like this.

He would take that flight someday.

After this trip, he would have all the time he needed.

He stepped onto the boat. His legs felt like compressed springs. Just one suborbital ride? If he continued growing his business, he would earn enough to buy his own suborbital.

An awning shaded the wooden bench seats. Courtney sat next to the boat's railing. Her head bobbed as she studied the water.

Liam set next to her. "We'll remember this like our wedding day. The kids' birthdays."

She turned to him. Her hat's wide brim made her eyes seem far away. "These treatments are banned in the US for a reason."

A pulse of annoyance tightened his lips, narrowed his eyes. This again?

He relaxed. The jet lag, ten and a half time zones and 14,000 flight miles in two days, made her cranky. "The reason is, the stem cell and telomere therapy industries didn't pay enough bribes to the FDA." Liam's voice sounded breezily confident. "The doctors here graduated from the best American medical schools. They know what they're doing."

"I'm sure," Courtney said, though her tone told him otherwise.

After everyone boarded, two boatmen shoved long poles into the water and pushed the boat away from the dock, toward the lodge. The folds of *dhotis* wrapped around their legs flexed with their motions.

Courtney spoke again. "What if the treatments fail?"

"The treatments will work. In a week, you'll feel decades younger. All this humidity, it'll be just like that spring break trip to Destin."

She ducked her head and wriggled her shoulder against him. Liam imagined memories bringing up an embarrassed but lusty smile hidden by her hat's wide brim. He put his arm around her and the boat went on. Kingfishers hovered over the lagoon. Splashes sounded the dives of turtles.

The boat pulled up to a dock near the lodge. Another boat bobbed there. The boatmen shoved their polls against the lagoon bottom and leaned on them. They chatted in the local language to the men of the other boat. The latter stretched out on their boat's cushioned benches, under an awning of thick fabric and fans buzzing like gnats. A luxury boat for VIPs.

He and Courtney would ride that on their next visit.

They debarked onto tight-packed paving stones. A broad pathway of the same stones led to the lodge. Courtney and Liam joined the crowd heading that way.

The lobby could belong to a resort in the US, except with more South Asians on staff. Spacers held the resort's name, The Malabar Coast, float-mounted on the wall behind the front desk. Men and women in khaki pants and horizon blue polo shirts bustled about the lobby and the concierge stand. The only sign of the resort's medical services came from one corner. A slender woman in a white lab coat sat in front of a video display showing energetic middle-aged white couples. Flanking the display, posters listed various medical service packages, omitting prices.

A short line of new guests, presumably freshly arrived on the VIP boat, already waited at the check-in desk. A youthful-looking man with a long, narrow nose, every strand of sandy brown hair in place, looked familiar. Liam blinked. He put his hand on Courtney's shoulder and guided her closer to the man.

"Honey?"

"It's okay." Liam raised his voice. "Sam Deckard?"

The man turned his head. His eyebrows crinkled, until he blinked. "Liam?"

"It's been a long time since college." Liam extended his hand, held it out for a long moment. Deckard's grip mixed supple skin with vise-like fingers. "You remember Courtney?" Liam asked.

"Of course." Deckard nodded in her direction. To Liam, he said, "Were you at the twenty-year reunion?"

"I wish I could have gone, but I was just getting my business off the ground."

Deckard asked, "Which industry?"

"Desktop manufacturing."

Deckard blinked once. "Really. I'm with UFabIt."

The biggest player in the industry, coasting on its founders' two-decades-old insights. It made sense. Deckard made solid grades in their chemical engineering classes, but his strengths and interest lay more in glad-handing and schmoozing.

"What do you do there?"

"I was recently named chief government affairs officer."

He couldn't hack real work? Liam clamped his lips together. If he said that, Courtney would glare sidelong here and give him an earful once they reached their cabin. Liam's cheeks tightened in a smile absent from his eyes. "It's a shame regulatory compliance is such a big part of the industry. All the paperwork about biological feedstocks, biodegradable products, emissions monitoring—"

"Regulatory compliance is just a fraction of my job," Deckard said. "You have someone to do that at, what's your company again?"

"SinterPrinter." Liam delivered his pitch with practiced ease. "We just went to market with our lead product. We combine 3-D printing and laser sintering to allow our customers to make plastic-cased electronic products in one fab round."

Deckard's eyebrows rose for a fraction of a second, then seemed to strike an iron wall and flatten out. "You made that work? UFabIt R&D has been pursuing that for a while. How'd you make it work?"

"You can read the patent."

"Why haven't we heard of you?"

"SinterPrinter is small," Liam said. "For now."

Deckard smiled. "We'll keep an eye on you. Maybe we'll buy SinterPrinter someday."

"Maybe." William bared his teeth, like a small mammal finding a nest of dinosaur eggs. "Or maybe someday we'll buy UFabIt." He laughed and clapped his hand on Deckard's shoulder.

Deckard's face, unnaturally smooth, blanked for a moment. Then he waved his hand to take in the facility the resort. "What did you come to have done?"

Liam put his hand around Courtney's shoulders and pulled her closer. "Oh, the basics. For this trip. You?"

Courtney chimed in. "We don't mean to pry."

Deckard flicked his fingers, as if he shooed away a fly. "A little of this, a little of that."

Liam's cheeks tightened, but the fake smile soon drained from his face. *A little,* but far beyond the basic longevity treatments on order for Courtney and him. Maybe one of the new, expensive gene therapy augmentations to increase IQ or reduce the need for sleep.

Motion at the head of the line drew Deckard's attention. "Time to check in. Great to run into you. Maybe I'll see around."

Liam bared his teeth again. "You will."

Next morning, 10 am, the veranda creaked and a sharp rap on the door heralded someone's arrival.

Liam wrote the last two words of an email to the office, hit send. He stood and smiled at Courtney. "Finally, time to get started."

Her lips pressed together. "Just get the door."

He did. An Indian woman waited on the veranda. Straight black hair fell to the shoulders of a white lab coat. Her hair framed an intelligent face, barely crow's-footed with the first touch of middle age. She extended her hand for a gentle shake. "I'm Dr. Thomas." She spoke a midwestern American flavor of English. "I'll guide you through your procedures."

Liam blinked twice. Maybe her ancestors had taken that family name when they built one of the Orthodox or Catholic churches driven by on the road from Trivandrum. "Where in the States are you from?" he asked.

"Iowa. My parents worked hard to get to the US and get my brothers and me through medical school. But when I got out, with all the prohibitions on longevity medicine being imposed back home, I had far more opportunities here."

Dr. Thomas flexed her fingers at the air. "Never mind. Have you recovered from your flights?"

"We sure did," Liam said. "The cocktail of, what's in it? Melatonin and—?"

"A proprietary blend of herbals and nutraceuticals."

"Did wonders. I feel no jet lag at all. Same for Courtney."

Courtney quirked her mouth. He knew her look. She still thought the clinic would sell them snake oil?

"I'm glad to hear it," Dr. Thomas said. "We have more good news. The eppendorf tubes with your buccal cells arrived in great shape. We have all the tranches of induced pluripotent stem cells we need."

Courtney sniffed out a breath. "You can really take cells from the lining of our cheeks, that we spit out, then make this stem cell business out of them."

"Court—" Liam's brows furrowed. The clinic's doctors knew what they were doing.

Dr. Thomas showed no offense. "I'm happy to answer any questions you may have, Mrs. Kleinschmidt. There are a lot of misconceptions about what we do, and I'd like to dispel any of those I can. Yes, the technology is well-established, despite the inexplicable ban in the US. We've been doing it here for about two decades. In fact, in a few months, I'll go through my third stem cell treatment right here in our clinic."

A gulp of air filled Liam's mouth. Her third treatment? At decade intervals, starting at the recommended age of 35—she was a decade *older*, not younger, than him—

If that didn't lead Court over her fears—

"No more questions?" Dr. Thomas asked. "The clinic is a short walk."

A stone path led from their cabin past a dozen others. Steep roofs, verandas, walls of clay-red bricks. After the cabins, the path turned and ran parallel to a high wall. Liam raised his hand. The wall stood just out of reach. Behind the wall, a stentorian voice spoke in an American accent. "No. I don't owe you a favor. *You* owe *me* one...."

Dr. Thomas led them past a yoga pavilion and tennis courts. The thwock of tennis balls still sounded when they reached a sprawling building of mirrored windows and straight lines. The doors opened and conditioned air spilled out.

Down hallways of off-white tile, they arrived at an examination room with two paper-covered tables. "Today, we'll do your preliminary workup. Assuming your workup checks out, tomorrow will be the day for the stem cell injections."

Courtney's eyes showed their whites. "Checks out?"

Dr. Thomas held up her palms. "For people your age, in decent health, it almost always does."

"If it doesn't? What are we supposed to do then?"

"You'll have a few days to enjoy the resort while we construct replacement organs for an autologous transplant."

"An organ transplant?" Courtney's hand rose to her neck. "US customs is starting to do body scans. If they see scars, they could arrest us—"

"Court," Liam said, "no one ever gets caught. I told you that. I told you they could do organ transplants and stem cell therapies. I told you all this before we got on the flight here. Too late to freak out now. So stop it."

Courtney glowered back. "Freaking out? Every time I had a question, you said *don't worry about it, no problem, everything will be fine*—"

"Over and over you asked the same damn questions—"

Dr. Thomas cleared her throat. "Mrs. Kleinschmidt, we appreciate your concerns. I assure you, we have world-class doctors, world-class nurses, and world-class facilities. We do world-class life extension treatments. As far as whether the US authorities would suspect upon your return, I can't promise anything, but as far as I know, no patient has ever been questioned by US customs. Questioned, not even arrested. Let alone convicted."

"See?" Liam said to Courtney.

Dr. Thomas lowered her eyebrows at him. To Courtney, she said, "Even though we'll finish the workup today, we aren't required to begin the stem cell procedures tomorrow. We could wait a day or even two—"

"Just get it over with," Courtney said.

Liam frowned. He let out a breath and his face relaxed. She might be unwilling now, but after she got through the tests, she would be glad.

Dr. Thomas nodded at two slumping pieces of thin fabric hanging near the door. "We'll give you a few minutes to change into your gowns. I'll be back with some nurses to start your workup." Dr. Thomas stepped out. The door shut itself behind her.

Liam undid a button of his polo shirt. "You heard the doctor." He pulled his shirt over his head and laid it aside.

They continued to undress, as unerotically as any couple married twenty years. He glanced at Courtney—a roll of belly fat obscured her c-section scar—then glanced at his own reflection in the mirror. Flabby gut, slouched shoulders, pallid skin from shoulders to knees. Both their bodies showed their ages.

For now.

As promised, the next hours passed in tests. Body scans. Detailed panels of organ activity. Assays for cancer markers. Maybe Court feared what the tests might find. Some cancer too advanced for the clinic's therapies to fight? Her father had died of cancer, but in his seventies. And prostate cancer to boot—

Later that afternoon, Dr. Thomas talked to them while checking notes on a tablet. "As I expected, you're both in average to above-average health for your age. The good news, of course, is no organ transplantation is required. Tomorrow we'll do the main panel of stem cell injections. Two days after that, you'll receive a molecular cocktail of telomere extenders." Her lips parted in a smile like tiled marble. "In a week, you'll feel a decade younger, or more."

"That's what I want to hear," Liam said.

Courtney didn't respond. She said little when they returned to their cottage and changed for dinner. They walked to the resort's restaurant as the tropical sun knifed between tall palms toward the Arabian Sea. He ordered an inexpensive bottle of red wine, then scrolled through menu pages on a tablet: soups, salads, entrées of chicken and lamb, then pages of Indian dishes. Chicken tikka masala he knew, but daal? Chana?

He ordered chicken breast and mashed potatoes. Courtney, a salad. He lifted the wine bottle toward her half-empty glass.

She waved her hand in the air above her glass. "We'll be under anesthesia tomorrow," she said. "One more glass, maybe, later."

He leered. "I'll hold you to that."

She showed no response.

They chatted, interspersed with long silences. A text message from the office led him out to the veranda for a fifteen-minute phone call. Not important, but urgent. When he returned to their table, their chatter held longer silences, and the message from the office remained on his mind, blocking out some of her words.

Back in their cottage, preparing for bed, he came up behind her, gripped her shoulders, turned her upper body toward his mouth. Her shoulders slumped when they kissed. "Hon, I'm so tired."

"We'll be more tired tomorrow." Fogged by anesthesia and aching from deep tissue injections.

"Then maybe in a few days."

"Court." He spoke with masculine power. Enough, at least. She leaned back against him. Acquiescent, not eager.

For now.

Stem cell implantation went like any other operation. Around 7:30, Liam and Courtney arrived at the clinic on empty stomachs. Chasing a preanesthetic with a glass of water, changing into gowns, lying on gurneys, looking up the noses of scrubbed-in nurses. While waiting in the hallway, he turned his head to flash Courtney an encouraging smile. She stared at the ceiling with drawn features.

They finally arrived in the operating room. Cool lamps and walls shaded in antiseptic white. Liam looked around at the masked and hair-netted faces. He found two exposed eyes belonging to Dr. Thomas. Someone set a clear, pliable plastic mask over his nose and mouth. Monitors beeped and pumps whirred. Shouldn't it kick in, the, what was it, anna seti…?

His eyes fluttered open. His body felt miles away. Billowing white sheets rose around him, floated above him. Squeaks below. Air comfortably hot. Nearby, thwock sounds. Running feet.

"Good shot." Voice familiar.

Another voice, like a king's. "That looked out from here."

"No, no, I was right on top of it. Clearly in. Good point."

Liam's eyelids became too heavy to lift. More squeaks from nearby. Courtney. Just sleep. Liam shut his eyes.

He woke in their cabin. A split adjustable bed elevated his upper body and bent his legs slightly at the knee. Next to him, her body mirroring his, Courtney slept.

A nurse stood up from a chair at the foot of the bed. "Here, Mr. Kleinschmidt." She held up a bottle sealed around a straw. Inside sloshed a blue liquid. "Drink as much as you can. Take your time."

Liam raised his arms and lifted his upper body from the bed. Everything ached. She handed him the bottle. He grunted and sagged back into the bed. A side of beef felt this way after being punched by a training boxer. Below his gown sleeves, his arms showed splotched skin.

"What—" A dry cough scraped out of his throat.

"You will mend in a day or two. Drink. It will help you recover."

Liam lifted the bottle toward his mouth. His arms wobbled. Bottle on his chest, he'd make it work. With awkward movements of his hand and head, he brought the tip of the straw to his mouth. He sucked and got only an ache in his throat. His lungs felt empty. He opened his lips and gasped.

Try again. Cool liquid flowed into his mouth. The second swallow hurt much less than the first.

Courtney stirred. "Wha—ugh."

The nurse gave her a matching bottle of the blue liquid. After a few sips, Courtney whispered, "I feel like hell. What did they do to us?"

"Court, they jabbed fat needles into twenty different organs. Of course it's going to hurt. It will heal."

"This was supposed to make us feel younger."

"It will. We'll notice results in a few days." That's what the website and the patient testimonials said. Courtney had read them too.

"Don't use that tone of voice with me." Courtney lowered her eyebrows. "I knew it would be uncomfortable but nobody said it would hurt this much. Something is wrong." She raised her voice. "Do you understand me? Something is wrong."

The nurse rose from her chair. "I will check you with the pain meter. It can gauge your pain level from skin electrical response and muscle tension in your face."

Courtney's pain would be normal. Liam wished he could bet someone twenty dollars on it. Why did she want their treatments to fail? The nurse dabbed sensors to Courtney's face, then spent minutes checking outputs on a tablet. "Your discomfort levels are normal."

Courtney's face looked like an infant's the moment after a parent took away a favorite toy. "But it really hurts."

The nurse puckered her lips at her tablet. "We can adjust the formulation in your recovery drink to reduce discomfort and aid sleep. By tomorrow, you should feel better."

"Tomorrow? But I hurt now!"

The next morning, Liam woke to the chirps of kingfishers. Sunlight passed in midmorning angles through the louvered shutters. The nurse's chair sat empty.

He felt much stronger than the previous day. His limbs ached, but he could move them, like a day after overexerting in the weight room. His bladder bulged. He pushed back the sheets and tottered on stiff legs to the bathroom.

Standing at the toilet, he lifted his gown. Despite needing to piss, his penis stood stiffly against his abdomen. A long time since he'd last had *that* problem. He turned his thoughts to Courtney's mother. Last Thanksgiving, the house she shared with her neckbeard husband, Courtney's stepfather. Dry turkey and gluten-free green bean casserole…. his penis detumesced enough to piss.

Bladder empty, he went back to the bed. Courtney shifted in her sleep. She brought one corner of the sheet with her, untucking the opposite one from the foot of the bed. He sat next to her, lifted a hand to rest on her rump. He pulled it back. Let her sleep. Let her aches subside.

Let her discover her newfound youth at her own pace.

A few days, a week, no matter. After she eased her mind about the treatments, they would have decades together. Perhaps centuries.

Courtney shifted again, opened her eyes. "Hi."

In that moment, erupting from dormancy like a volcano, his love for her burned hotter than it had in years. It glowed in his chest like a swallow of expensive liquor. "Hi back at you." Lame words, but his voice hinted at his emotions. "How do you feel?"

"Better." She twisted again, stretched her arms. A wince. "I still ache. But I feel better than yesterday."

Through the sheet, he patted her thigh. "Great. I know they recommend recuperative activities for the day after the stem cell injections.

We'll get a couple's massage, then sip Singapore slings on the veranda."

"This isn't Singapore," she said, voice barbed. She gave her head a tiny shake, then spoke again, more winsomely. "I know what you mean. Sounds lovely." Her smile made her face glow more than it had in months. "All of it."

They spent a day on massages, ice baths, cold drinks, room service, and a slow shuffling walk around the cabin.

The next day they felt better still. After breakfast and spiced coffee on the veranda, Dr. Thomas guided them to back to the clinic. "The stem cell treatment is rejuvenating your organs with new cells. Today's telomere treatment will cause your cells old and new to age more slowly. The telomere treatment will be much easier. The only common side effect are flulike symptoms—"

"You are injecting us with a modified virus, after all," Courtney said.

Liam's throat froze in a half swallow. *Not this again—*

"Mrs. Kleinschmidt, don't worry, the gene therapy vector has been rendered safe."

Courtney nodded. "All I mean is, a few days of aches and mild fever are a small price to pay."

Liam exhaled. Dr. Thomas smiled. "Of course." Mirrored windows dazzled sunlight into their eyes. "Here we are."

Inside the clinic, she led them a different way. At intersecting hallways, signs in English and the squiggly local script pointed arrows down the cross corridors. *Advanced Therapies. Neurocognitive Enhancements.*

Liam glanced down each cross corridor. Just like the main hallway. This one empty, then that one, then—

By the arms, two nurses helped Deckard walk. Liam raised his hand in greeting. Deckard started and barely lifted his chin in reply before Liam passed out of view.

Staggering on nurses' arms didn't look like a neurocognitive enhancement. Liam stood taller. Whatever you got, good luck, Deckard. An advanced treatment might help you better navigate the snake's nest in Washington, but it won't make you or UFabIt innovative. SinterPrinter will still bite your heels. Then it will overtake you.

The telomerase treatment involved an hour of IV drip. On the wall opposite their seats, a video looped through a description of the process. A few nucleotides were lost from the tip of every chromosome during every cell division. Eventually, chromosomes would lose important information and the cells would die. The gene therapy vector would insert copies of telomerase reverse transcriptase gene into the genome, which would somehow stop the problem.

During the video's third repetition, Liam squirmed in his seat. "Nurse, can we find something else to watch?"

The nurse pulled out her tablet. After a few taps, the monitor switched over to a US news channel. President Andrews-Hinojosa filled the screen. The president augmented his usual pout with lowered eyebrows.

"For far too long, the one-percenters have ignored the law in their arrogant and selfish quest for a fountain of youth. They fly to India for risky medical treatments completely unapproved by the FDA. They think their money gives them the right to pursue unnatural long life when millions of Americans still lack equal health care coverage. The one-percenters act like a breed apart." Andrews-Hinojosa shook his head. Disgust seemed to drip off the end of his long nose.

"But I tell you, we're going to reel them in. Today, I will sign executive orders authorizing greater scrutiny of travelers returning from locales known to be hotbeds for these illegal procedures. In the coming weeks, I will work with Congress to pass further laws to shut down the loopholes the one-percenters exploit. To do this, I need bipartisan support. I reach out to Sen. Bai, Speaker Ramachandran, Sen. Ramos, and others to preserve the dream of equal health care access for all Americans."

Courtney sucked air through her teeth. Liam reached over and squeezed her hand. To the nurse he said, "A new channel, please."

Over the next few days, his and Courtney's energy grew, along with their closeness. They played croquet, then tennis, then on their last full day he persuaded her to go on a zip line excursion. They waited their turns on a platform ringed by palm fronds. The ground lay fifty feet beneath them. As their turns grew closer, Courtney stepped back into him. Without thinking, his arms wrapped her waist. She angled her neck to rest her head between his neck, throat, and shoulder. Through his chest, he felt her heart slam.

"I've never done this before," she said.

"I haven't either. You'll do fine." He grinned. "People hardly ever fall out." She looked up, eyes wide in playful fright. He patted her rump toward the harness. While the attendants strapped her in, she glanced over her shoulder with an I-can't-believe-I'm-doing-this smile.

Her mood stayed festive until that night, at dinner, when the waiter poured from an expensive bottle of wine. Courtney reached for the stem and turned the glass in circles on the tablecloth. Light from the chandeliers glittered in the swirling red. The light drew her gaze for long moments.

Liam pulled a breath deep into his belly. Whatever troubled her, he would wait until she said it.

Courtney looked up. "I'm sorry I was so difficult when we first got here."

"You were worried the treatment wouldn't work? Side effects?"

She pressed her lips together and returned her gaze to her wine. "I wasn't worried it would fail. I worried it would succeed."

Liam smiled although he didn't understand.

"I don't talk much about my parents' divorce. Maybe I should have, over the years? Their divorce wasn't mutual. My dad got a promotion and a big raise and thought he could find a younger and prettier replacement for my mom." Her eyes moistened.

Everything seemed brighter. Liam wanted to notice everything about her. "Go on."

"Then we came here. You talked so much about regaining youth and going back to succeed in business—" Sobs like hiccups rocked her torso. "—I got afraid you'd leave just like my dad."

"I didn't know, Court." He turned his palm up and slid his hand across the table toward her. "I'm glad you told me. I love you. I'm not going anywhere."

Her fingers like spiders, her hand inched toward his, stopped short. "You talked about being twenty-five again...."

Liam shook his head, the motion slowed by the weight of wisdom. "I went to college hoping to find the love of my life. I did." He sat taller and raised his chest. "I only need to feel twenty-five again to threaten to punch all the men who are going to come onto you." He chuckled.

Her cheeks reddened. Her hand inched forward and her fingers slid over his.

He curled his fingers toward his palm, holding her fingers in a firm and warm clasp.

They talked for two hours over the courses of dinner. He received a text from the office and replied with a few words. *I hired you because I knew you would do the right thing for the company. Take care of it. See you in a few days.*

He angled his head. "Sorry, Court. Not important. Let's get back to us."

They talked about SinterPrinter, about its prospects for growth and expansion, about the fruits of success, about the kids' college expenses, about the money freed up afterward for travel, about the decades or even centuries they would have together. They walked back to the cabin through the early tropical dusk, serenaded by terns and cormorants. The veranda steps creaked under foot, and the door unlocked itself at their approach. Liam held it open, gestured her, then followed and shut the door behind him.

He turned. Courtney stood close, a leer on her lips. Her hands clasped his shoulders. She said, "We need to get to bed."

Liam grinned back. He felt like he could soar, as if his chest held helium and his back, wings. His hands slid down to her waist. He lifted her. She yelped in playful surprise.

He carried her toward the bed. "That's right. We do."

The customs line for general international arrivals stood dozens deep. Around Courtney and him, Liam saw familiar faces. Polo shirts stretched over thicker chests and arms. Shorts and sandals showed more slender ankles and more defined calves. Echoing off the linoleum floor and gray-green drywall, the squeak of robotic luggage cart wheels counterpointed the sullen grumbles of waiting travelers. At the screening station for VIPs, two customs agents with time to kill talked among themselves, a private conversation suddenly punctuated by cackling laughter.

Liam barely noticed. He squeezed Courtney's hand. They shuffled forward till they came to their turn before the customs agent. He peered at their passports through reading glasses aiding narrow, close-set eyes.

"Where are you coming from?" His head turned back and forth between Liam and Courtney. His jowls wobbled with each turn.

Liam stifled a frown. The exit visa stamp showed a date two days prior. "India."

"You went there for business or pleasure? Or something else?"

Liam stared at the bridge of the agent's nose. "Pleasure."

A frown troubled the flesh of the agent's upper lip and cheeks. "Wait here." He stepped back to a kiosk. The agent's gaze plodded across a display hidden from view, while one hand smoothed strands of hair across his balding head. "Mr. and Mrs. Kleinschmidt. Please step aside. The senior agent will come to ask you a few questions."

Courtney sucked in a breath. Her hand squeezed Liam's.

Liam deepened his voice. "What's this about?"

"I'm not at liberty to say," the agent said.

"If we're being accused of something," Liam said, "we have a constitutional right to know what. And why."

"You're not accused of anything. At this time." The agent's gaze pored over Liam's face and chest and arms. His upper lip hardened. Envy. "Please step aside and wait for the senior agent."

A cold shock flowed down Liam's spine. They knew. Out of dozens of people around them who underwent the same treatments, they somehow singled out Courtney and him. How did they know about their crime?

Crime? The crime of receiving medical treatment approved by the Indian authorities? The crime of ignoring decrees designed to send law-abiding Americans to an early grave?

Courtney gripped his hand even tighter. "Honey," she whispered. Her words came out as if someone held her at knife point.

Liam bent his head toward her ear. He whispered back. "When the senior agent asks us questions, we will decline to answer and ask to speak to our lawyer."

"We don't have a—"

"I'll call SinterPrinter's law firm and ask for a referral. We'll get a good lawyer."

Courtney's grip on his hand eased. She nodded minimally and pressed herself against him.

Liam stood tall again, but then a pit opened in his belly. Lawyers. If the feds pushed a case against them, he and Courtney would face years of legal battles. Not one good lawyer, but a team, of how many? At five hundred, a thousand dollars per hour? How many hours…?

His head wobbled. A deep breath managed to keep it straight. A million dollars in legal fees? Two million? Plus hundreds, if not thousands, of hours wasted meeting with lawyers instead of building SinterPrinter, hiring employees, providing customers the best value he could. All because some petty, low-level bureaucrat happened to single them out—

Two well-dressed figures walked past the line, bound for the VIP customs station. "I'm glad we had this chance to talk," Deckard said.

"I'm glad too," replied a familiar, stentorian voice. "Glad to hear the unfiltered truth from such a major player in our economy as UFabIt."

The man next to Deckard had warmly tanned skin and white hair like the mane of a platinum-blond lion. Liam recognized the man from news videos.

Sen. Ramos.

Gooseflesh covered Liam's arms and legs, as if an ant colony's soldiers launched a sneak attack. That's how customs knew—

Deckard met Liam's gaze. The corners of Deckard's mouth turned up slightly, under his pair of frigid eyes.

WORLDSHIP TRIPLETS

nstead of the fourth wall, one side of Henri's living room opened to the rolling plains of New Zimbabwe. The breeze warmed his face and neck and rustled the tall yellow flechettegrass. Burrs scritched across the tight spandex sleeve on his upper arm.

As he went further, his steps buoyant in New Zim's lighter gravity, avatars manifested around him. Women, men, machines. Impossible to judge from appearance whether the others came from another part of the worldship or someplace distant.

No matter. All belonged to the Unity.

Also belonging to the Unity: the rebel press officer. Speaking from a platform raising him above the flechettegrass, khaki cap at a jaunty angle, yellow-brown irises against his eyes' stark whites, the press officer's smile sounded in his voice. "Thanks to our friends in the Unity, our forces advance on all fronts against Tiánquán ground forces and New Zim's puppet government. Soon–"

"Papa, Papa!" Luc said from behind Henri. "Come see!"

Henri scrunched his lips together. What did the boy want? Over his shoulder, seen through the yellow stalks, Luc stood at the living room's picture window, fingertips on the plasma pane. From his rapt profile, he watched activity in the worldship's central tunnel. Probably a maintenance robot crawling on the tunnel's far side, 1200 meters away. Trivial, against news from one of the galaxy's many battlefields against the Tiánquán.

"Papa, come see!"

Luc's seventh birthday, when his brain would finally be nanolinked with the UEC, the Unity Electrotelepathic Community, could not come soon enough. Now, Luc was too young for the UEC, too old to be fooled if Henri let a software assistant guide his body while his mind remained in Virtual.

A thought slotted into Henri. *As the Unity is to its people, so parents should be to their children.*

He heeded the UEC's wisdom and went to his son.

The living room surrounded him with conditioned air and self-healing walls, proof he'd returned to full Verity. "What do you see?"

"The worldship is giving birth to triplets!"

What? Then the childlike logic made sense. The docks lay many kilometers to the left, past twists and turns, deep in the worldship's core. The tunnel was like the exogestator tube Luc's baby sister had emerged from.

So three ships came down the tunnel at one time. Small ships, then, tenders or light patrol craft. Henri put his arm around his son's shoulders and looked through the plasma pane.

Gooseflesh stippled his jaw. The three ships were cruisers. Saucers half the width of the tunnel and bristling with laser turrets and sensor arrays. The matter-to-energy conversion drives glowed dull red, not white hot, and the tunnel's hard vacuum limited the flow of heat from the exhaust ports. Even so, Henri squinted when the first ship passed. The plasma pane, tinted orange-red, shivered.

Luc yiped and pulled his fingertips away. He blew on his fingers yet his rapt gaze remained on the ships. "They're so big!"

Henri frowned. Three cruisers at once? Why?

"What kind of people crew them, Papa?"

Sensed through the UEC, flows of thought pulsed within and between the cruisers. Content obscured–the UEC knew he lacked any need to know military secrets–yet unease tugged at the back of his mind.

As if a switch flipped, the unease vanished. "All the sorts of the Unity's people. Verities, uploads, cyborgs, robots, and AIs."

Luc's gaze followed the last cruiser around the curve three kilometers to the right. His fingertips tested the plasma pane. "Where are they going?"

"I don't know." Stock images of space battles and ground support operations slid through Henri's mind. "But wherever their destination, they'll defend us from the Tiánquán."

Luc fell silent. In Henri's mind, blocks of thought shifted. Soon, pride in the Unity welled his chest. An odd emotion looking at the empty tunnel.

Empty, so why did they look at it? Had Luc gotten overexcited seeing another maintenance robot?

A reddish tinge faded from the plasma pane. Ah, a power surge must have excited the pane and caught Luc's eye. Call maintenance and have them check it.

Luc looked up. His toothy grin squeezed his eyes. "Papa, the triplets were so exciting!"

Triplets? What nonsense did the boy imagine?

Henri sloughed out a breath. Grant Luc his imagination. After he linked to the UEC, he would grow out of it.

He smiled and tousled Luc's sandy brown hair. "Yes, son. I liked them very much."

THE ULTIMATE WAGER

Under low, roiling clouds, the electric bus from New Madison crept down the streets of the alien city.

Near the front of the bus, holding onto a ceiling strap, Connor Little peered through the crowd. The Hspa Nki, seven feet tall with bluish-gray skin, walked on two backward legs. Thin glide membranes, translucent and veined, joined the two triple-jointed arms on each side. A light breeze rustled the dense patterns of beads, indicators of rank and role, tied to their tail quills. Their voices struck the bus like a downpour on a metal roof. From the din, Connor's comm implant could only extract the words *vacuum breathers*.

Never mind the planet's natives. Where were the explorers from Earth?

There had to be other humans nearby. A week ago, a ship had descended past the high plateau the human colonists called New Madison, toward this alien city in their planet's lowlands. An Exploration Consortium ship, it had to be. The descending ship must have seen the buildings, farms, and fabs of New Madison.

The crowd thickened. The bus lurched forward a few yards at a time.

No explorers from Earth showed amidst the Hspa Nki.

On an open field beyond a thinner part of the crowd, Hspa Nki threw flying discs made of some thin, pliable material regurgitated by one of the native bugs. The Hspa Nki were left-handed. Their backhand throws wobbled, but their forehand throws zipped and they plucked passes from the air.

Connor wavered on his feet. These Hspa Nki had failed to be picked for the aliens' ultimate flying disc team.

Explorers from Earth can't help you. You have to win this game on your own.

He rubbed his neck and shook out his free arm. The Hspa Nki had first seen a flying disc a week before, when they'd come up to the plateau to suddenly demand a retroactive land tax. Just because they had taken to throwing and catching the disc didn't mean they grasped ultimate's tactics—offensive stacks, defensive formations and marking, and more. The people of New Madison had played ultimate for thirty years, ever since *Bascom Hall*'s crash on this planet turned them from explorers to colonists.

A Hspa Nki drifted past the bus on spread glide membranes. Lucas, one of the New Madison all-stars, frowned. "Coach, if they can glide like that…"

Connor raised his voice to carry to all the players on the bus. "I insisted to Nednennik, the Hspa Nki's representative, that their players be forbidden from gliding to get open or catch a disc. Or catching with more than two hands. Nednennik agreed."

Lucas eased back in his seat, and the other players relaxed. Good, stay loose, ready to play.

Connor wished he could. Lose, and the New Madison colonists would be expelled from this planet; sent back to an Earth he and the other older colonists wouldn't recognize, and the younger ones, including all the players, had never known.

The bus' air conditioning labored as they approached a gap in a long, tall, knobby structure. Even after they went through the gap and parked in a cavernous garage, the air in the bus cloaked Connor like a steamy bathroom. Then they stepped out and the effect intensified. The air seemed almost chewy.

He inhaled. Chewy, but oxygen rich.

Outside the bus, a Hspa Nki lifted and spread its quills. Its haws blinked over its eyes.

Connor turned his palms up. "Honored host, I am Connor Little, son of…." He rattled off the names of his parents, still alive up on the New Madison plateau, and his grandparents, last seen before he left Earth as a teenager.

The Hspa Nki replied with a long list of ancestors, indicating low rank. "Honored guests, your fellows wait in the preparation chamber." It stretched all four arms toward a rounded doorway.

Connor's whole body quivered, like filings exposed to a magnet. Did the Hspa Nki mean—? "Fellows?"

"Yes." It held its arms in place. "They wait."

On unsteady feet, Connor led the team toward the rounded doorway. Lights inside pulled him closer, but part of him resisted. People from Earth, but why hadn't they come up the plateau to New Madison?

He went into the preparation chamber.

Flexible lighting panels, obviously human-made, clung to the regurgitated-brick ceiling. The panels illuminated two men.

"We've found our lost colleagues from the crash of *Bascom Hall*!" one said. He had thick black eyebrows curling down at the ends. Tall, with ropy limbs, he strode forward. Something about him seemed familiar. "I'm Vijay Rambard."

The room around Connor shrank away from his vision. Autumn evenings, the 3D in his parents' house on Earth. "I watched you when I was a kid. That championship series, against Denver, '72…" Connor's face warmed. A championship series Rambard's team lost.

A wince flickered over Rambard's face. "Always glad to meet a fan. But though I'm proud of my ultimate career, I've been a xenodiplomat with the Exploration Consortium for twenty years." He gestured at the other man. "This is Ernst Gonçalves. One of the Consortium's benefactors." A sour tone crept into his voice.

Benefactor? Some rich man salving his greedy conscience with donations to the Exploration Consortium. Connor's face tightened.

Gonçalves' head, neck, and shoulders flowed together, and his stomach lapped his belt. "You must tell me all about your colony,"

Gonçalves said around labored breaths. "Surviving a massive hyper-jump malfunction, the loss of your ansible and emergency beacon, and a crash landing on an alien planet. Earth's audiences will clamor for your story."

"And you'll take fifteen percent?" Connor asked.

Gonçalves' face soured. "Mr. Little—"

"They aren't here to sell 3D rights." Rambard's tone sliced through the air. "Not everything is about making money."

Gonçalves peered at Rambard through droopy eyes. "I don't need you to tell me that."

Rambard rolled his eyes. "You amassed five billion dollars—"

To Connor, Gonçalves said, "We'll discuss your story later. We have much else to discuss now."

Connor's comm implant flashed a fifteen-minute warning across his vision. "And not much time." He turned to the players. "Change clothes and get ready. Now!"

The players took their duffel bags to cubbies along the far wall. They changed into uniform shorts, jerseys, and cleats, and tossed bottles of sports drinks to one another.

"While the players ready themselves," Rambard said to Connor, "we'll tell you what we know or infer. As soon as our ship entered orbit, the Hspa Nki realized we had much more advanced technology than you were able to preserve from *Bascom Hall*'s wreckage."

Connor bristled. "We've done fine. A fusion reactor for power, a self-driving electric bus...." Obsolete toys compared to what Earth must have developed in the last thirty years. "Go on."

Gonçalves spoke, his words punctuated by heavy breaths. "The Hspa Nki only confirmed to us your colony existed after they imposed on you a tax you could not pay. But apparently they love to wager?"

"We're sure they never saw a flying disc, let alone an ultimate game, before they came up the plateau to New Madison and demanded all our technologies and almost all our production for the next decade."

"Their wager is a negotiating ploy," Gonçalves said. "They offered to waive your land tax if the Consortium paid them ten billion dollars."

Connor's mouth fell open. Finally he found words. "You didn't pay?"

Gonçalves' jowls shook with his head. "The Consortium cannot agree to so large an expenditure in a few days. We all wish it could."

Rambard chuffed out a breath. "Speak for yourself. We don't need to pay the Hspa Nki. Connor, your team will win this game. Because I'll be their coach."

Thick warm air flowed into Connor's lungs. Rambard might be a former star player, but—"I'm their coach."

"I played eight seasons in the North American Ultimate Flying Disc League. Decades later, I'm still in the top ten for many career stat categories."

Gonçalves cleared his throat. "In regular season games."

From under thick eyebrows, Rambard glowered sidelong at Gonçalves. "And I know firsthand how elevation impacts disc flight."

Connor's forehead furrowed. "Flight is flight, right?" Nearby, one of his players nodded.

"You don't leave your plateau, do you?"

Arms spread, Connor quickly said, "The Hspa Nki monitor anyone crossing the perim—"

"You mentioned '72. My last year with Houston. Yes, we lost the finals against Denver. Because there's a mile of elevation difference between Houston and Denver. Discs fly differently in the two cities."

He turned to the players. The young men paused in tying cleats and pulling on jerseys. "Right now, you're two miles below the elevation of the New Madison plateau. Down here, discs will fly differently than you expect. I can coach you through that. Connor, I'm sure he's a good mayor, has great amateur knowledge about ultimate, but if he coaches you today, you'll lose."

Mouths slack, Braden and most of the other players stared through wide eyes at Rambard. Lucas did too. Then he glanced at Connor and quickly turned his head.

As Mayor, Connor had long coached the team, but he could see immediately his players had already chosen their new coach. "I'd be a fool to turn down your offer," Connor said.

"You're no fool." Rambard pumped Connor's hand and slapped his back. "We're going to win this. You heard me, men?" he called to the players. "We're going to win! Hit the field!"

The players cheered and filed out of the chamber. Their cleats clattered on the regurgitated-brick floor. The sound loosened a knot of unease in Connor's gut. He had good players, and luck in having a former pro coaching them. New Madison would win this game.

Only Gonçalves remained in the room. He cleared his throat with a liquid rasp. "Mr. Little, I can't add any value to your team's play. I'll send a report now to Earth via the ansible on our ship. I'll join you on the sideline in a few minutes."

"Take your time," Connor said. "We don't need you."

Gonçalves wheezed in a breath. "A time may come to reconsider that." He waddled away.

Alone, Connor left the preparation chamber. His footsteps echoed off the chewed-and-hardened walls. Hspa Nki with thinly-beaded tails guided him to the field with sweeping gestures of their four arms.

He emerged from the tunnel into the largest enclosed space he'd ever seen on the planet. Scalloped grandstands surrounded the field, rising like the walls of an eroded canyon. Hspa Nki crowded the grandstands. Thousands of clinking alien voices echoed. *Vacuum breathers.* Connor hunched his shoulders, as if the voices were rain falling from the low gray clouds.

At the stadium's far end, a tall wall held panels with gargantuan, unreadable alien script and a twisted structure of curved, nested arms. Three Hspa Nki clung to railings under the text and structure. Connor's comm implant labeled various objects. Team names. Points. Time remaining.

Connor went to the New Madison sideline. Most of the players stretched or made short, soft warm-up throws, all with wary eyes on the steep grandstands.

"We've never played a road game before, have we?" Connor said. He squatted near the players, ran his fingers through the coiled, green-black ground cover, then beckoned for someone to throw him a disc. Though fabricated by the Hspa Nki, and as yellow as the barely-remembered sun of Earth, the weight and feel filled his hand and slotted into decades of muscle memory. "But wherever we play, it's the same field, the same disc, and the same spirit of the game."

Smiles and nods showed among the players. Braden closed his eyes and bobbed his head at some music played through his comm implant.

Rambard, Connor, and Lucas went to midfield for the opening toss. Two Hspa Nki players accompanied Nednennik, whose tail quills bore a thousand multicolored beads. Nednennik's haws peeled back and it stared at Rambard while its quills rustled.

"Good to meet you somewhere other than the negotiation chamber," Rambard said with a smirk.

Connor stepped forward. "Honored host, are all the rules clear to you and your players?"

Nednennik's voice sounded like a bag of pebbles rolled from hand to hand. "Yes," Connor's comm implant translated to his auditory nerves. "A player scores a point by catching the disc in the opponent's end zone. The possessor of the disc may not run and may only pivot on one foot and throw. The defender guarding the disc's possessor calls out ten seconds. If the possessor holds the disc for ten seconds, or throws an incomplete or intercepted pass or one landing or caught out-of-bounds, possession goes to the defending team. Contact is forbidden. Players call their own fouls, in the spirit of the game."

The humans nodded. The Hspa Nki won the toss.

Back at the human sideline, Rambard told the team, "We're throwing off. Remember! Down here, the disc won't carry as far as you're used to. Who's throwing off?"

Players nodded at Lucas. Sure hands and strong arm, a handler.

"Throw harder on the throw-off," Rambard said to him. "Trust me. It won't go for a touchback. And everyone, on deep passes, the same applies. Throw harder than you think you should. Starters, get out there!"

Braden raised his hand. "Which side do we force them to throw on?"

Since an opponent with the disc could only pivot, and most throws came sidearm, the player guarding the disc-handler would generally stand in one throwing lane to force the disc-handler to throw down the other. Announcing the forced side let defenders marking receivers know from which angle to expect a pass.

A brief frown, dispelled by a shake of Rambard's head. "They're left-handed, aren't they? Force to their left." Their forehand side.

Players nodded. The starting seven ran a couple of steps toward their own goal line.

"No!" Connor shouted.

The players stopped running and jostled together.

"Have you seen them, Rambard? They throw strong forehands. Their backhands are weak. Force to their right!"

Rambard stared at Connor, then turned to the starting seven. "As I said. Force to their left."

Connor's chest burned. Then a firm voice burst through his comm implant. "Honored guests, are you ready to begin?"

"We are," Rambard said. He slapped Braden on the shoulder. "Get out there, men!"

The players ran out to their own goal line. Lucas stood in the center and raised the disc to show his readiness. The golden disc contrasted starkly with the blur of Hspa Nki in the far grandstand. The disc commanded the eye, like a ship at a launch station with the whole galaxy to be explored.

At the far end zone, amid a line of gray-blue figures, the tallest Hspa Nki raised its hand.

Lucas lined up for a backhand throw-off. "Game on!" He swung back his arm.

Connor's throat tightened. Too big a backswing. Rambard must have it wrong. Lucas would throw the disc through the end zone for a touchback.

Face tight, Lucas grunted and whipped his arm forward. The disc came out fast from his hand—

—and flew wrong. Too slow for the power behind it. And though discs curved a little in flight, this one banked like an airplane turning hard to the right.

Connor's stomach fell.

Rambard was correct.

The disc arced toward the right sideline and dropped through the thick air. Hspa Nki loped toward it. Most passed it. The disc landed only a few yards beyond the center line, great field position for the aliens. The humans rushed up to play man-to-alien defense.

A Hspa Nki picked up the disc with its top left hand. Braden guarded the alien, standing in front of the alien to its right and waving his arms. Blocking its backhand passing lane, just what Rambard had called for. "One!" Braden counted. "Two!"

The Hspa Nki pivoted left and snapped a forehand pass. An effortless motion of its elbows and wrist. The disc curled over the sideline, then zipped toward a corner of the end zone. A Hspa Nki strode to the corner and raised its left hands. Lucas matched the alien stride for stride, but the disc curled inbounds past his stretching fingers.

The Hspa Nki squeezed the flying disc between its left hands. Connor's face scrunched up. Good catch, great throw.

The crowd rustled its tail quills and cheered like concrete rattling in a mixer. The human team's shoulders and heads drooped. They trudged to their goal line to receive the next point.

"Rambard!" Connor shouted. "Force to their right!"

Rambard stood stiff-backed. He lifted his palm toward Connor, yet kept his back to him, and his gaze on two players substituting in. He spoke quietly and the two players hurried onto the field.

The Hspa Nki throw-off landed three yards in front of the human goal line. Lucas made a short forehand pass to Tanner. The disc slid through the air to the left—Tanner stretched to catch it. Connor let out a breath. *The team is getting the hang of this—*

Tanner threw a backhand to Dustin. The disc curled away from Dustin and clacked into the ground. Turnover.

One Hspa Nki sprinted for the center of the end zone while a second went to the disc. A high forehand pass and the sprinting Hspa Nki caught it easily. The crowd cheered.

Cold oozed down Connor's throat.

The next human possession ended the same way, turnover and quick score. Hspa Nki 3, New Madison 0. The crowd sounded even louder this time, as if they'd thrown Connor into the mixer with the concrete.

Labored breathing suddenly cut through the noise. Gonçalves took up position next to Connor. "My regrets for my lateness. What is our situation?" He looked at the scoreboard. Hspa Nki scoreboard operators glided from perch to perch. "I see."

The world spun. Connor shut his eyes. "We're getting humiliated."

Gonçalves rested his fleshy hand on Connor's shoulder. "The game has barely begun. The winds of fortune may yet turn."

In a lull of the crowd noise, Rambard's words to the next substitutes carried to Connor. "Short passes on offense until you get a feel for the air density. On defense, force to their right! Make them beat us with their backhands!"

The Hspa Nki throw-off landed four yards in front of the end zone. Lucas picked up the disc while his teammates formed a stack, a line running toward midfield. Everyone looked more assured. One by one, human players broke from the stack to give Lucas passing opportunities. He flicked a forehand eight yards to Dustin, Dustin to Jacob past the fingertips of a lunging Hspa Nki. Back to Lucas. With more short passes, they advanced.

Braden made a sharp cut in the end zone and ran alone toward the sideline. Lucas tossed a soft forehand into the air ahead of Braden. Connor groaned. A throw that soft would drop to the ground before Braden could catch it… if they played up in New Madison. The disc seemed to levitate as Braden ran to it and cradled it in both hands.

Now, the only cheers came from the human sideline.

On the next Hspa Nki possession, the human defense forced them to their backhands. Tail quills rippled, signaling unease. The Hspa Nki backhands traveled slowly and curled off-target. One bounced off a Hspa Nki's right hands. Turnover and quick score for New Madison.

Momentum shifted for the rest of the first half. At halftime the scoreboard showed Hspa Nki 8, New Madison 6.

Connor stared at the scoreboard, looking past the players returning to the sideline. Within striking distance, but could they close the gap?

The players drank water and toweled off sweat. Rambard clapped and aimed an intense gaze at them. "Men, you're getting the hang of disc flight down here. And because you're conditioned for thinner air, you'll have stamina for the entire second half. Keep playing your game, and you'll win!"

New Madison received the throw-off to start the second half. The players sprinted to their positions. Crisp passes sliced through the thick air. Players made sharp cuts toward the disc-handler or into the corners of the end zone. On defense, they hustled to guard the disc-handler and deflected throws off their fingertips. The Hspa Nki managed several points, but with four minutes left in the game, New Madison tied the score at 13. One quick turnover later and Lucas fired a deep pass to Braden in the end zone. Connor's heart soared with the disc.

Braden caught the disc and tapped both feet a few inches inside the sideline.

New Madison 14, Hspa Nki 13. Three minutes to go.

On the next throw-off, the Hspa Nki raced to the disc. Their handler launched a long but wobbly backhand toward a streaking teammate. The Hspa Nki receiver dove. Its glide membranes rippled, then air stretched them out. Its dive seemed to last forever. With its top left hand, it plucked the disc from the air an inch above the ground.

Connor's arm snapped up and his index finger jutted at the play. "Hey!"

Lucas ran up to the Hspa Nki, then swept his head from side to side. His comm implant relayed his words to the sideline. "No gliding. You agreed."

"I didn't glide," the Hspa Nki said.

"Yes, you did." Lucas pulled his arms up, as if to stretch out glide membranes.

"I didn't glide."

Lucas' face turned red. Human players ran up.

"Don't lie!"

"We all saw you glide!"

Hspa Nki huddled around their player. "She did not glide," one said.

Another alien waggled its tail quills and spoke into the ears of nearby teammates. The Hspa Nki soon argued among themselves. Rapid clattering voices and waves of rippling quills erupted, but soon died down.

Connor found himself standing next to Rambard, two yards onto the field. The Hspa Nki wouldn't blatantly cheat—

The Hspa Nki receiver set the disc on the ground, then dragged its tail quills. "Honored guest, my teammate saw my actions better than I could feel them. The disc is yours."

Lucas nodded, then looked at the still-running clock. "We're willing to add thirty seconds for this stoppage."

"What?" Rambard muttered. "Don't offer that." Thirty seconds more for the Hspa Nki to tie the score.

"That is most generous," the Hspa Nki said. "We agree."

"No!" Rambard shouted.

Connor scowled at him. "The Hspa Nki needed time to realize Lucas was right. It's in the spirit of the game to give them time back."

"We wouldn't have done that in the NAUFDL playoffs. Let alone when a human colony on this planet is at risk." Rambard clawed the air, then flung his hands forward. "Lucas offered, they agreed, we can't back out now. Damn." He retreated to the sideline.

Connor followed. His voice flowed like a wide river. "It's the spirit of the game."

"You think because I got paid to play I don't appreciate the spirit of the game?" Rambard shook his head and peered past Connor at the scoreboard. The clock stopped, ratcheted back around its spiral, then restarted.

Gaze darting between the field and Rambard, shoulders hunched, Lucas picked up the disc. "Game on!" he shouted.

Lucas' throw left his hand. The disc quickly turned over and knifed along the ground. He gaped after it.

Don't let Rambard get in your head. Just play—

The Hspa Nki formerly guarding Lucas broke toward the end zone. Mouth gaping, Lucas ran after it, but a second too slow.

Catch in the end zone. Tie game.

The next throw-off went to Lucas. A Hspa Nki with wide arms and quick feet guarded him just outside the end zone. Lucas faked a backhand, then made a soft forehand throw.

The Hspa Nki lunged for the disc. It slapped the side of the disc, keeping it spinning and deflecting it to the end zone.

Eyes wide, Lucas ran after it, shoulder to shoulder with the Hspa Nki. It stretched its top left arm toward the disc while boxing out Lucas with its right elbows. Its fingers clamped around the edge of the disc.

Connor's stomach flopped. Gonçalves' labored breath roared in his ears.

The Hspa Nki led by one.

On the next throw-off, the disc landed between Lucas and Dustin. Lucas shook his head and backed away.

Come on, Dustin, you're a good handler. Connor's thought sounded like a lie told to a child.

Three Hspa Nki raced forward, one to guard Dustin and two to stand five yards back in his passing lanes. Not a double- or triple-team, therefore legal. Dustin's head jerked around, looking for open teammates.

The guarding Hspa Nki's translated shout came through Connor's comm implant. "Eight. Nine. Te—"

Dustin tried a hammer throw to Lucas over the guarding Hspa Nki. The disc dropped like a shot bird.

Two Hspa Nki broke for opposite end zone corners. The third tossed a backhand over Lucas' outstretched hands to its teammate.

Hspa Nki 16, New Madison 14, ninety seconds to go.

Lucas hung his head. He shuffled to a stop and looked to the sideline.

"We should pull him," Rambard said.

"No," Connor said. He caught Lucas' gaze and gestured for him to calm down. "Play your game!" he shouted. To Rambard, he said, "He's the best handler we have. You've seen that?"

Rambard frowned. "That's true."

Connor filled his voice with assurance he did not feel. "Play your game!" he shouted again.

Lucas nodded at Connor, then jogged with growing intensity toward the goal line.

"Men!" yelled Rambard, "you have time to tie the game if you score quickly!"

The Hspa Nki throw-off landed three yards in front of the goal line.

Lucas picked up the disc and surveyed the field. Despite the Hspa Nki guarding him, he fired a curling backhand to Jacob near midfield, then hustled up for a drop pass. He zipped a long forehand to Braden in the end zone.

Down by one. A minute to play.

Rambard sent in substitutes with fresh legs. A tie at the end of regulation would send the game to sudden death overtime. New Madison's best chance was a deep throw-off, a quickly forced turnover, and a disc to the end zone.

Lucas raised the disc in readiness. A Hspa Nki matched the gesture. Lucas threw off.

The disc headed toward the right corner in front of the Hspa Nki end zone. Connor gritted his teeth. If the disc landed over the goal line, touchback for the Hspa Nki. If it landed out of bounds, the Hspa Nki would start in the field's middle.

Braden, Quillen, and Waters raced after the disc. It landed inbounds four yards in front of the goal line. Perfect place to crowd the Hspa Nki handler.

Quillen guarded the handler, jumping from side to side and waving his arms. Braden remained five yards upfield, a foot from the sideline, blocking the forehand throwing lane. The Hspa Nki handler pivoted to forehand, to backhand—

"Seven!" Quillen counted. "Eight!"

—to forehand, and threw. Braden leaped. The disc hit his open palm and tumbled to the ground.

"Turnover!" Connor shouted.

Quillen and Waters had already broken for the end zone. The Hspa Nki player dropped back to cover Quillen heading toward the middle, leaving Waters unguarded toward the back corner. Braden picked up the disc.

Connor's breath hitched. Had Braden thrown at all today? *Come on, easy, a firm throw, float it in the thick air—*

The disc spun gently out of Braden's hand. The right throwing lane, but too soft. Like Lucas on the game's opening throw-off, he used muscle memory tuned for the thin air of New Madison. The disc glided downward, far too short for Waters to catch it in stride.

Waters' blue eyes widened. He angled back toward the disc. His cleats dug into the ground cover. The disc sank through the air. Waters stretched. Dove—

The disc clacked against the ground. It rolled on its edge over his arm and bounced into his face, then settled upside-down on the ground.

The crowd's cheers erupted. The Hspa Nki players all looked at the clock and lifted their tail quills in dominance. The human players looked too, hands on knees, eyes haggard.

Three seconds, two, one.

Zero.

The human players trudged to the sideline. Braden turned his shoulders away from his teammates. Tears flowed down his face.

"I lost the game," he said, voice choked.

Connor's arms enveloped him. "We played as a team and lost as a team."

"That's right," said Lucas, his eyes moist. Other players nodded in agreement.

Braden buried his face in Connor's shoulders. "We're going back to Earth because of me."

A labored breath heralded Gonçalves. "The winds of fortune may yet change."

Braden backed out of Connor's hug. His brows crinkled at Gonçalves. Connor glared at the lying billionaire. "Change? How?"

Gonçalves raised a palm. "I must first talk with Nednennik."

Nednennik loped across the field, glide membranes rippling. "A well-played game, honored guests," it said. "You nearly proved yourselves our equals. You must vacate our planet within thirty local days."

Older New Madisonites hadn't asked to be marooned here, but to lose the only home the young generation ever had… Connor shut his eyes. "We wi—"

"A word," Gonçalves said. "Nednennik, you told Rambard and I you would waive New Madison's land tax if we paid you ten billion dollars?"

Nednennik's tail quills flattened. "I did."

Gonçalves heaved out a breath. "I will pay it."

Connor's head swam. His comm implant caught Nednennik's skeptical reply. "You said the Exploration Consortium could not pay that amount."

"It can't. *I* can."

Rambard scowled. "What are you doing?" he hissed at Gonçalves. "Your net worth is only five billion."

"No. It *was*," Gonçalves said. "Just before the opening throw-off, I ansibled our situation to Las Vegas, on Earth. The sportsbook computers gave New Madison odds of 1:2. I wagered almost all my holdings that the Hspa Nki would win."

Nednennik writhed its quills. "New Madison would either win the game or you would pay its debt. Wisely chosen. You, of New Madison and of Earth, are truly our equals."

Amid the knot of players, Braden watched with red-rimmed eyes. His mouth parted in a newborn smile. A wave of understanding flowed from face to face.

The Hspa Nki spectators filed out of the grandstands. The scoreboard operators took down the score panels and spun back the clock's nested arms. Nednennik and the last Hspa Nki players entered the tunnel to the aliens' locker room.

Rambard stared at the coiled, green-black ground cover and shook his head.

Connor went to him. "You coached well."

"Not well enough." Rambard turned his head. "We started off forcing the wrong way—"

"You understood what the thicker air would do to the disc. I had no idea." Connor rested his arm on Rambard's shoulder. "You coached us better than I would have."

Rambard nodded yet pulled away.

Nearby, the New Madison players huddled together, again with tears. Now, though, their tears rolled down faces lifted to the sky and trickled past giddy smiles and laughing mouths.

Connor blinked at Gonçalves. For a man who barely knew them to pay so much… "You spent your entire fortune?"

"Not *entire*. I'll live comfortably enough—"

"But why? For us?" He widened his arms to indicate the players behind him.

"The Exploration Consortium will want to lease base facilities from New Madison, which benefits us both. I will win acclaim on Earth, something a fortune alone cannot buy. And a colony of human beings will keep its home of thirty years."

Pressure welled behind Connor's eyes. "Thank you."

Gonçalves shook his jowly head. "You don't need to thank me. I acted in the spirit of the game."

—The author thanks David Abmayr, Jr., Ph.D. for technical consultation regarding altitude effects on flying disc dynamics and ultimate gameplay.

ABOUT THE AUTHOR

I'M **RAYMUND EICH.** I use my Middle American upbringing as a launchpad for journeys to the ends of the Universe.

Growing up in the Midwest prepared me for my academic career, culminating with a Ph.D. in biochemistry from Rice University. It helps me help inventors around the world prosper from their innovations.

Above all, it inspires me to write science fiction and fantasy about ordinary people facing extraordinary wonders and horrors, battling enemies both foreign and domestic, and building better lives for themselves, their families, and their societies.

My last name has one syllable and is pronounced "eye-sh." I live in Houston with my family.

Connect with me at **www.raymundeich.com** or follow the QR code below.

Online and brick-and-mortar bookstores around the world list millions of books, with thousands more published every day.

I'm glad you discovered this one.

If you'd like to learn more about me and my books, join my Readers Club. To thank you, you'll immediately receive a collection of five short stories unavailable anywhere else.

After that, I'll email you monthly with exclusive content reflecting my interests in science, fiction, and related subjects. Plus short personal updates and publishing news.

Yes, please! I'll go to **www.raymundeich.com/mailing-list** or scan the QR code below.

No thanks. I'll take my chances next time I look for your books.

OTHER BOOKS BY THE AUTHOR

Available wherever books are sold.

Learn more about these titles at our website, **www.cv2books.com,** or follow
the QR code below.

THE INCEPTI CATACLYSM

The entire galaxy knows about the Incepti Cataclysm. The occupation force from Vela destroyed a planet with nanotechnology. Only a few Inceptis fled the wave of death in time to join their brethren scattered across the Democracy.

Everything the galaxy knows is a lie.

Anara Orden. Daughter of survivors. Recruited by fellow Inceptis to join Democracy intelligence. Though young and good of heart, she kills without qualms. She knows her employers only order her to terminate Velan agents threatening the Democracy.

But when her next target is a fellow Incepti, she questions everything and chooses a new mission. She will share the truth with friend and foe alike.

Yet powerful forces across the galaxy will do whatever it takes to cling to power. Even if millions of innocents must die.

Escape from Conatus (Book One)

When Anara learns the truth, a simple mission becomes a flight for survival.

Revelation in Vela (Book Two)

Instead of a refuge, Anara and her companions end up in the cross-hairs—of two sides.

Victory for Carina (Book Three)

As war comes to the galaxy, only Anara's desperate plan can bring a just and lasting peace.

THE FALSE FLAG WAR

Concordia's mission reflected the best of the human race. Crew and scientists from both of Earth's rival factions, Humanists and Traditionalists, journeyed for years at relativistic speeds to reach Bravo Charlie, a life-bearing planet orbiting Alpha Centauri B, to expand the frontiers of knowledge for all.

Concordia's mission also reflected humanity at its worst. Corrupt bureaucrats and ambitious political leaders in both factions maintained a status quo backed by weapons of mass destruction. The faction commanders on the mission each sought to seize advantages for their side alone.

Then the ship received transmissions. Signs of an ancient, powerful alien presence on the planet below.

Exploration 2127

Sent to explore, **Jaeger** and **McIlroy**, born and raised in a Texas divided by razor wire and minefields. Men torn between the mission's ideals and orders from their respective faction commanders, oily Varanathan and domineering Sandford.

Then Jaeger and McIlroy discover how to bring Earth's factions together... using knowledge given by aliens dead over a million years.

Invasion 2132

Concordia fell silent. Mission control now detects an unknown ship leaving the Alpha Centauri system. Heading to Earth at relativistic speeds. Silent about its purpose. Its crew unknown.

Earth's one chance: Its rival factions must work for mutual defense, against shadowy figures who strive to use the unknown ship for their own faction's gain.

STONE CHALMERS

Earth barely survived the 21st Century.

Biotechnological and nuclear terrorism, civil war, famine, and ethnic cleansing killed billions. Thousands fled on warpdrive ships to colonize planets around distant suns.

In the 22nd century, after Earth unified under one world government, it opened wormhole links to the distant colonies, to prevent a repeat of the previous century's chaos on a galactic scale.

Enter operative Stone Chalmers. Spy. Assassin. Instrument maintaining Earth's dominion over all human worlds.

Opposing him are hostile forces on colony worlds… and within the Earth government itself.

When Stone clashes with those forces, Earth—and every human world—will be transformed forever.

Learn more about the Stone Chalmers series at **www.cv2books.com/stone-chalmers**, or follow the QR code below.

The Freeland Vendetta

On the newly rediscovered colony world Freeland, a conspiracy plans a powerful blow against Earth's control of the planet. A blow supported by treacherous forces inside the government of Earth.

The Trinity Deception

From the religious colony world of Trinity come clues of a long-lost prize. The last warpdrive ship outside Earth's control.

The Minerva Conspiracy

Expecting a mission beneath his talents, Stone fights for his life—and soul—against a terrifying conspiracy.

The Terra Betrayal

Schemes and plots from the colonies and the capital converge in the halls of power on Earth itself. Only Stone can fight his way through a web of intrigue and bring freedom to all human worlds.

THE CONFEDERATED WORLDS

The purpose of all other combat arms is to put the infantryman in sole possession of the battlefield.

A thousand years from now, while Earth sleeps in virtual reality, three polities—the Confederated Worlds, the Unity, and the Progressive Republic—strive to connect the scattered, terraformed worlds of humankind by artificial wormholes.

When they meet, they clash, in a decades-long struggle of arms that will embroil every human world, in which dedication to duty liberates worlds—and oneself.

Learn more about the Confederated Worlds series at **www.cv2books.com/the-confederated-worlds**, or follow the QR code below.

Take the Shilling

The Confederated Worlds implanted in his brain the skills to make him a soldier. Tomas Neumann had to learn for himself how to survive interstellar war.

Operation Iago

The Confederated Worlds lost the war. Can Lt. Tomas Neumann win the peace against elusive, deceptive foes out to turn the Confederated Worlds against itself?

A Bodyguard of Lies

Assigned to the halls of power, only Capt. Tomas Neumann can save the Confederated Worlds from the ultimate treachery.

OTHER NOVELS

The Blank Slate

Neuroscience entrepreneur Clay Shieffer must stop a tyrannical president… because he unwittingly gave the tyrant power over the human mind.

New California

After New California's founder committed suicide, two men vied to rule the colony.

Ashwin George, supported by the colony's elite and the Chinese company dominating half the settled galaxy.

Against him, Desmond Park, nanotechnology engineer, armed with the most formidable weapon of all.

A single idea.

The Reincarnation Run

Skeptical spacejock Landry Krieger knows exactly how to smuggle the "reborn" spiritual leader of an oppressed people past their conquerors... but the boy's priests—and governess—shake up his orderly plans.

Azureseas: Cantrell's War

Ross Cantrell joined the animal control mission on the newly-discovered planet Azureseas to earn the money to start married life together with his girlfriend.

Then Ross discovers the truth about the planet's "animals."

SHORT NOVELS

Love and Death in the City of Bone

He had a month to learn the planet's mysteries—and Juliette's.

- His cover story: return to Elard to dismantle his sect's missionary work to the planet's natives.
- His true mission: investigate decades-old mysteries of love and death.
- His objective: return to Earth with his discovery.

If he can.

A Mighty Fortress

Theodore and his team from the Lutheran Interstellar Terraforming Society would transform a barren, rocky world into a refuge of faith and life.

Or die trying.

Winner and the Poacher

A Portia Oakeshott, Dinosaur Veterinarian Short Novel

As a consultant to law enforcement, Portia confronts stark evidence of a rich young man's crime: the mounted head of a massive herbivorous *Wintonotitan*. A winner.

A dinosaur the company never granted a permit for hunting.

SHORT STORY COLLECTIONS

The First Voyages: The Complete Science Fiction Stories 1998-2012f

From 21st century asteroid settlements to World War II Romania, from an Earth dominated by immortal aliens to Christ's empty tomb, a fresh, distinctive voice in science fiction will take you on journeys to the photosphere of the sun, the coding regions of DNA, and the complexities of the human psyche.

Orbital Maneuvers: The Complete Science Fiction Stories 2019-2020

In these pages, you can join–

A mission to terraform a lifeless, rocky planet | A private detective uncovering the ultimate crime | A woman called by an ex-boyfriend… who's been dead twenty years | A President breaking his country's highest law | A star athlete discovering the true price of a championship

–and enjoy five more tales, in the latest installment of the Complete Science Fiction Stories of Raymund Eich.

Extravehicular Activities: The Complete Science Fiction Stories 2021-2022

Leave the safety of your space capsule for the dangers of billion-year old alien derelicts, intelligent insects with mysterious motives, espionage in an alternate 1920s Paris, and rogue reconstructed dinosaurs.

These wonders and more await in the fourth volume of the Complete Science Fiction Stories of Raymund Eich.